KEEP IT SECRET

Snehaprava Das

KEEP IT SECRET

Snehaprava Das

BLACK EAGLE BOOKS
Dublin, USA | Bhubaneswar, India

Black Eagle Books
USA address:
7464 Wisdom Lane
Dublin, OH 43016

India address:
E/312, Trident Galaxy, Kalinga Nagar,
Bhubaneswar-751003, Odisha, India

E-mail: info@blackeaglebooks.org
Website: www.blackeaglebooks.org

First International Edition Published by
Black Eagle Books, 2025

KEEP IT SECRET
by **Snehaprava Das**

Copyright © Snehaprava Das

Cover & Interior Design: Ezy's Publication

ISBN- 978-1-64560-699-4 (Paperback)

Printed in the United States of America

DEDICATION

In the hands of my Beloved Parents

A secret is a kind of promise….It can also be a prison…

Jennifer Lee Carrell

Acknowledgements

I owe a debt of gratitude to all those nice people around me without whom the book would not have happened. My sincere thanks go to Dr. A. J. Thomas, eminent translator and critic and former editor of Indian Literature for reading my stories and commenting on them from time to time, to the renowned fictionists Chandrahas Choudhury and Hansda Sowvendra Sekhar for their appreciation and for writing the beautiful blurbs, to Akshay and Satabdi of Walking Book Fair for always being ready to provide a platform for the reading and discussion of my books, and to Mitra Samal for always being there to inspire and encourage me. Last but not the least I extend my sincere thanks to Black Eagle Books for accepting the book for publication.

CONTENTS

From the Author's Pen...

In one if his most famous lyrics Randall Stuart Newman says, 'It is a jungle out there--- A very appropriate observation indeed. The world outside our self-erected walls of impassive nonchalance, is a jungle infested by creatures guised under the mask of civility, lying in ambush, ready to pounce upon us at our weak, vulnerable moments. 'There is chaos and confusion everywhere and violence and poison...,' and thus the lyrics project a bleak and grim picture of the modern world we inhabit. But he does not stop at that and moves on to sing 'It's a jungle in here, too,'… he is right there, too. We all, deep inside ourselves, carry our individual jungles, where atavistic passions guised in gentility invade the territory of the subliminal.

The evils that throng the jungle outside, perceivable usually in the form of human cruelty, violence, envy, avarice, frustration and many such instincts and detectable through logical reasoning, influence our conscious thoughts and action. They expose the bitter realities of human existence and the struggle for survival in a world ridden with such negativities. They in a way impact as well as condition our socio-cultural existence. They also influence our mood and behaviour, and the change makes itself manifest on the surface realities. But the jungle each individual carries within houses raw, volatile passions, universal and archetypal. They lie muted, repressed under the layer of rational thinking in the form of dreams and memories, and illusions,…...as blurred reflections on the shadow of time, elusive phantoms that haunt our lonely, unguarded moments.

There is actually a very thin, floating borderline that keeps the two jungles apart, and life goes on apparently easy and undisturbed as long as they do not happen to converge on certain specific points. When they do, our illusive emotions, memories, traumas, hallucinations lying hidden in the dark depths of that jungle slip out to the open like bubbles surfacing on the waters of a dark well. And we stand helpless and crumbled, staring in helpless agony at the bleak, naked face of our private truth. They are the moments of our epiphany, of the interfacing of the real and the unreal and of shedding the artificial faces off our persona.

Keep It Secret, a collection of ten stories has in its agenda an effort to cross over the flimsy and floating border between the substance and the shadow, to explore into the jungle within, to study the secrets carefully concealed behind the mask of pretense and shamming of an agreeable and acceptable facade.

In the words of Andre Malraux, 'Man is not what he thinks, he is what he hides.'

The aim, thus in a way, is to unravel the truth man hides and strives to protect it under a falsehood, that, at times projects, reveals itself through a behaviour pattern which may appear absurd. It intends to push aside the deceptively glossy screen of fake complacence, and traverse into that murky, elusive terrain beyond the ordinary logical perceptibility.

Hence a character may believe he was wronged by someone's action in the past, and would set out to avenge it in the present, because as Freud observes that beliefs are the conclusion our inner conscious draws through reconnoitering the memories of experiences of the past, because not just our conscious behaviour, but even our moods and temperaments are controlled by our subconscious beliefs. If we are to accept the views and observations of Chad Chesmark, the famous performer, speaker and mind-reader from Las Vegas, as he puts forth in his 'How to Predict the Future by Creating it Yourself,' this action of the present may have an overwhelming effect on his future. The trauma one passes through can build up a set of beliefs which could influence the mind to predict a future-scenario often construed by the presumptions and perceptions derived from the past as well as the present happenings. A guilt-stricken mind can in the same way, through misleading beliefs and perceptions could act in an abnormal way. Regina Pally, the renowned psychiatrist and therapist from Los Angeles comes forth to explain that for most of what we perceive occurs non-consciously and effortlessly, and according to her the process could be termed as a 'survival-instinct'. This may prompt the guilt-ridden mind to construe and condition a future for recompensing the wrong done in the past. This 'survival-instinct' that allures one to assume and perceive things, could even give a mental twist to the real impact of a real happening, conjuring up multiple and bizarre versions of one individual incident which may tend to verge on the surreal.

'From error to error, one discovers the entire truth,' observes Freud. Some of the stories aim at exposing the errors man is forced to commit lured by compulsive emotions, which leave life irrecoverably difficult, and could at times prove fatal in that self-destructive process of discovering the truth. There are stories that make an attempt to study the complex and shifting patterns of human relationship, that hang precariously balanced between trust and distrust, and to observe the reaction of the characters while confronting the secret of that relationship which was kept closely guarded till the end. The experience of that confrontation could be subversive in that specific moment of anagnorisis. Some stories, therefore, may not always offer a seemingly logically definable or happy ending. Does not Camus say that 'Maybe it's not about happy ending. Maybe it's about the story?'

The stories, I believe, besides just offering a superfluous reading experience, may also guide a sensitive reader to the secret world within through a narrative style that hovers between first person and third person to delineate the changing moods of the characters, between past and present tracing a journey across different layers of time, and between truth and untruth examining the complex, overlapping emotions lying there in obscurity.

Snehaprava Das

The New Year Gift

Everything that you love you will eventually lose, but in the end love will return in a different form…
> **Franz Kafka**

The loud giggles of Rohit and his friends filled the house as they barged into the drawing room. It was followed by an excited cry from Rohit. 'Mama, see what I have brought.' I was making fruit-milk-shake for him in the kitchen. 'Coming darling. Go and wash your hand and feet first,' I called back loudly over the sound of the whirring juice blender.

My husband had asked me and Rohit to get ready by six thirty. It was the evening of thirty first December and we were to attend a New year Eve dinner party at his club. I was in a hurry to wrap up the remaining kitchen-chores and make the milk-shake for Rohit.

'You come here first and take a look…' Rohit shouted back. I switched off the blender and scuttled out of the kitchen, curious to know what made him so excited.

'What is it?' I asked and saw the thing he was

clutching in his small arms almost simultaneously. It was a baby animal… perhaps a puppy, looking white and soft as a curled ball of cotton wool. The two other kids too looked eagerly at the thing cuddled up in Rohit's arms. All three pairs of eyes were sparkling with the joy of making a rare discovery.

'What is that? Didn't papa ask you to get ready by six thirty? What have you been doing till this late?

Very carefully, as if he was handling an expensive and very fragile piece of glass, Rohit put the thing down and raised his eyes gleaming with a beatific smile to watch my reaction. I looked at the tiny creature. It was a kitten, hardly a week old. So soft that I was afraid that it will be crumpled even at a light touch from my hand. The kitten was all white except for a deep black spot under its tiny nose.

'It is a milk-sucking newborn. Why did you take it away from its mother?' I asked.

'I will feed it milk in a bottle Mama. We will get a feeding bottle for it. And we will celebrate its birthday tomorrow on the New Year.' Rohit urged. I did not have the heart to get angry with him so keen was he on keeping the kitten. 'But it is born a few days before,' I smiled amusedly. 'Why should we celebrate its birthday on the New Year Day?'

'Because it will be admitted into our family as a new member on that day. Please Mama! Do not say no!' Rohit implored, his small delicate arms encircling my waist.

'Ok. Ok. Now go and get yourself washed and have your milkshake. Let me think where we will keep it tonight when we will be away for the party. I will call Mina to get an old feeding bottle of her son. We will manage for the time being with that. Tomorrow we will make some permanent arrangement.' 'Love you Mama,' Rohit ran towards the washroom. I asked the other two kids to go back to their homes and come the next day to celebrate the kitten's birthday.

Slumped on the cold floor the kitten looked as if it had no life in it. But the gentle rise and fall in its body testified to the fact that it was breathing. There was no one in the drawing room now.

I squatted down on the floor close to the creature and squinted at its face. It seemed I had known this tiny animal closely, and long since. As if I had some intrinsic connection with it since years. And suddenly a long-forgotten name that had created an upheaval in my childhood came alive like a flash of lightning.

Domii!!

Now I realized why this baby cat looked so familiar. *It was an exact replica pf Domi... the same snow white furs and the same tiny black spot under the nose!!*

A small shiver, I was not sure whether of excitement, or happiness or of apprehension ran through me as I peered at the furry white ball of a creature lying still by the leg of a couch.

I clicked the number of Mina on my mobile

phone. 'Get me an old feeding bottle of your son, Mina and make it quick.'

Domi!

The forgotten days of childhood came back to me in an overwhelming onrush.

***

It was a day of celebration for me and my brother when Rani gave birth to four kittens under the drumstick tree at the far corner of our backyard. I was in class seventh and my elder brother was in class ten. Rani had been living with us for more than a year and was a great help in driving the notorious, obdurate rats away who damaged books and papers and ripped the clothes and quilts to tatters. That way Rani had become the favourite of all of us, especially my father. She too never hesitated to extract advantage of our love for her. She would settle stubbornly in front of the plate when any one of us sat down to eat and demand her share of food with an obstinate and constant mewing until some food especially fish, was put before her.

I was overjoyed when mother revealed that Rani was going to have babies. 'How many babies Ma and when?' I asked eagerly, finding it difficult to wait to see the baby cats. It was an effort to hold on to my patience. 'In a month,' mother said touching my head fondly. Rani was given fish almost every day, and a small bowl of milk. Days seemed to be dragging painfully slowly as I waited for the babies to arrive and then in one cool November morning, I woke up to the happy announcement of mother that Rani had given birth to four kittens. I jumped out of the bed and ran to the drumstick tree that stood aloof in one far corner of our backyard like an abandoned soul and looked. There she was! Rani, lying under the tree on a heap of ash, contentment in its half open eyes as the four kittens sucked at her udders as if they had been hungry for an eternity. I did not want to leave the spot and would have stood there for hours watching the babies curled up together in a grey and black bundle but for father's angry admonitions. My elder brother, concerned that the babies would catch cold put a piece of a torn blanket on that pulsating bundle.

The real problem came up when a robust and aggressive looking male cat made its disturbing appearance in our backyard. 'Male cats kill the newborn babies. We have to be careful.' Mother warned. So, I and my brother kept guard over the kittens outside of our school hours and father put them in the abandoned junk room at the far end wall of the backyard and bolted the door from outside preventing the entry of the male cat.

A month passed. I and my brother now fed the babies with bread and biscuits soaked in milk. The kittens grew up healthy and strong only except the smallest one who remained skinny and weak even with the healthy diets. They came out to the open to play in the back garden. It was one of their favourite sports to bit and scratch at one another. Sometimes they rolled about on the ground and over one another. At other times they would try to climb up the trunk of the drumstick tree clawing at the bark. It became an engaging pastime more for me than my brother to watch them playing, clawing and chasing one another.

'Two are male and the other two are female..' mother said. 'I will name them Ma, I claimed. 'I have already thought of the names,' Father smiled fondly. 'And what will they be?" he asked. 'Romi and Domi for the two male ones and the female ones will be called Julie and Lily.' 'Nice names. So, we will call them by those names,' my brother remarked.

I liked them all though I was a bit disappointed at Lily's sickly physique. But it was Domi who had the lion's share of my love and concern. He was the healthiest and cutest amongst all four. He looked like a small bundle of glossy white fur, the whiteness enhanced by the contrasting tiny dark spot under his nose. He will run to me the moment I entered the front gate and twine itself around my legs wiggling its tiny, furry tail and making a soft purring sound. I would fling my schoolbag across the veranda and lift it up in my arms. 'You, naughty girl,' mother would yell at me. 'What are you doing? The dirt of its feet will soil your school uniform. The furs will get into your nose and mouth. Put it down and get yourself washed clean with Dettol and water.' I would not listen to mother and run about the front yard cradling Domi in my arms. After that I would put a bowl of milk before it. I would not budge until he had licked away the last drop of milk. I would change my school uniform, wash myself and sit down to eat only after he had finished his milk.

***

I and my brother spent the whole of the Christmas vacation playing with the four of them. Mother made delicacies at home on the new year day. It was one of the best New Year Day in my entire childhood as far as I could remember.

I was more indulgent in my love and care, especially for Domi, than my brother who seemed to have developed an interest in Romi. The school reopened after the vacation and I had to go to school leaving Domi alone for about six hours a day. And he would circle around me happily licking at my legs and purring nonstop when I returned.

Another month passed.

One day Romi did not show up at the meal time. He was not there in the backyard nor was he found roaming about the house as he always did. Romi was my brother's pet and he was expected to quell the anxiety.

'Where is Romi?' Father asked my brother who sat burying his head in a book, apparently oblivious to the commotion relating to Romi's absence.

'Bibhu had taken him to his home. He replied without looking at father. 'Taken him? Why? Where does Bibhu live?'

Brother did not say a word.

'I am asking you.' Father demanded. 'Where does this Bibhu live? Why have you given Romi to him?'

'He gave me twenty rupees and took Romi away. He wanted to keep it.' Brother said at last, in a voice that quavered in fear.'

'You have sold it for twenty rupees?' Father stared at brother. 'What a despicable act!! Why did you take money from him? Where did you learn making such deals? He can keep Romi if he promises to take good care of it. Give the twenty rupees back to him first thing when you meet him tomorrow. No body in our family sells animals this way, and get that deep into your thick skull.' Father stamped away.

'How could you sell Romi, bhai? I asked accusingly.

'Now, don't you get started. Mind your own business. Take Domi to your in-laws' house as your bridal gift.' Brother sneered.

I did not like to argue with my brother.

The three other cats were growing up fast. Julie looked cute with the small brown patches on her white skin. Even Lily was beginning to look glossy despite her black sin. But it was Domi who was the cutest amongst all and had the maximum claim over my love. Julie was now spending most of her time in another Bengali family living in the neighbourhood. 'That Julie has a preference for fish, ' father remarked laughing. 'She has chosen to live closer to the Bengali family because they fed her fish every day.' I did not mind Romi or Julie leaving home. I did not bother much about 'Lily the blackie' too. It was Domi that my mind was totally focused on. Except for that six or seven hours spent at school I kept Domi by my side all through the day. He sat by my leg when I studied and ate from my hand. Given a choice and the chance I would never have let Domi out of my sight even for a moment. 'That cat had cast some magic on this girl.' Mother would complain thoroughly vexed when I put Domi on my bed while I studied. 'It is shedding furs everywhere contaminating the bed and the clothes. Keep it out of the bedroom.' I did not pay much heed to her admonitions. I knew she too liked Domi and would not want to harm him in any manner.

'You were perhaps a cat in your previous birth, and was somehow related to Domi's family.' Megha, my friend teased. 'Why talk of previous life?' Ginny joined, 'She will be changed into a cat in this life. Look at her eyes, they have become round in shape and green-tinged; her teeth are getting sharp and pointed like those of a cat. You will one day hear her mewing during the roll call and the teacher would wonder how a cat has entered the classroom.' And all of them would laugh boisterously at the joke. My face flushed in anger and embarrassment. 'I won't speak to you if you say such things.' I retaliated. Then they would coax me. 'It was just a joke dearie' don't be so serious.'

'But it is true that your Domi loves you a lot, just the way you love it.' Ginny said sincerely.

***

My annual examination was drawing near. I had to attend tuitions and extra classes. Father warned me not to while away time playing with Domi and to focus more on my studies. Domi seemed to understand the seriousness of the situation and kept himself a bit aloof. He was growing up fast and was now roaming about in the neighbourhood during most part of the day. But he would never miss to greet me with his soft purring and wagging of tail whenever I came in from outside and would not deviate from his routine of eating out of my hand every night and sleeping on the foot-mat by the bed.

The annual examination was finally over. I was relieved and happy that there would be no time restrictions for playing with Domi. But Domi was now more interested to play outside. Often, I had to take him outside the front gate while he scampered about here and there, excited at exploring the world beyond the big iron gate. I stood by the gate chatting with the girl who lived next door but studied in a different school. But my gaze followed Domi constantly, never letting him out of sight. It was early summer and the warm breeze blowing from south made the afternoons pleasant. I would come back with Domi before the sun set and close the gate behind us.

I had joined a private tuition center for an advance study of the next year's course. The timing of the tuition class was from morning seven to eleven. As usual Domi would wait for me on the inner side of the iron gate and would instinctively know when I reached and begin mewing and purring and would twine itself around my legs the moment I stepped inside.

My school reopened after the summer vacation. It was monsoon time and rained most of the days. Domi did not prefer to go outside the gate when it rained. He would squat on the heavy doormat closing his eyes, enjoying the warmth of the mat. My brother was now in class eleven and was seriously preparing for the school finals. He had joined more than one coaching classes for different subjects and had not much time to spare for other engagements.

Days moved on.

And then Domi went missing.

***

That day it rained nonstop. I returned from school early. Domi was not there by the gate. It was obvious since there was water all around and the ground was sloshy. I came inside and stepped on to the veranda. Domi was not there on the doormat. My eyes roved around searching for him. May be he was somewhere inside, or in the kitchen with Ma. I walked to the kitchen. Ma was busy cooking some afternoon snack. Domi was not around. 'Where is Domi?' I asked mother, anxiety dripping from my voice.

'It must be somewhere around. Why are you so worried? Get changed. I am making fritters and chutney.'

I had lost interest in fritters now, though it was one of my choicest snacks and more so in the wet climate. My mind filled with premonitions. I searched all the rooms and also the abandoned shed adjoining the far wall of the backyard even though Domi never goes there. Domi was not found after a frantic search of half an hour or so. Where had he disappeared? I slumped down on the bench that stood against the wall of the inner veranda, still in my damp school uniform. Helpless tears ran down my eyes. Mother came out of the kitchen to soothe me. 'He may be somewhere in the neighbourhood and will come back when it gets dark. He is growing up and does not like to remain confined inside the house. Come on, get changed and have something to eat.

'I will not eat until Domi comes back,' I whimpered. 'Don't behave like a two-year old,' mother snapped. He will come back.'

But Domi did not come back. Father returned from office and brother from the coaching class. 'Perhaps he had taken shelter in someone's house,' Father said trying to explain Domi's unexpected disappearance but there was no conviction in his voice. He stroked my head. 'Let us wait for the night. He will surely come back in the morning.'

Mother's reasonings and father's assurances did not do much to quell my fear. I knew instinctively that Domi would never return. I could not eat even a morsel of food that night despite my parents' coaxing. I lay down in the bed staring into the darkness, my thoughts around Domi. Where must he be? What had happened to him? Did he come under an automobile? I tried desperately to fight the frightening thoughts away but they came creeping back, haunting my sleepless night, making me tremble all over.

After a seemingly endless night, the dawn broke. I climbed off the bed and ran down to the gate. There was no sign of Domi. I woke up my father and implored him to go searching for Domi.

'I shall come with you,' I urged father as he mounted his bicycle.

''There is no need for you to wander around with me. I will search every possible place where he could be.' He assured me.

'Possible place? What possible place is there for little Domi to go? He had hardly crossed past the front gate in months,' I wanted to cry out loudly. But no sound came out of my mouth that felt dry as if it was filled with sands.

Father returned around midday. He looked tired and drained out. He must have been moving around in the sun searching for Domi. I was waiting impatiently without taking my breakfast. I ran to the front gate as he opened it. He cast a lingering glance at me before he turned back to close the gate. The sadness and frustration in his eyes answered the question before I voiced it. I had nothing to ask now. I heaved my stiff legs back to the front veranda and sat down on the bench staring blankly at the heavy foot mat where Domi used to squat and dose dreaming of some happy hunting grounds where he chased elusive grasshoppers.

'Somebody must have taken him,' mother said.

'Could be. He is a cute one.' Father agreed.

My tears had congealed into a lump that stuck at my throat that obstructed the swallowing of the food. It was a torture to sit by the plate and go with the pretense of eating while my whole body revolted at the sight of food.

'I will go again in the afternoon and search some more places. Eat properly and stop worrying. Cats and dogs always remember the way to their homes. Domi too will come back in a day or two.' Father said consolingly.

The search in the afternoon yielded no result as it did not in the morning. The only hope rested on Domi's choice and chance to make a voluntary return.

***

It was on the third night after Domi had gone missing that the fever came. My head ached like someone was hitting it with a sledge hammer. And there was a violent churning in my stomach which made me throw up whatever little I had eaten in the evening. Then came the rigors, shaking me from head to feet. One moment my body felt as if it was set on fire, and the next I was drenched all over in sweat. I moaned and whimpered and blabbered and my own voice sounded strange to me.

'I am getting Doctor Sinha,' I heard father saying. I could hear mother saying something but could not make out what it was. I shut my eyes tightly and there he was!! Domi!

Perched comfortably on the edge of the compound wall, looking at me with his round greenish eyes, mewing loudly. I wondered how could he climb up the high wall.

'Come down you silly cat,' I shouted 'Or you will fall and hurt yourself.'

I heard mother's voice.. 'Calm down my baby,' Everything will be fine. The doctor will be here in a minute.

Then I heard voices. May be, it was my father speaking. There was another voice that sounded unfamiliar. I wanted to make out who could that be but my head reeled. I felt something cool and heard pressed to my chest and a hand trying to lift my eyelids.

And then there was Domi again, running along a partially deserted street. I ran after him but he ran very fast as if trying to escape me. A vicious looking dog emerged from a large gate of a bungalow on the roadside and began to chase Domi. 'Hey you, stop.' I screamed but the dog pounced upon Domi who mewed frantically. I ran towards him as fast as my legs could carry me. But by that time Domi was mauled so badly that he was reduced to a crumpled ball of red and white. I began to tremble uncontrollably and then someone put a big blanket on me suffocating me. There were voices everywhere, low and gentle at first then rising to a crescendo threatening to burst open my eardrums. I felt a prick just above my hip and the sounds died down almost immediately. I saw myself in the park near my school. Domi springing and bouncing around chasing the tiny birds that came swooping down from the trees. I laughed out loudly. And then Domi was gone. The park had vanished too. I was in a vast desert standing alone, my throat burning in thirst.

Something that felt cool and wet was placed on my forehead. Once again I felt the prick at the right side above my hip. I felt relaxed and light as if something weighing a ton was taken off my head. I was feeling sleepy and the noise around me had subsided.

***

A bird, a koyal probably, cooed in a distance. My body was no longer burning. The thirst had gone too. I liked the bird's song and wished it would never stop cooing. A soft hand touched my forehead. A cool, glass filament like object was thrust under my tongue. 'Normal. The fever is gone. She is fine now. The weakness will go in a few days.' someone said. I was feeling hungry. 'Ma I am hungry.' I said feebly. 'Yes, darling,' mother's voice glistened with tears. I was made to sit on the bed propped up against pillows and mother fed me some semi-solid thing that was a blend of salty and sweet. It tasted good. Then mother adjusted the pillows and lay me down straight. 'Enough of your antics,' I heard my brother saying, sounding happy and relieved. 'Now be a good girl and get back to your routine,' he added. I wanted to smile at him but my lips felt stiff and dry. I shut my eyes.

I found myself in a garden of exotic flowers. Birds chirped and a cool breeze blew from the south. I sat on a bench and watched small kids darting around, chasing the butterflies. Then I saw Ginny and Megha in the swing laughing happily. They waved animatedly at me. I wanted to play with them but had no strength to get up from the bench. But I was feeling happy and relaxed and hungry again.

***

'You had given all of us a fright, sis!' my brother said. I had recovered fully now and had resumed my routine. Surprisingly enough no one in my family mentioned Domi, and still more surprising was that I had stopped missing him. I seemed to have lost interest in Domi somehow and any other pet animal for that matter. I could feel that a change had come over me.

***

Days turned into months and months into years. My brother had joined college after completing school. I was in my final year at school and was heavily preoccupied with my studies. During the months before the pre-board examination, I, Ginny and Megha were attending different coaching classes for different subjects.

'Hey! Look at that.' Megha said, her voice loud with surprise and excitement. I and Ginny turned almost simultaneously to look at the object she pointed at. It was a big sized cat, perhaps a male one, with very white furs and a deep black spot under its nose.

'Doesn't it look exactly like your Domi?' Megha asked, sounding enthusiastic.

I glanced at the big cat. It waddled towards me confidently as if it knew me before. I stepped back. 'Hey, get back', I said and began to move faster.

'What happened dear?' Ginny asked me. 'You should have been happy that Domi has returned. It has grown up but it still remembers you.'

'Yes, it could be Domi. Often the people and things we love a lot and are separated from by compelling circumstances, return to us acquiring new looks and shapes. Like it happens in the story of 'Kafka and the Doll' we read last year. Perhaps your Domi was travelling around, exploring the world and now has come back.' Megha added.

I stared hard at the big white cat.

Domi?

Could it really be Domi?

What is the big deal even if it was Domi? I did not want to fall into that kind of temptation any longer. Love, whether it is for people or animals and birds, or even plants, always brings pain. The cat looked a little like Domi but I decided to believe it was a different cat. Love had not returned to me like it did to the girl in the story of Kafka and the Doll. Nor was I deluded by the semblance of Domi this cat carried in its looks.

'Forget it. I do not like this cat even if it looks like a bigger version of Domi. Ma will get worried if I am late.' I pulled Megha by her hand and strode forward, Ginny at our heels. After we had walked about a couple of meters, I stole a glance behind. The cat was gone. A sigh of relief escaped me. 'I was right. It was not Domi.' The incident of meeting a big cat that resembled Domi was soon forgotten.

And time moved relentlessly on.

***

And after years, my son had brought me a replica of Domi! What an amazing new year gift!! I remembered the story of Kafka and the Little Girl's Doll and the famous lines

'Everything you love will probably be lost, but in the end, love will return in another way.'

I was no longer ashamed to admit that Domi had never gone out of my mind. I was just pretending to reason with myself that I had lost interest in him. I was shocked to see the big white cat which Megha announced to be the bigger Domi. I had secretly believed in Megha and that was the reason why I boldly denounced her assumption. The sight of the tiny snow-white cat my son had picked up and which looked like a mirror image of the Domi I had lost years ago was like the doll in Kafka's story, …. a thing loved earnestly and lost! But love had returned in another way.

It was the best New Year Gift for me.

'Shall we name it Domi?' I asked Rohit that evening as I was dressing him up for the New Year Eve party. 'Why, yes mama,' Rohit exclaimed happily. 'That is such a cute name. Do you like the kitten, mama?'

'Very much!' I smiled and kissed his forehead.

FAN

Rationalization may be defined as self-deception by reasoning...

Karen Horney

'What is it?'

I looked questioningly at Lakshmi who stood in my front, holding her head down.

'I want to ask something from you, Ma, if you do not mind.' She said looking like an image of abject humility, her eyes downcast.

'Here, look at me,' I said. Do you need an advance on your salary?' I was now feeling pretty sure that she needed money. Now that Raju has returned, she might be in need of some extra money for refurnishing her house, or cook some of her special dishes for him.

It was, however not unusual for her to ask for an advance on her salary. In fact, she had always been in a bad need for money when her sons, Krishna and Raju were small kids. 'You deduct the amount from my salary Ma' she would say on every such occasion but I never adjusted it from her salary nor did she insist on that. But she had stopped asking for money for the last few years, since her elder son Krishna had started working at the construction sites and her husband had overcome his drinking spree in a reasonable degree. It is not about an advance Ma,' she muttered, fidgeting with the end of her saree uncomfortably.

'Not an advance? Then what is it?' It was now difficult for me to suppress the suspense mounting within.

'Raju wants your cassette player for a day.' She mumbled, looking pathetic and absurd in her embarrassment.

'Cassette player? You mean the DVD player?' I asked, very surprised now.

She nodded without a word.

***

Lakshmi was with me for about one and a half decade, since my younger son was only two months old. The period of my maternity leave had expired and my mother-in-law who had arrived from village for the delivery of the baby was anxious to go back. I was desperately looking for a babysitter cum nursemaid to take care of my infant son in my absence. My elder son, who was a little above six at that time and was in class two also needed someone to be present at home when he returned from school at about two in the afternoon, to help him with changing his uniform and to feed him lunch. These days one can post a job offer for such posts in the social media and could afford to be selective. It was not so at that time. One had to explore difficult possibilities for finding out a trustworthy house-help or a nursemaid. I had requested my friends, colleagues and other contacts to search for a good babysitter who could also look after my elder son. I was ready to make all possible compromises on the financial front.

And then one of my South-Indian colleagues discovered Lakshmi for me. She lived in a slum that was at a little distance away from my home with her husband and two sons. 'My housemaid told me about her today,' my colleague said. 'She happens to be a good, trustworthy woman. Her husband is a rickshaw puller. But he squanders whatever he earned during the day in the local liquor shop in the evening. Instead of shouldering the responsibilities of his family of a wife and two kid sons the drink-sodden villain tortures the wife when she refuses to part with the meagre sum she saves from her own paltry earning The poor woman works in houses of people as a housemaid and feeds her children with whatever little she earned from that. Now she finds working with different households strenuous and taxing and looks for a fulltime job in a single family. I have asked her to meet you. I think she will be, for the time being, the best solution to your problems.' She remarked.

The news helped a lot to relieve the desperateness I was living my days through. And then Lakshmi made her entry to my house like a godsend.

She came as a housemaid but later became

more than a member of the family. She not only took charge of the cooking and cleaning but she became a caring nursemaid for my younger son.

Years rolled by and my sons also grew up. I could not remember an occasion when Lakshmi had given me a reason to be dissatisfied with her or distrust her.

She had proved her worth and dependability in all these years and had become indispensable for our family. It was because of her I could discharge the parallel responsibility of taking care of my family and becoming a sincere employee of the office successfully.

My younger son had become four and I had got him admitted in school. Lakshmi's husband, Ramu, despite his addiction to liquor, was a good man when he was not under the influence of alcohol. Most of the days he took my son to school in his rickshaw and I brought him back while returning from office. My elder son rode to his school and to his coaching center on his bicycle. But on the afternoons when it rained, Ramu took my elder son to the coaching center in his rickshaw and brought him back home in time in the evening.

There was no computer or internet those days. No question of visiting countless social media sites like people do at present. Children used to play outdoor games like football, cricket, hide and seek and kabaddi after school hours. The one luxury we had at home was a Video Cassette Recorder, shortened as VCR where my children watched cartoon shows like Tom and Jerry and Donald Duck and Pop Eye. In the leisure time, which was very rare for me and my husband, we watched a movie.

On the festive occasions like the Dusshera and Diwali or Makar Samkranti the friends of my sons, living in the neighbourhood, gathered in our house to watch movies and cartoon shows. I asked Lakshmi to bring her sons too. The elder one Krishna, who studied in a nearby a vernacular school was a docile and shy boy. He would sit in front of the television watching the cartoon show or the movie silently while others jumped and hopped and squealed and made my drawing room a bedlam. But Lakshmi's younger son was a keen movie watcher. He would goggle at the screen, fascinated, the contours of his face changing keeping pace with the shifting scenes and actions. He was very fond of Telugu movies, and especially the movies of Cheeranjivi, the famous South Indian hero. He was some five years older than my younger son but much advanced in his knowledge of cinema. Given a chance, the boy would gurgle out a detailed account of the names of Cheeranjivi movies and the songs too.

Raju was about nine at that time, and my younger son was a few months under five.

'My Raju is very cooperative,' Lakshmi would say at times. Her eyes would go soft when she spoke about her cinephile younger son. 'He never complains if there is no curry to go with the rice. Give him one big green-chilly. He would hold it in his left hand and finish his bowl of soaked rice just looking at it.

'Just by looking at it?' My elder son who was very fastidious and choosy about food and always troubled me on account of that, would ask in surprise. I had to hold an amused smile in check fearing it would offend Lakshmi. 'But he has just this one flaw,' she would add, 'whenever a Cheeranjivi movie runs in a cinema hall he will pester me to let him watch it. He is not old enough to be sent alone to watch a movie. So, I ask the son of my husband's brother, to take Raju with him. Obviously, I have to pay for both the tickets.'

'Anna,' Raju would entreat my elder son. 'Please play a Chiranjeevi movie on the VCR.' My sons, who did not understand much Telugu, nor the scrolling English subtitles, got easily bored, but not Raju. He would sit there, his gaze fastened to the screen, his body stiffening and relaxing from time to time as the movie progressed. He would not budge from his place before the television until and unless Lakshmi admonished him and pulled him away and took him home with her.

Time moved on.

My elder son, after the completion of higher secondary was doing his pre graduation course in the college and the younger one was in class nine at school. Raju too had grown up and was doing sundry jobs at different places, sometimes as a helping boy in a motor garage, a waiter at a tea stall and things like that. Krishna worked at different construction sites as a daily wager and earned good money. Lakshmi, now, no longer lived in financial constraint. Even her alcoholic husband Ramu, was now having a pretty well income from rickshaw -pulling. But Lakshmi still was with us, a dedicated and committed house-help as she had always been.

It was a fine, sunny morning of early winter. I and my husband were sipping our morning tea from steaming cups when Lakshmi ran in, disheveled and breathless, tears streaming down her eyes.

'I sprang up to my feet. 'What happened? Why are you so upset?' I asked in a quavering voice. My husband, too looked at Lakshmi in concern. 'Something has happened to Ramu?" he asked Lakshmi. 'No baboo,' Lakshmi swallowed a sob. 'It is Raju.'

'Raju? What about him? Is he sick or something?'

'He has run away.' Lakshmi blurted out through convulsive sobs.

'Where?' Why?' I and my husband asked at the same time.

'He has written a letter mentioning that he is going to Chennai to try his luck in Telugu movies.'

I stared at Lakshmi in shock and disbelief. 'Chennai? Alone?'

'What I am going to do now Ma?' Lakshmi sobbed uncontrollably. I solaced her and promised her to find some news about Raju using the help of some of my contacts at Chennai. She calmed down after a long time.

I was in luck. The brother of one of my colleagues had a friend who worked as a cameraman in a film studio at Chennai. He tracked down Raju after a lot of effort who, he said kept visiting studios, meeting the agents, seeking roles in a movie. Raju had not succeeded yet in achieving his purpose, but was pursuing his goal with some sort of a devout tenacity. He had met Raju and asked him to go back home, but Raju had made up his mind to settle at Chennai and seek a role, however small and insignificant, in a Cheeranjivi starred movie. He had written a short letter to his mother mentioning his purpose and asked her not to be sad.

After about a year the next letter came from Raju. He was now driving an autorickshaw, Raju wrote and was still pursuing his goal. He had not given up hope nor his determination was shaken in a bit.

Lakshmi and Ramu had got over the initial shock and had let their lives fall in a pattern. She came to our house routinely, did her chores, gossiped and sipped tea. Ramu pulled rickshaw and Krishna worked as an assistant to the chief mason at a construction site.

My elder son was now studying medicine in another city, and my younger son had joined a reputed college in our hometown and was doing his pre-graduation.

***

And then, in another fine, warm morning of

early summer Lakshmi came much before her usual time. 'What is the matter, Lakshmi?' I asked curious to know the reason that brought her here at that unexpected hour. Her tired, dull face lit up with a smile. Without her saying so I could immediately guess that she had some good news about Raju. 'Is it Raju?' I asked.

'He has come back.' The hard lines in her face dissipated giving it a delicate look as she said it.

'Is it?' I was so happy that I took Lakshmi in my arms, 'When?'

'Last night.'

It is such a good news, ' I exclaimed excitedly. 'Ask him to come and meet me.'

'I will, Ma,' Lakshmi said and stood holding her head down.

'What is it?' I asked. Feeling oddly curious since she kept standing there instead of going back to her house.

'Do you want to say something else, Lakshmi? Need an advance?' I asked sensing instinctively that she had something more to say. And finally, after a little persuasion she came out with her request to borrow our DVD player for one evening.

We had in the meantime got rid of the old VCR and bought a fancy DVD player at the demand of the children whose choice had gone past the cartoon shows to the Science Fiction movies in English.

'It is alright Lakshmi,' I said, conciliatorily, 'it is not a problem. Why must you feel so guilty about it? You know you are like a family member. So are Krishna and Raju. But Raju can always come here and watch movies on our coloured television. It has a large screen too. You have a small black and white TV. Tell Raju that he can come with his friends and watch the movie or anything else he wants to watch, here. You can, of course, take the DVD player if he feels shy or uncomfortable to do so.'

'Raju wants to watch a recent Cheeranjivi starred movie.' Lakshmi said, still a bit contrite.

'What's new about it? He has been a great fan of Cheeranjivi since he was a child.' I said pleasantly and smiled to allay her embarrassment.

Lakshmi did not say anything. 'Is it a special movie?' I asked.

Lakshmi nodded, still looking down. 'He says he has acted in it.'

I stared at her, speechless for a brief moment, letting the words sink in.

'Is it? What a marvellous piece of news!' I said, overjoyed. 'What do you say? Our Raju has finally succeeded in his mission and has acted in a movie, that too a Cheeranjivi-starrer! How did this miracle happen?'

Lakshmi's embarrassment was ebbing slowly away. Finally, she came out with the whole story. She said that Raju had approached a number of film agents in Chennai but everywhere had confronted disappointment. Some agents had suggested him to make an acting portfolio. Raju had used all the money he had taken from home in doing the photoshoots. When he was utterly broke, a friend, who too was struggling for a livelihood at the city, and slept in the same dormitory, arranged for him the job of an autorickshaw driver. Raju was in luck and earned well from driving the autorickshaw. He had saved a reasonable amount in a few months. But he had not given up hope and kept approaching the agents and smalltime movie directors. One agent, out of sympathy had helped him join an acting school and recommended him to the director while Raju was doing a two-years course at the school. The film agents were picking up students from different acting schools for performing small roles in the movies from time to time. The payment was small but could not deter them from their pursuit. The agent who had suggested Raju's name to a director had finally selected him for performing a small role in a big budget movie with Cheeranjivi as the hero. Raju's dream had finally come true. It was this lifetime chance he had been waiting for all these years. This movie is released last week and Raju has not watched it. They have paid him five thousand and he had decided to come home with this surprise.' Lakshmi paused. There was a brief silence.

'Great!' I said, feeling happy more for Lakshmi that her son. Acting or no acting, he had learned, though in a hard way how to earn money in an unfamiliar, apathetic city. He, at this young age, had learned the art of facing life alone and deal with its adversities on his own.

I asked Lakshmi and Krishna to shift all heavy furniture in our drawing room to the hall, making space on the floor in front of the television, leaving back only a long settee. I asked my elder son Sonu, who had come home on a brief vacation, to bring some snacks. After all, munching popcorns and fritters add an extra charm to the joy of movie watching. My sons, especially the younger Monu, was bursting with enthusiasm at the prospect of seeing Raju on the silver screen.

At about four in the afternoon some friends of Sonu and Monu, who lived in our street made their entry to our house in ones and twos. After a few minutes Lakshmi and Krishna wandered in, followed by a shy looking Raju. Raju was no longer the skinny boy who sat wide-eyed in front of our television watching Tom and Jerry and squealing in joy at the funny gestures the characters made. He had grown up to be a handsome young man, though the faint hard lines on his face that testified to how he must have struggled to survive in a strange place, gave it a slightly matured look. He touched my feet, and I ran my hand affectionately on his head. 'Arey Raju, you have become a big boy now! And a movie actor.' I said fondly. He gave a brief smile, and touched the strand of hair behind his left temple shyly.

'Come on in!' I opened the door wider to let him in.

A few young boys of the slum where Lakshmi lived and were Raju's childhood friends too brisked in laughing and talking loudly. After everyone took their seats in front of the TV set my son took the CD of the movie from Raju and inserted it in the DVD player. A hushed but electrifying excitement hung in the air of our drawing room. I turned to look behind and found Ramu standing quietly by one of the pillars in the porch adjacent to the drawing room. I motioned him to come in but he shook his head. The movie began. All eyes were riveted on the screen.

It was a good action thriller and soon the young mass was watching it in rapt attention captivated by the incredible chutzpa of the swashbuckling hero and the charms exuded by stunning south Indian heroine. 'When will your scene come, Raju?' my son Monu, asked unable to hold back his curiosity.

'Sometime later, in a song. The third song perhaps. It will come after the interval.' Raju said.

Most of the spectators had now forgotten they had come to see their Raju on the screen and were totally gripped by the thrill and excitement of the noisy fights and the scintillating romance.

The word 'Intermission' flashed boldly on the screen.

The movie resumed after a brief commercial. The plot was getting more and more complex and serious. The acting of the veteran hero Cheeranjivi had made us keep our eyes glued to the screen.

The eager spectators were so involved that they had, it appeared to me, forgotten why they were watching the movie. And then Raju said, 'the song will come after this fight scene.' Every one became alert instantly.

The song began. It was picturized on the hero and a group of co dancers as it mostly happens in the movies of modern times. 'I am one of them,' Raju said proudly pointing to the group of dancers that skillfully emulated the steps of the hero. The co-dancers of the hero, in the first cut were clad uniformly in red and yellow sherwanis, and turbans. In the next they were in skintight jeans and snazzy tops. Their costumes kept changing as the song progressed.

We waited, holding our breath, for a close up of Raju. But the camera focused most of the time on the hero. It swept past the dancers from time to time resting for brief moments on the face of different dancers but it was not possible to identify Raju from the crowd. 'Which one of them are you, Raju,' Monu asked, his enthusiasm giving way to impatience. 'They all look alike.' 'The third one from the right, with the purple turban,' Raju said, not taking his eyes off the screen. 'Where? I can't see you?' Monu prodded him. 'Watch quietly,' Sonu, my elder son, who had grown reasonably sensible, pressed Monu's shoulder lightly, forbidding him from querying further. 'Yes, yes, I can see him, the third one from the right. It is my Raju alright.' Lakshmi exclaimed, her voice wet and suffused with joy and excitement. I turned to look at Ramu who was still standing by the pillar by the steps that went down to the porch. There was a sparkle in his eyes. The song ended. Raju turned at the spectators, his face beaming and let his proud glance sweep past the eager faces. I could notice some of the boys looked vaguely skeptical. Some of them exchanged curious glances, as if they were not sure enough about what they were asked to believe.

Sonu embraced Raju. 'That was a great performance, Raju. You can really dance well.' He said effusively. 'You are so lucky to have this chance to perform with the hero you are such a great fan of.' He added.

'Wow, Raju, when did you learn to dance so nicely?' I patted Raju fondly. Tears of joy were streaming down Lakshmi's eyes. Ramu's freckled face was lit up with a wide smile. Monu looked at his elder brother dubiously. He was about to say something, but fought it off at the stern look in Sonu's eyes.

The boys requested Sonu to replay the song. After it was replayed two times the doubt that haunted them had eased out considerably and they too were abuzz in their admiration of Raju.

The movie finally came to an end and the audience dispersed. 'Well, Lakshmi aunty, how are you going to celebrate?' Sonu asked. 'Rice and chicken curry.' Krishna laughed. Lakshmi swept and cleaned up the drawing room and left. Sonu gave Raju a fond smack on his back as he was moving out of the door. 'Congratulations, buddy,' he said. 'Your dream has been fulfilled at last. Not everyone is lucky like you.' Raju grabbed Sonu's hand affectionately. 'That is so sweet of you Anna,' he smiled politely and moved out to the street. He stopped, turned to look back and waved at Sonu and Monu. They waved back.

***

'Are you sure bhai, it was Raju?' Monu looked at Sonu across the dinner table, an incredulous look in his eyes. 'Yes,' Sonu said with emphasis and a finality.

'Forget it, both of you. Concentrate on eating.' I admonished. There was no more discussion on the topic.

My husband called from Hyderabad where he was on an official tour. 'Did you watch the movie where Raju featured? Tell me about it. Ramu and Lakshmi must be very excited. Weren't they?'

'Yes. I too am very happy to see our Raju performing. He danced like a professional. Sonu and Monu too were very excited.'

***

I lay on the bed gazing at the ceiling fan that whirred softly, thinking about the third young man from the right wearing a purple turban who danced with Cheeranjivi. Did he look like Raju? I wondered. 'Must be. If Raju says so.'

It was difficult even for me to identify him amidst all those dancers in similar costume. But I was very happy that the little Raju who was so understanding that he could finish a bowl of watered rice just looking at a green chilly he held in his left hand had finally proved his mettle. I was happy that this little fan of Cheeranjivi could make his dream come true with his dedicated pursuit.

I smiled to myself and closed my eyes.

ALWAYS YOURS

I love you without knowing how, or when, or from where.
I love you simply, without problem or pride...

Pablo Neruda

She looked up again at the sky. It was getting darker. The pale November sun, after struggling hard through the accumulating layers of clouds had finally given in and had gone into hiding. She will be in trouble if the school bus did not turn up in time, and the trouble will be multiplied twofold if the boy on the bicycle turned up before the school bus did and found her standing alone in the rain. She took a few steps back and squirmed under the asbestos gradient inclining over the porch of the small departmental store where she used to stand waiting for the school bus. She desperately wished she had not forgotten the umbrella, and wished more desperately for the boy on the bicycle not to show up. 'The rain will stop him,' she thought and wondered if she really wanted the boy not to show up. She was unable to decide. She felt her heart had been split into two, one part secretly expecting the boy to turn up and the other wishing, rather prudently, just its opposite.

It was a fortnight or so since she was seeing the boy. Almost every day. He would cruise past the departmental store by which she stood waiting for the bus. She knew instinctively that he came there to see her and was filled with apprehension. At the same time, deep inside her there lurked a secret, irrepressible curiosity to know about him. He would flick a naughty smile at her when their eyes met and pedal away, only to return and have another look at her. Her heart would beat erratically and sweat beads break out on the back of her neck when he swished past her, smiling that naughty lopsided smile.

A thunder rumbled startling her out of her thoughts. Then she saw him emerging out of the curve where the street turned to left. And almost at the same time the school bus slithered in. She hurried out of the porch as the bus made its brief stop and the boy on the bicycle squeezed himself between her and the steps of the bus she was about to climb, shoving a folded piece of paper into her hand, and rubbed past her in one quick, flitting movement. She clutched the piece of paper instinctively, not knowing what she was doing and why, and scrambled into the bus. Another thunder crashed overhead and the sky opened up pouring a torrent of rain down as she took a seat by her friend Mala. She cast a furtive glance out through the window glass now hazy with the splatters of rain.

The boy was there, astride on the bicycle, looking straight at her, drenching in the heavy downpour. Their eyes met for a fraction of a moment and the bus rolled forward.

***

The demography of the small, nondescript township comprised mainly of the two major communities that though belonged to separate religious cults, lived in peace and harmony with hardly any discrepancy or disagreement. They had been doing that for years, as their forefathers did until recently and had never had even an exchange of offensive remark. But times have changed and so too the minds. She had not much idea what exactly it was except that some unexpected and untoward incident which happened during the ceremonial immersion of the idol of Goddess Duga had led to a skirmish between the two communities. May be some act or remark of one group that was considered blasphemous by the other had scratched a cut on the flawless polish of professed brotherhood and tolerance. Every one guessed that a tension was brewing deep underneath but it was kept all hush hush. 'Be careful, Rupa,' her grandparents had warned her more than once. Do not roam around here and there with friends and come straight home from the school. There was, however, not a chance for whiling time away with friends since she commuted in the school bus. Hop into the bus that stopped at the departmental store at a quarter to ten and step out from it at the same spot at half past four in the afternoon. That was her routine--unvarying and undeviating.

She had spent most part of her schooling years in this town, with her parents and elder brother. Life was easy and cheerful with her maternal grandparents staying close by until her father got his order of posting in a city outside the state and her family shifted there leaving her with her grandparents. It was her final year at school and she was supposed to join them after the pre-board examination. 'It is just a question of a few months,' father said consoling her. 'Study seriously and do not trouble your grandparents. Ask uncle if you need anything special and never go to the market on your own.' There was no belying of the fact that she loved her grandparents and uncle but to stay away from her parents for months was an ordeal which she was not sure she could smoothly pass through because now she had to grapple with not just the tough syllabus of the final year and the long, laborious study hours but the frustration resulting from living away from her parents.

And now, adding to that, there was the boy on the bicycle.

He was, she admitted to herself gingerly, a handsome boy and looked decent. Every day he cycled past the spot where she stood waiting for the school bus but never came close or behaved in a way that would have seemed offensive. He just smiled at her and moved away without making any overtures.

The fear that haunted her in the beginning at the thought of seeing the boy was slowly replaced by an embarrassing shyness which gave way to curiosity. The boy seemed to have become a habit with her in the last fifteen days or so and she was beginning to miss him if he did not show up in time. She admitted to herself reluctantly and a bit guiltily too, that the pang of living away from her parents had lost its brunt in a remarkable degree after she had met him. Amazing!!

***

'Nasty weather,' Mala said, interrupting the flow of her thoughts. 'Rain in early winter! I would like to spend the day in bed, tucked under a blanket watching a movie. Won't you?'

'Oh yes.' She blurted out absently, her mind not registering much of what Mala said, her fingers tightening around the crumpled piece of paper the boy had shoved into her hand as she scrambled into the bus, desperately wanting to find a little solitude to take a look at it. 'What are you thinking?' Mala asked probingly, determined to hold her attention. Rupa did not have an immediate answer to that. 'About the growing tension between the two communities in our area.' She said for the sake of saying something.

'Why are you so serious about it? These are passing phases. Brief skirmishes and rows occur now and then during religious festivals but they do not take a serious turn. By the way did you watch the new movie? It is a historical romance. I watched it on my sister's phone... simply loved it' Mala's eyes sparkled as she mentioned the movie.

'Not yet,' she said distantly, her thoughts centring around the folded paper in her clammy grip.

***

She cast a furtive look around to ascertain no one was watching her and took out the piece of paper from the book of English prose where it lay hidden, pressed between a couple of pages. She put it on the book and smoothened it with her fingers. It looked like a page torn from a writing pad, glossy and a faded green in colour. There were only a few lines written on the paper that held the muted smell of some perfume. The boy had sprayed it on the paper, she guessed and ran her gaze on the contents, holding her breath.

'Dearest,' it began. 'I do not know how you will accept it but even as I tried my best, I could not resist the impulse to express my feelings on pen and paper. Neither you nor I have a mobile phone in our possession to make the communication easier. Hence this letter. I have no compunction in admitting that I have fallen in love with you on the very first day I saw you standing in the porch of that shop. You are the loveliest thing I have ever met. I do not want to ask you if you feel the same way about me. I would like to remain under the impression that you do. It is better this way. Love......lots and lots........

'A Y'

'A Y'?

What is A Y?

Must be the first and last letters of his name, she decided. There are a number of names beginning with the letter A and ending with Y. Is it Ajay? Atrey? Amiy? Abhay? ...She wracked her brain making guesses at the name of the boy. 'He wants to keep his name a secret,' she thought. 'As if I am dying to know his name…!' she said to herself and tucked the letter back between the pages of the book.

'Hey, Rupa, come here and join us.' One of her friends shouted from near the compound wall where they sat clustered gushing over the pictures of film stars in a movie magazine. She let out a deep breath and wandered over to the spot.

***

Several names beginning with the letter A and ending with Y came crowding into her mind as she lay in her bed that night, open eyed, ensnared in the magic of the words the boy wrote. Later when she finally slept, she dreamt of him.

He stood in the bright sunshine holding something like a small mirror that captured the reflection of the sun and turned it between his thumb and forefinger to make the light fall on her face. She hid her face with her hands to block the light and he laughed, a naughty, amused laughter.

She woke up, rubbing her eyes. The light of the morning sun that had climbed quite some distance up filtered into the room through the chinks of the window panels.

***

She left home earlier that day.

Her heart was beating unusually fast as she waited for the school bus.

Was she waiting for the school bus? Or the boy on the bicycle? The boy whose name begins with A and ends with Y. She asked herself. Did she or did not she wish to see him? A tricky question and she had no answer to that. Her reasoning mind advised her not to, but her heart was prodded on by an urge that was irresistible. It was all so confusing!

Then she saw him approaching, pedalling rather lazily, unhurriedly as if he knew she would be waiting for him. He flashed his naughty, playful smile at her as he rode past the shop, and her lips parted involuntarily in an answer. He rode on a few meters and then made a U-turn. Again, he smiled at her, and again she smiled back.

The bus rolled to a stop and she clambered into it hurriedly. She took a seat by the window and looked out. The boy stood at the same spot where she had been standing, his gaze fixed at the window of the bus. She turned her face away.

***

It rained again the next day. She stood in the porch of the shop. Rain in November is not unusual though. But it made the weather cold and bleak. She shivered a little. 'He will not venture out in the rain, 'she thoughts, feeling slightly disappointed.

Rain could be a magic at times as it was now… she wished to stand next to the boy whose name was AY, inhaling the wet earthy smell in the air, her body sipping in the warmth of his closeness. Her face flushed and she felt a hotness behind her ears as she imagined herself standing close to him in the rain. She tried to fight the thought off her mind.

And then she sighted him at the curve to the left of the street. He was in a raincoat, most part of his face hidden under the rainproof cap. He rode straight to the shop, got down the cycle and hurried into the shop without flicking a glance at her. 'Why didn't he look at me and smile?' She was surprised and felt ignored and that made her upset. She had come early today just to see a bit more of him, and here he was, behaving as if she was not there! She thought angrily and wished for the bus to reach soon. The boy strode out, carrying a polythene bag that looked stuffed, she guessed, may be with grocery items. He wandered over to her casually, careful not to rouse the interest of the man at the counter of the shop who looked out at the rain impassively, pushed a folded paper into her hand, and strode away, not stopping.

The bus rolled in lazily through the rain. She ran to the bus and got in, tightly clutching the folded paper he gave her.

***

'Love,

I will be waiting for you at the post office square at five in the afternoon tomorrow. The public library is at a few meters walk on the street that goes to the left from the square. We will go there. The library is a safe place to meet. Get down from the bus and walk in the opposite direction on the main road to reach the square. Can't wait to meet you.

AY'

She folded back the letter and tucked it between the pages of the same book where she had kept the earlier one. The English teacher was explaining the lines from a poem..

'all day the rain has glided, wave and mist and dream

drenching the gross and heather, a gossamer stream....

Yes, she was drenching in a gossamer stream ....of Love ..' she thought and smiled secretly.

***

'There had been a scuffle between two young men over a small accident. The accident was nothing serious. No one was hurt and no damage to either of the vehicles. But the two fellows had a heated exchange of offensive words. There was some angry mention of the earlier clash during the immersion of the goddess's idol last month, too. The hostility is lying dormant now but I fear it might surface any time. The tension is written large on people's faces.'

Her uncle announced on returning from the market.

'I am worried about Rupa,' her grandfather said. 'Of course, she is safe in the school. The school bus is okay, too. I am concerned how safe it is for her to walk down from the bus stoppage to the house. The distance is about two hundred meters or so.'

'That part of the road is safe. Not much crowded.' Her uncle said, trying to alleviate his father's fear. 'It is the market area that is most sensitive. Better to avoid crowded places till the issue is peacefully settled.'

'Better for her to stay out from school for a few days.' Grandmother said, looking worried.

'We are having extra classes for clarifying doubts,' She protested. 'I cannot afford to miss them.'

'It is all right.' Her uncle said. 'I will pick you up at the bus stop from today onwards.' She was dismayed. She had to meet AY at five in the afternoon. 'But I will be late today. Our last class is at four thirty..' she lied, not looking at her uncle.

'Well then. Do one thing. Make a call from your school phone to me before you start. I will reach at the stop to pick you up.' He wrote down his phone number on a piece of paper and gave it to her.

'I remember your number,' she said. 'Keep it.. in case you don't remember at the right time.'

'All right, uncle.' She said accepting the paper.

***

She got down from the bus at four thirty and walked to the porch of the shop. There was not much traffic on the street at that hour. The shop too was practically empty. No one was there in the counter. The boy who signed his name as

AY would be at the post office square by five. It would take her about eight to ten minutes to walk in the opposite direction on the road that led to her home to reach the post office square. She had to kill a little time somewhere before making a start. She looked around to decide where to wait. A few meters ahead of her, across the street there was a stationary shop that sold notebooks, pens and pencils and other such items. She had never visited that shop before. She decided the stationary shop would be the most ideal place to while away a few minutes and moved towards it. She bought a notebook and an inch scale though there was not much need of them. She started off exactly at four fifty and headed for the post office square.

She had walked not more than a hundred meters when she smelled the smoke in the air.

And in the next instant saw the thick columns of black smoke mushrooming up to the sky. 'Must be the municipality people. They have set fire to a heap of garbage on the roadside.' She thought and moved on. Then she heard the noise of glasses breaking and angry screams. A loud uproar accompanied by harsh, terrifying metallic rattle. She saw men and women running towards the direction she was walking from, panting hard. 'What is happening?' she inquired, feeling a frisson of fear. ' Run away to some safe place,' one woman who strode ahead pulling at the hand of her kid son warned her. 'They are setting fire to the vehicles and vandalizing the shops. Go back to your home, girl. Go back, at this very instant!' the woman ran away dragging along the kid.

She knew instinctively that she could not move any farther. It would be dangerous. She decided to return home, her heart heavy with a deep sadness.

Even as she turned to walk back home, she heard the heavy, trampling footfalls behind her and almost within a minute the street was thronged with men. An angry, ugly mass, who shouted and sloganeered in an ear-splitting cacophony. Some of them were brandishing sticks and batons and cycle chains.

She ran off the edge of the road and hid herself behind a massive tree. She stood there shaking from head to foot, her heart thumping, breathing in wild, scratchy gasps.

She did not know how but suddenly she was swept out from the shelter behind the tree and was flung into the tossing, rushing currents of a frenzied humanity. She struggled frantically to find a support to steady herself. But they were all around her, angry, shouting people, closing in on her, crushing and smothering her.

And before she was sucked in and was bludgeoned by the raving mob a hand pressed hard over her shoulder and pulled her out to the safety of a narrow alley branching off the right side of the road.

'Hop on the backseat,' the boy on the bicycle said in a voice throbbing in anxiety and urgency.

She stood undecided for a brief moment wondering what to do, caught in a terrible dilemma. 'Don't think so much. We must move out of this place fast.' He handed her a black scarf. 'Cover your head and face', he said impatiently and mounted the saddle seat. Finding no alternative, she obeyed him, wincing slightly at the discomfort of sitting on the bare bars of iron, not able to see properly where they were going, but not complaining. She did not know why but she trusted him and was confident that no harm would be brought to her when she was with him.

He rode up to a circuitous path, leading away from the main road, with almost no traffic. The noise faded away as they moved on. The dust-laden narrow street they rode along was fringed on both sides by wild hedge plants and sand patches. It curved to right abruptly at one point, and slithered to the old railway station. They rode on. There was not a soul in sight. It seemed all the people of the town had thronged in the market area and the post office square, fighting, vandalizing shops, setting fire to the vehicles which were trapped there, and shouting blasphemous slogans.

He stopped by a tiny, rundown place that was somewhere between a cabin and a shed located under the ramp of a pedestrian bridge that sloped down to an unpeopled platform, no longer in use. A few rusted bogies of an old engineless goods train stood on the track like a behemoth silhouetted against the darkening sky. She looked uncertainly at the cabin or if it could be called so, a room. It was a murky, derelict place, abandoned may be for months. They peered in. In the slowly inspissating darkness of the advancing evening they could just make out a stack of soiled and dusty benches against the back wall, which perhaps once were used in the railway coaches but now were rendered useless, their cushions peeping out brazenly from the slashed and torn out upholstery. There was perhaps a toilet adjacent to the place. The smell of urine assailed their nostrils with an outrageous impudence. But the place seemed a safe haven in the given situation. They stepped in, pressing their hands to their nose in a vain effort to hold back the stench. The gravels in the cracks on the cement floor grated and crunched under their feet as they walked guardedly inside.

***

They stood plastered to the damp, musty wall of the dingy room, in the thick, pulsating darkness, breathing hard. They stood quiet and stiff, afraid to make even the slightest noise, let alone talk, their hot breaths coiling and twisting together like a couple of snakes, and feeling each other's presence in an intimacy that was unfamiliar yet exciting. Some animal, may be a mouse or a mole went scurrying by her feet. She stifled a scream. The grip of the boy's hand on hers tightened in a gesture of assurance.

After a long time, may be half an hour, but which seemed like an eternity, they could hear the siren of the police vans followed by the sound of angry, shrill whistles at a distance.

More minutes passed. There was silence everywhere. Even the sound of the siren from the police vans had died away.

Cautiously, casting furtive looks around to ensure no one was there, they tiptoed out of the narrow, ramshackle room. A naked bulb that hung from a post at a few feet away from that old platform, scattered a dim light on a small patch of the deserted lane. The boy pulled out his bicycle that he had stood against an old, broken wall, hidden amidst wild growths of weeds and bushes. 'It seems safe now,' he whispered. 'Let's go.'

She watched him as he mounted the saddle seat. 'Climb on to the rear seat', he said. 'I will drop you at your home.'

'What is your name? She asked without making a move. Her voice was unsteady.

The boy chuckled into the darkness. 'Guess', he said naughtily.

'You signed AY. What does AY mean?' she asked again, persistent.

'AY for Always Yours.' The boy laughed shortly, reached out for her hand and pressed it lightly. 'Now get up on the bicycle,' he said dismissing the conversation. Perhaps he was still apprehensive and that was why did not want to talk much, she reasoned with herself.

Without protest she took her place on the carrier-seat at the back and they rode away from the place. She knew it was not the right time to wish so, but she wanted the ride to go on forever.

He stopped at the entrance of the by-lane that led to her grandparents' house. She got down as if stepping out of a dream, a 'gossamer stream' as in the poem, she thought, and strode ahead, repressing the blind urge to take a look back. She knew he was there, standing by his cycle, waiting to see she had reached home safely.

She saw her uncle and grandfather standing outside of the house, panicky and desperate. 'There she is,' her uncle ran towards her, her grandfather at his heels. In the next moment she was in the arms of her uncle. 'Oh God! Where were you dear? Are you alright? We were worried to death ...' He stroked her head as the questions gushed out of him unstoppably.

'Let her come inside first,' her grandfather said and cradling his arm around her led him into the house. Only then she cast a brief look behind and saw him riding past her house towards the main street.

***

She did not go to the school the next day. Not the day after. Her pre-board examination was drawing close and soon after the classes would remain suspended for enabling the students to prepare for the school finals.

'You will not commute by the school bus anymore. I will drop you at school and pick you back till the classes were dropped.' Her uncle announced. 'These are crucial times. Any untoward incident might happen any time. We cannot afford to take any risk now.'

Peace had returned to the town and everything had got back to normal in a week. But she was not allowed to go out anywhere alone, not even to the house of her friends for group studies.

She did not, could not, find a chance to meet the boy who called himself AY for once thereafter. Her pre board examination was over soon and she had to remain indoors preparing for her final examination. Her parents made a visit a week after.

'I have spoken to the college authorities there. There won't be any trouble in getting a seat in the science stream if you score just eighty percent in the finals. But I know you would do better than that. Do not worry. You would be joining us in just a month or two.' Her father assured her before returning.

***

They stood queued up before the counter waiting for their turn to fill up the forms for the final examination. It was almost mid-February… the month of spring and the song of the koyal.

The month of love!!

Girls of junior classes stood in clusters giggling and chatting and making their plans for celebrating the days of love. But the final year students looked serious, edgy and anxious. They talked about the possible questions, and the right ways of answering them and their worries and their premonitions. The fear of the ensuing final examination that lurked on the horizon of their thoughts had cast an ominous shadow over the rainbow ecstasy of love. A koyal began to sing somewhere from a tree in the corner of the large compound wall and a waft of cool south breeze swept past her face, ruffling her hair delicately. She felt a prick at her heart. She had not seen the boy, AY, since the evening of that nasty clash.

She came out of the gate of the school with Mala discussing a complicated sum of Mathematics and saw him standing under the big tree across the road. Her heart gave a lurch. Her feet refused to move forward. 'What happened?' Mala asked. 'I will wait for my uncle here,' She lied. 'But you said he would not be reaching till four pm. Come, let us have some ice cream before we part. You will be leaving this place for good after the examinations. God knows when will we get another chance to spend some quality time together.' Mala pulled at her hand.

'I won't be leaving immediately after the examination. We will have enough time to spend in each other's company. Do not worry. I do not feel like having ice cream now.'

'Mala's face registered disappointment.' 'Okay. I will leave then, see you during the examination. Bye.' She waved at an autorickshaw and got in. 'All the best,' Mala said and waved at her as the autorickshaw moved away.

She glanced at her wrist watch. It was a quarter to four. Her uncle would not be arriving to pick her up until after four. She looked around to ensure nobody was watching and wandered towards the tree across the road. The boy looked deep into her eyes. The earlier sparkle in his eyes had given way to a shadow of gloom. He smiled at her. It was not the naughty smile he used to flick at her earlier, but a sad, rueful smile, an effort at camouflaging the agony within. 'I missed you.' He said in a strangled voice after a long moment. She did not say anything and stood still fixing her eyes on an invisible something on the ground.

'Did you miss me?' He asked sounding anxious as if his life depended on her reply. She raised her eyes and looked steadily at him. 'Yes.' She mumbled incoherently. His face lit up for a brief moment. 'I have brought this for you,' he held out a small envelope that looked slightly bulged. She took the envelope and stowed it carefully into her sling bag. It was almost four. 'Uncle would be reaching. I must leave,' she said. 'When shall I see you again?' he asked eagerly. A hard and hot sob stuck at her throat, threatening to choke her. Her lips moved but no words came out. She turned and walked away, crossed the road in quick steps and went inside the school gate about just the moment her uncle brought his motorbike to a halt.

As they drove away, she stole a glance back. The boy AY was still there, standing under the tree. He waved at her when he saw her looking back. She turned her face away and wiped the drops of tear that trickled down her eyes with her left hand.

She opened the envelope after ensuring that everyone had gone to bed and took out the contents. There was a half-bloomed red rose inside and a folded paper of green as usual, torn out from a writing pad. She unfolded the paper and read the letter.

'Love,' he had written, 'I had missed you like crazy. The memory of the evening in that smelly, dingy room will forever keep my dreams fragrant. Strange that our first meeting was in such a place and in such a situation. We could not even talk. I want to meet you again and again, talk to you, hold your hand. Please let me know when and where could we meet again. I will wait for you near your school on the last day of your examination. Please make some excuse at home and meet me. Love you more than my life!!

AY

But she never met him again. On the last day of her examination her father had reached at her school, before the final bell rang. She could not think of a possible excuse to move across the road to the other side. She knew he would be waiting under the tree across the road.

With a tremendous effort she checked the impulse to look back. She left for the place where her father was posted the next day.

***

'We should try this one.' Rohit said. 'My colleagues at the office had strongly recommended this joint. It happens to be the best biryani centre in the city, they say.'

Rupa smiled fondly at the boyish eagerness of her husband.

She had moved in to this city to join her husband who worked as an IT professional in a multinational company there. Getting a transfer in her job was not easy but her father had some connection in the upper circle. That, and her uncle's political clout had finally made it possible. So there she was, finally settled here in this city, with her husband, after almost three years of their marriage.

And it was Rohit's plan to celebrate the entire month of February, the month they were married, in visiting places, dining at different restaurants and watching movies and theatres.

She looked up at the neon sign above that flashed the name of the place. 'ALWAYS YOURS' and under it written in comparatively smaller letters *'A. Yaseer's Specialities'*

'An uncommon name for a restaurant, isn't it? Hope the biryani would be unique too.' Rohit said, and laughed shortly. Rupa stared at the name, wondering why it struck a chord somewhere deep in her.

'Let's go in,' Rohit said. They entered pushing back the large glass door and stopped short. The ambience inside was something out of a dream; soft music and concealed, diffusive lighting; chandeliers suspended from the ornate ceiling, and elegant table settings with fine China, crystal glasses and silverware. Thick, expensive brocaded draping across the walls cut the place off the rest of the world giving it an ethereal look. The place was designed and decorated to provide the customers a luxurious dining experience. She looked at Rohit, who seemed to be quite impressed by the lavishness of the atmosphere.

A waiter in an elaborate uniform hurried in to receive them. 'Welcome sir, welcome madam,' he said effusively. 'Would you like to dine in a family room? They are on the first floor.' He pointed to a flight of stairs at one end of the spacious hall that went curving up to the first floor.

'Yes. We would like that. 'Rohit said and moved towards the stairs, beckoning Rupa to follow him. As they reached the landing a man, dressed in an expensive two-piece suit emerged from a door across the wide dining space. He stopped abruptly at the sight of Rohit and Rupa, as if he was not expecting them there. In the next instant he managed to get hold of himself and flashed his professional, amiable smile at them. 'Welcome to Always Yours, sir!' He greeted them politely. 'This way please!' He guided them to a corridor leading off the landing, to a row of tastefully designed rooms at the far end of it. 'You have a fine joint here,' Rohit exclaimed, in genuine admiration. 'Do you serve only biriyani?' He inquired. 'Biryani is the speciality of this place, sir, but we try to cater to the tastes of our heterogenous diners. We serve here multiple non-vegetarian dishes including seafood. You can have ice creams too.'

The man looked vaguely familiar. Rupa wondered if she had seen him somewhere before.

He stopped outside a room with a glass door. 'Please come in. He pushed the door open and stood aside to let them in. It was cosy and cool inside, not so lavish as the dining hall downstairs but quite comfortable and inviting.

'Are you the manager here?' Rohit asked holding out a friendly hand. The man shook it warmly. 'I am the owner, Ahammad Yaseer is the name. Happy Valentine's Day to both of you.'

'Happy Valentine's Day to you, too,' Rohit wished him back in his usual convivial manner.

'Thank you, but I don't happen to have a Valentine of mine!' the man chuckled, an easy, naughty chuckle it was.

'Not married yet? Never in love?' Rohit asked through an affable smile.

'No' to the first one, 'yes' to the second,' Ahammad Yaseer laughed. A short, mysterious laugh.

Rupa's heart gave a start. It was the same naughty, amused chuckle! Her thoughts raced back to an evening in a dingy, smelly, rundown room under the slope of a footbridge of an old railway platform, the hot, assuring grip of a clammy hand over hers, her hot breath mingling with the breath of the boy who called himself AY, and what he had said when she asked him what the initials AY meant.

A Y!

Ahammad Yaseer!

Always Yours!!

She now knew why he hadn't revealed his name to her, why in that fateful evening, he had reached the spot where she stood concealing herself behind that tree, and rescued her from the clutches of the angry mob. She knew that he had anticipated the dreadful event and had come prepared to carry her away along that circuitous path leading to that unused railway platform, in case anything went wrong. He was sure that the road was safe and nobody from his community would suspect or attack her if she was found with him. And she knew the reason now why he had asked her to drape her head in the black scarf!

She looked up at A Y and their eyes locked. And she could not take her eyes back, as if she was under some kind of a hypnosis.

'Is this a family business? Or your personal choice to be a hotelier?' Rohit asked.

The spell lifted. Rupa looked away.

'My father had a small restaurant in my hometown. I had always been a fan of good food. I did a course in hotel management after completing graduation in commerce and came here to try my luck.' AY replied, his gaze hovering still over her.

'It seems luck has favoured you,' Rohit smiled.

'Yes, at least in this.' He said, a cloud of gloom crossing his face.

'I must ask you to excuse me sir,' Ahmmad Yaseer said abruptly, swung on his heels and strode out of the room.

'Nice gentleman! Isn't he?' Rohit remarked looking at the glass door he had gone out through.

'Yes,' she said lamely.

***

The biryani was lavishly delicious and so also the dishes of chicken. But she had lost her appetite, and went through the pretence of eating just to satisfy her husband. 'Why don't you eat? 'Rohit looked searchingly at her. 'I have developed a nasty headache suddenly,' she said. 'That's too bad. The biryani is just divine. I won't want you to miss it. I will ask the waiter to pack it for us to take back home.'

A waiter arrived carrying a small bouquet of roses and a glossy, scented card where, embossed in golden letters was the greetings ….. 'Happy Valentine's Day… AY'. 'Our boss wishes you a happy Valentine's Day sir,' he said politely. Thank you,' Rohit said and rose to his feet. They climbed down the stairs and reached the dining hall on the ground floor. 'Where is your boss?' Rohit asked one waiter. He moved behind the counter to enter a chamber where perhaps his boss was. And she saw him walking towards them, his face beaming in a broad, cordial smile. Rohit shook his hand again. 'All the dishes were fabulous, and a big thanks for the lovely roses.' Rohit said. 'Visit again, sir. I will be delighted.' 'Sure,' Rohit walked up to the glass door. Another waiter came hurrying, handed the parcel of packed food to Rohit and held the door open for them.

Rupa turned to look behind. AY stood by the door his gaze fixed on her. The smile had vanished and a shadow of melancholy had taken its place.

She hurried out to the street.

***

She lay in the bed, wide awake, gripped by a strange unrest. Rohit had gone to sleep long back and his light snoring rippled across the room. She looked out. A pale, half-moon floated lazily in a misty sky. She walked over to the wooden closet built into the wall and carefully pulled out a small suitcase that contained the certificates of her academic qualifications. Stowed away under a couple of files and a small stack of papers there was a small folder inside which was a leather-covered diary. She drew back the small zip on its inner flap and took out the letters. There were only three of them. They had gone a bit smudgy but the writing was clear. She rummaged inside the flap and took out a few dried -petals of rose. They too had gone brittle, browned, and dark at the edges. She breathed out a heavy sigh. 'Forgive me!' She mumbled indistinctly, and tore the letters into tiny bits. Carrying the pieces of the paper and the wilted petals she went to the washroom, flung them into the toilet pan and flushed.

She waited briefly as the bits of papers were sucked into the rushing water, wiped her tears and lumbered back to the bedroom. She now knew that nothing would have come off the dream, a gossamer dream, she had chased years back, but still her heart felt unusually heavy.

She lay on the bed and glanced at the glossy card AY had given them with the Valetine Day's wish embossed on it, and at the bouquet of roses on the bedside table. She would not destroy them. They were for her and her husband.

A mysterious smile crossed her face as she snuggled over to Rohit and closed her eyes.

THE MISSING BOY

The true mystery of the mind is the visible, not the invisible...

Oscar Wilde

Nikhil stood irresolutely in front of the old wooden gate that was painted black may be many years ago but had pathetically faded to a dark slaty under the tyranny of changing weathers. He asked himself for the second time if he would enter or go back and return later in the day after ascertaining from his friend Sudhir Kumar if it was the right address, or Nikhil had misinterpreted it. The solitude and silence around made him wonder why must Sudheera and her husband who was an officer in a government institution choose such a secluded area of the town to settle.

Sudhir, who worked as a business analyst in Delhi was a close friend of him since their college days and despite that they lived in places distanced by many miles from each other the two friends had remained in touch. Night before last he received a phone call from Sudhir.

'I need a little help of yours, buddy,' Sudhir said.

'What is it? Why must you sound so formal? You know that I will always be there for you.'

'I know, I know bro,' Sudhir laughed. 'The thing is that it is a bit personal. You have to deliver a gift to my sister, who is now in your town.'

'Your sister?'

'Yes, my younger sister. Sudheera is her name. You have seen her when you used to visit our place during our college years.'

Nikhil tried to remember. He perhaps had seen Sudhir's younger sister while they were in college. But that was years ago. She must have changed in many ways in course of time. He could not recollect Sudhir's sister clearly now. But he did not tell that to Sudhir.

'She is here?'

'Yes. Her husband who works as an accounts officer in a government office is transferred there. They have taken a house on rent in Shakti Nagar. You have to go there and deliver a gift to her.'

Nikhil thought for a moment. Shakti Nagar was at the other end of the town. Some ten kilometers away from where he lived. But he could not refuse his old friend.

'No problem there,' Nikhil assured him. 'Give me the details.'

'You know the Raksha Bandhan festival is in next week. This time I won't be able to reach her. I will be in Singapore next week on an important business deal. I wanted to gift her a white sari of silk with a wide red border this time. But it appears that will not be possible since I will have to leave for Singapore day after tomorrow. I want you to do me a favour. I will transfer the money to your account. Buy a white silk sari with a wide red border and take it to her on the day of Raksha Bandhan. I want it to be a surprise gift this time.' Sudhir said.

'Buy a sari?' Nikhil knew he sounded hesitant, but he had not much experience in buying or choosing a sari. 'I do not know much about a sari,' he said uncertainly.

'I somehow do not trust this on-line shopping. They would show you one picture and send another.' Sudhir said to justify his request.

'But, will she appreciate my choice?' Nikhil's voice still held a note of doubt.

'What is the big deal in choosing a sari? Just tell the salesperson at the counter to show you a white silk sari with a red border.' Sudhir said encouragingly.

***

But it did not prove as easy as Sudhir had pronounced. Nikhil had to visit nearly half a dozen sari shops before making a final selection. But the sari was a good one and Sudhir was effusive in his praise when he saw the picture Nikhil had sent to his WhatsApp. Now the task remained to locate the house and deliver the gift to Sudheera.

He knew Shakti Nagar was at about ten kilometers distance from where he lived, a relatively less peopled area inhabited mostly by old generation people who had their own individual houses or bungalows. A calm, tranquil locality, away from the hubbubs of downtown area, not yet invaded by the outrageously smart and swanky apartment culture.

A light rain had started. He looked up at the overcast sky and grimaced.

The house that stood a little behind the blackish wooden gate, a small two-storied one, partly hidden by the dense growth of a couple of deodar trees in the front compound, wore a forlorn look. The abraded walls of the compound, their plaster peeling off at several places revealing unabashedly the cushions of moss on them, were a picture of decay. He looked around to inquire if a person called Mahesh Singh had moved in to the house with his wife recently but there was no one in the vicinity. He was still hesitant about entering a house of someone who he was not sure would recollect him, a character from distant past. It began to rain heavily and that decided him. He unlatched the rickety gate and stepped in. A narrow, cemented path that led to the front door of the house was lined on both sides by closely spaced clumps of jasmine that had grown blossoms in a scented, white profusion. There were also a few bushes of roses and cannas against the compound wall. Sudhir's sister, if at all it is she, who lived in this house, must be tending the plants with love and care, he thought admiring their healthy growth.

He stepped on to the small veranda and

looked for the doorbell. He could not see one. After searching some more, he finally discovered it sandwiched between a hanging flowerpot wherefrom a money plant climbed up to get itself coiled around a rafter supporting the tiled roof over the veranda, and the fringe of the door curtain that hung heavily over the closed front door. He pressed the doorbell gently and waited listening to the soft chime inside the house. He did not have to wait long. The front door opened and a young woman appeared. Nikhil, gave her an embarrassed smile.

'Excuse me,' he asked politely. 'Does a Mr. Mahesh Singh live here?'

The young woman smiled. It was not a small, discomfited one at seeing a stranger, but broad, friendly and welcoming. 'Please come in,' she stood aside to give him way. 'I am his wife Sudheera Kanchan.' She smiled again.

Nikhil was surprised. Not many young women would welcome a total stranger with such cordiality.

'My name is Nikhil. I am your brother's friend. You might not be remembering but I used to frequent your house at Sonepur.' Nikhil said thinking it would be wise and courteous to introduce himself before getting in the house.

'Is it? What a nice surprise! You are doubly welcome!' Sudheera Kanchan flashed her pleasant smile once again. Nikhil found her smile infectious. And this time he smiled back as he entered a cool, dimly lit room.

'Please sit,' she pointed to a comfortable looking settee. Nikhil looked around the room. It was large and spacious but poorly lit. The furniture, though a bit old fashioned and heavy had an aura of aristocracy about them. Everything in the living room looked impeccably neat. The house that looked shabby from outside was actually had an immaculate interior, tastefully decorated with wall hangings, and freshly cut roses and colourful cannas and bunches of jasmines in a brass vase that stood on a glass topped circular table. There were figurines and statuettes of silver as well as of ceramic and glass on the shelves. A cabinet with glass doors, lined with rows of books stood against the wall to the left. A peaceful tranquility pervaded the room. His eyes fell on a flight of wooden stairs by the glass cabinet which led up obviously to the upper floor.

'This is a big house for two people,' Nikhil said.

Sudheera Kanchan smiled again. 'Yes. It is. But I like the peaceful environment, away from the crazy bustles and noise of the main town. The neighbours are quite amiable and involving in nature. Of course, most people here are senior citizens. Their children are settled abroad and they have to live alone in the big houses they had built investing all their savings. I feel really sorry for them.'

'This is an isolated spot,' Nikhil said thoughtfully. 'I have a feeling it is not safe for you to stay alone most part of the day. There is always the fear of theft and burglary.'

Sudheera did not say anything to that.

'You should never open the front door so readily to strangers as you did today. Imagine what would have happened had it been some notorious character instead of me!' He added putting up an air of a protective big brother.

'You have a point there, Bhaiya. I should be more careful.'

'That is right,' Nikhil said and dismissed the topic. He held out the giftwrapped packet to her. 'Take a look at this. It is a Raksha Bandhan gift from your Sudhir bhaiya. You must be aware that he won't be able to come personally this time since he is away at Singapore. He had entrusted me with the job of selecting a sari for you. If you do not like the sari we can always get it exchanged and buy one of your choice.'

'I know. Sudhir Bhaiya called me yesterday. But he did not say that you would be bringing the gift.' She said as she tore open the gift wrapping. 'Wow! What a lovely sari, my favourite colour combination, and the texture is so soft and smooth! Have you chosen it?'

'Yes,' Nikhil smiled, enjoying her elation.

'Superb! Simply splendid!' She exclaimed happily, excited as a small girl.

'Sudhir wanted it to be a surprise. How I wish he could see your reaction!!'

'I am so, so happy. I will tie a band of *rakhi* around your wrist too. Wait,' she said and ran inside.

She was, Nikhil thought amusedly, like a rollicking countryside brook, carrying broken fragments of sunlight in her easy flowing laughter. She came back almost immediately, carrying a *rakhi* and some flowers, a few pieces of burfi, a little parboiled rice and a burning *diya* on a small brass plate. She sprinkled some rice and loose petals of flowers on Nikhil, put a small vermilion spot on his forehead and tied the band around his wrist. Then she put a piece of burfi in his mouth. Nikhil put his hand on her head blessing her. 'I haven't brought a gift for you,' he said and taking out a couple of five hundred rupee notes from his wallet, put in her hand.

'What is the need of this, Bhaiya? Give me a hundred rupees as a token of your affection.'

'You have to. You cannot say no to a brother's gift. Can you?'

She broke into a silvery peal of laughter. 'I cannot win you with words,' she said and took the money. Now that you have seen the house you can come any time. Mahesh will be very happy to meet you.'

'I too would like to meet him.'

'I still think you should shift to a more populated area. This place does not look safe enough for a young woman like you.' He added after a short pause.

'What about young men? Is the place safe enough for them?' The inoffensively mocking undertone was not lost on Nikhil.

'Men are different.' Nikhil remarked, ignoring it, a faint note of pride creeping into his voice.

'You mean they are not easily scared,' she said provokingly.

'You can say that,' He laughed.

'Men are always so pompous!' Sudheera Kanchan wrinkled her pretty nose.

'That is the way it is, my dear! Men are stronger.' Nikhil teased.

'Oh! Really!' she smiled her infectious smile again.

'Maybe you are right,' she said compromisingly. 'But I have come to like this place. The calm solitude, the peaceful ambience is so soothing,' she said after a short pause. 'The owner has given it nearly fully furnished for only ten thousand a month and it is pretty cheap at that. Actually, this house is rented out for the first time after the owners, a young man and his wife, left here some years back.'

'Why did they leave here? Did they choose to live in some posh area in the center of the town?'

'They are out of the state now. They would never come back to stay here. They did not care much if it was rented out or not. We got it through an agent. And got it cheap because they never quoted any specific amount.'

'What is the cause of such disinterest? Nikhil asked, slightly curious.

Sudheera Kanchan's cheery face clouded. 'It is a sad story, Bhaiya,' she said sounding dull and gloomy. 'I have heard it from Leela aunty. This is the ancestral house of Swaraj Patnaik, the present owner, who lived here with his wife and son, a handsome, playful kid of six. They had come to settle here following Swaraj Patnaik's posting here as a program manager in some reputed company. The house was left abandoned and uncared for since the death of his father. He had entrusted the responsibility of housekeeping to some distant relative. But the fellow proved not to be very sincere in discharging the responsibility. The lack of proper care sent the house sliding down the road to decay. Swaraj Patnaik was glad when he got a posting here. He came to live here with his family. They got the house partially renovated before moving in. They decided to demolish the broken compound walls and raise new ones in their place once they had settled here. The work was about to begin when disaster struck the family.' Sudheera paused and looked at Nikhil.

'What disaster?' Nikhil asked, his curiosity growing.

'It was the boy, Somu. He was a very animated child, loved to play football all the time. Not much interested in studies. It so happened that the father received a complaint from the principal of the school where he had joined his son. You know that the boy was new in the school and was not yet ready to blend in with his classmates. There was a nasty fight between Somu and another boy of his class over a cricket game and Somu hit the boy. Jabbed a heavy punch at his nose. Blood came out from the boy's nose and his father, an influential person of the town, complained to the principal. Swaraj Patnaik was called in to the school and was warned to teach manners to his son. The humiliation of asking for an apology to the principal of a school on behalf of his son had made him terribly angry and he took it out on his son. 'He must be punished for his irresponsible conduct' he decided.

Somu was asked to sit alone in the compound for the whole day, morning to evening. He would be given his food from time to time, but no one, neither his father nor his mother would speak to him during that period.'

'Then?'

'The boy did not say a word, nor did he make any promise to mend his manners as most children would do in similar circumstances. He just took his football and went out of the house and sat under a tree in the compound. This arrogant indifference made his father even more angry. And now there was no expecting of any possible leniency from the father which an earnest apology might have elicited. But the son, a sensitive and stubborn kid, would neither ask to be forgiven nor promise to behave in the future. His mother, after his father left for the office, asked the boy to come inside but the boy did not. Nor did he touch the food despite all the coaxing and cajoling of his mother.'

This was getting more and more interesting. Nikhil found it difficult to resist the urge to know what followed next. He looked expectantly at Sudheera.

'Swaraj Patnaik might have been feeling guilty for having consigned his only son to exile this way. He called his wife and learnt about the boy's stubborn refusal to take food or drink. He returned home early, accusing himself all the way for being so impulsive and erratic. His wife, distressed and panicky, ran down the path to meet him at the gate. She told him that she had seen Somu, their son, playing football in the compound about half an hour before. She got busy in the household chores after that. The boy was not there in the compound when she came out to see. The front gate was open. She searched for the boy in the neighbourhood but no one seemed to have seen him. She had called his office, she said, and was told that Swaraj had already left for home.

Assuring his wife that he would find the boy soon who he thought must not have gone very far in such a short time, he rode away on his bike to make a thorough search for the boy. He inquired in the school which was closed that day following a function in the previous evening. He went to the home of some of Somu's classmates, and asked them about him. No one had seen Somu that day. The exhaustive search for Somu proved to be an exercise in futility.

The light of the afternoon began to fade as the sun neared the western skyline. Soon it would be evening. There was no sign of Somu. Swaraj Patnaik was terribly upset. A strong premonition gnawed at his heart. His wife, dishevelled and weeping stood by the front gate along with a few sympathetic neighbours when he reached home, defeated and spent.

'What happened then? Did they find him?'

Sudheera Kanchan shook her head sadly. 'After spending a sleepless night waiting for Somu, they reported in the local police station next morning. A missing case was promptly filed and an organized search operation was carried out. They went about all possible places looking for a boy of six in a yellow T-shirt and blue shorts, but Somu was not found. Nor did the police have any lead or clue that could have helped to pursue the matter from a new angle. They suspected kidnapping but there was no ransom call. Inquiries were made in the local hospitals for possible accident cases. But they drew a blank everywhere. The six-year-old Somu had just vanished into thin air.'

The mother of the boy was inconsolable. The unexpectedness with which the blow had struck, affected her mind and left her disoriented. A dejected Swaraj Patnaik opted for a transfer to some distant place, preferably outside the state and left this place for good. After so many years he finally decided to put it on rent and posted an advertisement through an estate agent. That is how we got it at a cheaper rate.'

'This boy Somu, he was never found?' Nikhil asked, feeling dismayed at the tragic fate that befell a happy family.

'Never found and never returned. That is what Leela aunty says. I am sure the boy is no longer alive.'

'Why?'

'There would have been some news of him if he were alive. He would have come back. After all he was a six-year-old school going boy. He could have given the address to someone and that someone would have helped him reach here.'

She breathed out a deep sigh.

The rain had stopped. 'I will leave now.' Nikhil rose to his feet a little languidly.

'Wait, Bhaiya. You have come to our house for the first time and that too on such an auspicious day. You can't leave just like that. I will get you some snacks and coffee in a jiffy.' Once again, she ran into the house, sprightly and frisky like a mountain stream.

***

Nikhil glanced at his wrist watch. Sudheera was gone for more than five minutes. He looked around the room. It was a rainy day and there was no sun. The window that overlooked the compound was shut. Sudheera had not switched on the ceiling fan probably because the weather was cool. The room was dimly lit from the feeble streaks of day light that came through the open front door. The wispy darkness that hung in the room and the total silence made him a bit uneasy. He wondered why Sudheera was taking so much time to make a cup of coffee. He could not call out to her. That would not be decent. He had nothing to do but wait. He picked up the newspaper from the glass topped center table and let his eyes stray across the pages.

Then he heard it.

A gentle thump—thump sound. As if someone was hitting the roof lightly with a rubber hammer or something of the sort. The sound was coming from the upper floor. He knew Sudheera was in the kitchen. And he also knew that she was alone in the house. She was married for a few months only and had no children. Her husband was out at his office. He was instantly alert.

What could be the sound?

A cat jumping about? Pillows falling down? Some thief hidden in a room upstairs?

But the sound had a rhythmic pace, as if it was made with a deliberate regularity.

The hairs on the nape of Nikhil's neck bristled. His eyes darted to the flight of stairs and then upward where the steps seemed to disappear into the darkness above.

Nothing! Absolutely nothing to rouse a suspicion.

The thumping sound stopped as suddenly as it had started.

Nikhil looked at the curtain over the door that perhaps, he thought, opened to the hall and the kitchen, wishing Sudheera to come in. This place was not as comforting as Sudheera believed. Let her stay in this house if she liked it here. He wandered to the door to call Sudheera and say he was leaving.

Nikhil felt his presence before he saw him. His body felt suddenly rigid and taut and an electric shiver ran through his nerves. As if he knew intuitively who and where he was. Slowly, as if it was an effort to move, he turned to look.

The boy, in a yellow T-shirt and a pair of blue knickers, stood in the middle of the staircase, grabbing a dullish white big football in his small hands, looking straight at him!!

Somu!! The boy that had gone missing!!

Nikhil stood rooted all his reflexes paralyzed. He tried to call out to Sudheera Kanchan loudly but his tongue was stuck to the roof of his mouth. He just gaped at the boy with the football. And as he looked, the boy climbed down the rest of the steps and went out through the open door to the compound and then out through the dull-black rickety front gate.

Nikhil stared at the disappearing frail figure, his heart doing summersaults, his knees buckling.

A minute passed.

Sudheera was still somewhere inside the house. Not caring if Sudheera would mind if he left without informing her, Nikhil stumbled out of the house, crossed the veranda and the narrow path lined with jasmine bushes in quick, long strides and walked out of the old and rickety front- gate to where he had stood his motorbike. He stood there for a moment, flicking furtive glances in all directions to find the boy. He was nowhere. Like Sudheera had said, just vanished into thin air!!

He struggled on to his bike, made a turn and drove away fast. It was when he arrived at the crowded market area some five hundred meters away, he stopped, mopped his sweaty face, and waited to get his breathing back to normal.

***

The boy ran down the stairs carrying a dullish black and white football under his arm. 'Come back Somu,' Sudheera Kanchan called loudly and ran after the boy. She wore a silk sari with a wide red border. The boy flung open the rickety wooden gate which had once been black but now had turned a dark slaty under the tyranny of changing weathers. Tears rolled down Sudheera's big, beautiful eyes and she waved her hands frantically trying to stop the boy. The boy disappeared into a wooded patch thronged with thorny shrubs, beyond the narrow, cobbled road. He stopped for a fraction of a second to turn and smiled at Sudheera. As she blundered across the path to catch up with the boy a lone motorbike that was vrooming past the road hit her. She fell headlong and rolled into the mass of straggly bushes. The man on the bike braked hard and stopped, and climbed off it in utter panic. He stared at the young woman sprawling awkwardly amidst the spiky bushes, face down, her red bordered white silk sari smeared in blood at places. The man looked desperately around and swung on his feet. He was facing the black gate. Nikhil peered at him from behind the curtain that hung on the front door of Sudheera's house. The face of the man on the bike came into full view. Nikhil drew in a sharp breath. And the next moment his whole body went stiff in a cold, primeval terror. The face of the man on the bike was his own!!

He sat up straight in the lounging chair, letting out a startled gasp, and almost synchronously his mobile phone sprang into life. He recalled he was relaxing in a lounging chair in the balcony of his apartment after returning from office. The morning at Sudheera's and the busy office hours had left him drained out and he had no idea when he had snoozed off. He touched his face. Sweat beads had broken out on it and his hands were clammy. The ringing had stopped and as he picked it up to see who had called it began ringing again. The phone dropped from his hands but he grabbed it back before it fell on the floor and looked at the display screen.

It was Sudhir Kumar; he must be calling from Singapore.

'Thank you, buddy,' Sudhir's ebullient voice floated in from the other end. Sudheera called me to tell that she was delighted to have the gift. She was all praise and admiration for you. But she said you left without letting her know, while she was making some snacks for you. What was the hurry? She would have called you but she did not have your number. I have given her your number. She may call you some time.'

'It was a pleasure to meet her.'

'I wanted to meet Mr. Mahesh but he had already left for his office when I reached there around eight thirty. Sudheera was alone. She is a very cheerful and pleasant-tempered person. Wish I had a sister like her.' He added after a brief pause.

'She is your sister too, buddy,' Sudhir laughed.

'Who was the boy, Sudhir?' Nikhil found it difficult to hold back the urge any longer.

'Boy? What boy?'

'I saw a boy in the house. He came down the stairs with a football. I think the house is haunted. Try to convince Sudheera to shift to another house in the mid-town area.'

'Haunted?' Sudhir's voice reflected his astonishment. 'Why do you think so?'

'The house owner, a Mr. Swaraj Patnaik had a six-year-old son who went missing one day and was never found. The police and the people believe that the boy must have fallen a victim to some crime or an accident and is no longer alive. That was the reason why Swaraj Patnaik had never returned to his ancestral home and rented it out through an estate agent. That was how Mahesh and Sudheera got it so cheap.' Nikhil narrated what he had heard from Sudheera.

'Wait. There must be some misunderstanding. Mahesh and Sudheera live there alone. But I remember now Sudheera telling me about Mahesh's sister visiting them for the occasion of Raksha Bandhan. She has a son, around six or seven years. Ankur. You must have seen *him*.'

'Was the boy Mahesh's nephew?'

A confused and puzzled Nikhil asked more to himself than Sudhir.

'What about the story of Somu, the missing boy?'

'Now I understand,' Sudhir exclaimed breaking out into a boisterous laughter. 'Sudheera must have played a prank on you. She is very keen on concocting such imaginary tales. She must have conjured up the story when you have advised her not to stay in a secluded house!!'

'An imaginary tale? Concocted by Sudheera? That playful, innocuous young woman who looked so vulnerable?' Nikhil found it difficult to believe that Sudheera could play such a prank.

'I will ask Sudheera to speak to you. And, buddy! Remove this idea of 'a haunted house' from your imagining mind.' Sudhir said.

Nikhil sighed. 'Okay, brother, bye and good night,' he said and broke the connection.

He was not prepared to believe that a young woman like Sudheera Kanchan could narrate a fictious incident so glibly and so convincingly. He was still pondering over the morning's happenings when the phone rang again.

It was a video call from Sudheera Kanchan. She wore the white silk sari with the wide red border and looked innocent and pretty. She flicked her infectious smile at him from the screen.

'Hello Bhaiya! Why did you leave in such a hurry? When I came in with the snacks and the coffee I found you gone.'

'I remembered some urgent work at the office.' Nikhil lied.

'Do not lie Bhaiya,' Sudheera said, her eyes dancing. 'You were frightened at the sight of Ankur. Weren't you?'

The boy Ankur made his appearance on the screen. He still cradled the football under one arm. There was an innocent smile on his face.

'Say hello to uncle,' Sudheera asked Ankur and the boy waved at Nikhil from the screen.

'You are so mischievous,' Nikhil said to Sudheera finding nothing else to say.

'Will you say now that men are not easily scared, bhaiya?' Sudheera Kanchan broke into her silvery flow of laughter

'You win, I lose!' Nikhil said through an embarrassed smile.

'Come again bhaiya. Your coffee waits for you.'

'Sure,' Nikhil agreed and waved back at Ankur and Sudheera.

'Bye,' both of them said together as Nikhil clicked the connection off.

THE PURPLE SCARF

The only regret I will have in dying is if it is not for love...

Gabriel Garcia Marquez

He cast a surreptitious glance around, to ascertain no one was looking in his direction, ran a quick hand on the backpack and mounted the steps cautiously. The bus was nearly packed with passengers, college students, office goers, traders, salespersons, vendors, shoppers and other occasional travelers. The conductor was prodding them down the aisle to make more spaces for the new passengers. Anwar stood by the door, his hand securely gripping a grab-handle, watching the steady inflow of passengers as they climbed into the bus and made their way along the aisle. The inside of the bus felt unusually hot and the backpack was heavy. Abbu had advised him several times not to speak to any of the passengers and put through a call to him when the bus stopped at the Globe Supermarket area to receive the instruction regarding the next move. He was also warned not to leave the backpack alone and keep a close guard over it. Anwar tried to guess what could be inside the backpack, and he was scared at the guess, but he did neither have the courage nor the heart to question Abbu. He knew if it had not been for Abbu he would have died of starvation like a stray dog alongside an anonymous street. He did not know who his real parents were, nor did he want to know. Abbu had reared him up with love and care. He cooked for him, took him to the school, sat by him through sleepless nights when he fell sick. He had put him in a college where Anwar did his Bachelor in Commerce. Anwar knew that one lifetime wouldn't be enough to do things to pay Abbu back for what he owed to him. He would lay down his life for Abbu without turning a hair if the need arose. He liked Abbu's robust personality, the kindness camouflaged under his rude exterior, the rigid reservations and laconism with which he dealt with people around and the openhearted, frank smile that lit up his stubbled face when he saw Anwar. There was just one small thing which he disliked about Abbu. The odd glint in his otherwise benevolent eyes at the sight of that group of strange men who came to meet him from time to time. And the way he hedged when Anwar asked him about them. Abbu became a changed man when he was with those seedy and suspicious looking bunch. As if he was another person, unknown, hard and bitter.

He remembered the moment when he bade

farewell to Abbu this morning. His face was heavy with some hidden sorrow and there was a queer look in his eyes. He hugged Anwar tightly and kissed his forehead. 'This is a very important job, beta. Everything depends on your alertness and foresight. I will pray for you. *Inshallah*! You can pull it off without hassle.' He mopped his face and looked away as if to avert his eyes. Anwar felt uneasy at such a strange emotional response. As if he was not going to meet Abbu again. It was after all, he thought, a simple task of transporting something in the backpack and delivering that to a person who would be waiting in the Globe Supermarket area. Last night two men had come to meet Abbu, and they sat talking in hushed voices in the corner room till late in the night. Anwar had no idea why but he was feeling somehow restless that night. He lay in his bed in the large room adjacent to the one in the end of the open corridor. He could overhear snatches of indistinct conversation as the two men came out of the corner room along with Abbu. He could faintly hear words like 'Azim *maqsad*, '*shahadat*' and '*Inshallah*' and the familiar voice of his father saying resignedly 'If that is the how it has to be!' And, they went out of the gate of their small compound. He heard the heavy footfalls of his father outside his room a little later. Then the door opened gently and Abbu entered. Anwar closed his eyes. Abbu wandered over to his bed, stood for a while and then bending down he kissed his forehead. Then he turned abruptly and strode out of the room closing the door behind him. Anwar's eyes moistened. How deeply Abbu loved him!! He will never turn him down, come what may. Anwar promised to himself and drifted into a peaceful sleep. In the morning Abbu asked him to take a bag to some friend of him at the Globe Supermarket.

***

The driver sounded the horn interrupting his flow of thoughts. A young man who had occupied a seat suddenly sprang up to his feet and scrambled out of the bus. 'He has perhaps got into the wrong bus,' Anwar thought and breathing a sigh of relief occupied the seat the young man had vacated before any one made a claim over it. He felt relaxed. The backpack was still a handicap. He took it off his back and slid it under the seat. He recollected Abbu's warning never to let the backpack out of his close reach. 'Whatever is there inside it,' he thought grimly, 'will remain secured under the seat.' He looked furtively around. No one was watching him or the backpack. The engine was revving and the bus had started to crawl forward when she climbed into the bus, her lovely face flushing crimson.

***

Apoorva climbed into the bus and was instantly filled with dismay at the sight of the crowd of the passengers. For a brief while she thought if she should get down and wait for the next bus, but that would mean waiting for at least another hour. The next bus to Bharatpur, her hometown will not be arriving one hour before, and she had to reach

Bharatpur by early afternoon anyhow to collect the printouts of some photos she had selected from an internet website for her project work in the college, from a cybercafe. The bus was packed with people and the sweltering heat was terribly discomforting. On any other occasion she would have felt irritated and repelled by the discomfort but not today. Today was special. Yesterday, she had come here with her parents to attend a marriage function at one of her father's friends, Bikash uncle. Bikash uncle was a close neighbour of theirs at Bharatpur a couple of years ago and had shifted to Silarkot on an official transfer. She had guessed that attending the function was an excuse for something else, a camouflage to conceal the real purpose. She knew, without being told that a marriage alliance was getting secretly negotiated between the two families. Her marriage with Bipul, Bikash uncle's son. Apoorva and Bipul had played together as kids of neighbouring houses do though they went to different schools. The childhood friendship had grown intimate as they stepped on the threshold of youth and this had not escaped the eyes of the elders. Bipul had left town to pursue higher studies outside the state, but the two were constantly in touch.

Apoorva touched again the pendant of the gold chain around her neck. It was a gift from Bipul's mother. She had herself put it around her neck as Bipul watched, a knowing yet mischievous smile in his eyes. 'You are my daughter now, an integral part of our family', aunty had said and kissed her forehead. An informal, modest event but it had cemented the bond between the two families. Later, in the evening, when everyone was busy in the function Bipul stole into the room and took her in his arms. He let the length of the gold chain roll along his fingers, and holding the pendant gently pressed to her throat, he kissed it. A wave of ecstasy flooded into her as she recollected the warmth of Bipul's lips exploring her throat.

She remembered she had to buy some foodstuff for dinner as her mother had stayed back at her uncle's. 'I would get it from the Globe Supermarket.' After all it was where she would get down. She looked around and then into the inside of bus hoping to find a seat, but the crowd of passengers blocking the passageway obstructed her gaze. A young boy, looking handsome in a pair of gray blue jeans and a black shirt, the full sleeves neatly rolled up, and fashionably trimmed hairstyle occupied the seat just by the door. An elderly lady sat next to him, by the window, a bored, indifferent expression on her face. As she made a brief survey once again still not losing hope of getting a vacant seat, she saw the young man on the seat by the door looking at her fixedly. There was something oddly intense about the look. It was like an overpowering urge, compelling her to turn her gaze back to him. Their eyes locked for a fraction of a moment and she felt, guiltily enough though, that the world has come to a standstill and there was no one else in the bus except for the two of them. Even Bipul and the magical ecstasy of the closeness with him were erased off her mind like an unwanted line is erased from a drawing sheet. It was difficult to take her eyes off the young man. The driver honked the horn again and the bus jerked to a start. The spell broke.

***

Anwar had never seen a girl like the one that got into the bus in a desperate hurry. It was as if she had some magic about her that took him in its power. He could not take his eyes off her. She was beautiful in a different way, not like the tallish girls with big black eyes, sharp nose full mouth, and creamy complexion. She was rather petite, her complexion a blend of glossy brown and white, her hair luscious, and she had a small but sharp nose over a well-shaped mouth. But there was something about her that made her look special even in a simple outfit of a white salwar suit and a purple scarf around her neck. Sweat beads glistened on her face giving it a dewy look and her eyes were wary as she turned a desperate gaze around looking for a vacant space in the over crowded bus. Then she looked straight at him and their eyes met, and were locked for a brief, hypnotic moment. And everything went out of his mind, the noisy bus, the moist heat, the backpack his father had warned him repeatedly never to leave alone, and all the doubt and apprehension veiling it. His mind was now filled with the girl with the purple scarf who stood leaning hard on the post by the door, clutching a small handbag that slung from her shoulder. She was so close Anwar could smell her, an intoxicating smell that kept swirling and coiling around him like a fragrant helix. Should he ask her where she would get down? Should he offer her his seat? But the backpack was under the seat and he could not afford to keep it away from him. The girl swayed gently as the bus rolled on a patch of bumpy road.

'You can sit here,' Anwar said to the girl, getting up. The girl smiled at him as she muttered an indistinct 'thank you' and slid on to the seat he had vacated. Their bodies touched as she did so and an electric tremor ran through Anwar. He no longer cared about the mission his Abbu had entrusted him with. He did not bother about losing the backpack. May be there was something which his Abbu considered valuable and important in there, may be drugs as he had doubted earlier. Drugs it must be, he was sure now, or else why his father was so particular about the backpack? Anwar had felt the outlines and guessed there was a heavy, rectangular box like object. May be, the drug packets were inside that parcel. He did not care a bit now; his thoughts were around the girl. Once the bus reached the stop by the Globe Supermarket, he would call Abbu and someone would come to take away the backpack.

He looked at the girl again, and again their eyes met. There was a semblance of a smile on her face. Anwar's heart began to beat faster. He felt the girl had a magnetic charm that dragged him towards her. It was as if time had stopped and become an eternity, the world around him had become an enormous emptiness where he and the girl levitated around interminably, endlessly, securely locked in each other's arms.

***

'Court Square' the helper-boy who stood by the door hollered as the bus crawled to a stop at the District Court area. Passengers got down and a few new ones made their entry. There would be two more stops before the bus reached the Globe Supermarket area. He was feeling slightly dizzy. He was not sure whether it was because of the apprehension that something untoward might happen while the man collected the backpack from him, or because of all the fantasizing involving himself and the girl. His eyes were keeping straying back to the girl who sat cradling her handbag on her lap, looking out of the window. A lock of hair over her left eye wantoned in the wind that wafted in through the window. As if she could instinctively sense he was looking at her, she turned her gaze to him.

'Where will you get down?' he asked, not able to resist any longer the urge to talk to her.

'Near the Globe Supermarket,' she smiled shortly.

'My stop too,' he exclaimed, feeling immensely happy within that he could now know more about her. He could even accompany her to her home, he thought hopefully. All depended on the man who would collect the backpack or the drug, or whatever his father wanted to smuggle out. He did not care anymore about it.

The bus was slowing its speed. The Globe Supermarket was a hundred meters or so away now. The girl stood up and moved closer to the door. He could feel the caress of her purple scarf across his arm and her warm breath over his shoulder as she inched closer to him. Anwar bent down to get his backpack from under the seat but the girl stood obstructing the way. He decided to get it after the girl stepped out of the bus. 'I will make the phone call first.' He took out his phone from his back pocket and dialed his father's number.

***

He tried to turn on his side and felt a sharp pain like a knife stab ripping through his left side. He groaned and tried to open his eyes that were swollen and bleary, a bit more. He discovered himself lying on a metal cot. The mattress was thin and knobby and he could feel the hard and cold springs underneath. His mind was in a whirl and he was not able to think soberly. His hand went up to his head that felt unusually heavy and was buzzing inside. He grimaced and raised his hand to touch his head. The effort of lifting up the hand made him wince in pain. He closed his eyes and remained still to let the waves of pain recede, and tried to remember. But he was relieved that there was no injury to the head or face.

He remembered the bus he was travelling in crawling towards the stop in front of the Globe Supermarket. The girl too had got up from her seat by the window adjoined to the exit of the bus, and stood just behind him emitting that enchanting smell that held him captivated in a world of euphoria. He had bent down to pull out the backpack under the seat but the girl was in the way. He waited for the girl to get down. The bus was about to stop and he took out the mobile phone from his back pocket to make a call to his father. He selected 'Abbu' from the contact list and clicked the dial icon, and the bus erupted into a gigantic blast, amidst a blaze of red and black and orange.

And all the hell broke loose. There was a tremendous roar and almost instantly he and the girl were flung out of the door as if pushed by enormous hands. The bus turned into a pandemonium of hissing flames licking at its seats , windows and the supporting bars and the ugly crackle of the wooden structures as the flames ate into them, the loud groans and the wild, frenzied screams and the pieces of glass, molten iron and human flesh spattered across the floor and the walls, and the mushrooming smoke -clouds. He felt himself falling into a scorching vacuum and in a desperate effort to clutch at a support he had grabbed at the girl as they were thrown off. The last thing he remembered was both of them getting flung into a thick smoke haze and his head hitting the concrete sidewalk. Then there was total darkness.

The girl!!

Where was the girl who had a gold chain with a

pendant around her neck and a purple scarf over her slim shoulder?

He sat up abruptly on the bed. All the blood in his body seemed to rush up to his head as he did so. He shut his eyes once again and kept still to let the feeling wear off. A few minutes later his mind cleared a bit. What had happened to the bus? Why did it blow up? Was there a bomb hidden somewhere inside? The backpack carrying the parcel of expensive drugs must have been reduced to cinders, he thought regretfully.

What about the person he was supposed to deliver the parcel? Had he arrived there to collect the parcel from him?

Then it came to him with a sudden startle, like a blinding flash of lightning.

Why did the bus blow up the very instant he click-dialed Abbu's number?

Did the parcel inside the backpack he carried have actually drugs inside it, or…..? he flinched away from the thought.

But it came creeping in with an obstinacy he found difficult to resist.

He remembered the fragments of the conversation among Abbu and the men who came to the house he had overheard last night, words like azim *maqsad ,shahadat* . What did they mean? He had a vague idea that shahadat meant something like martyrdom, laying down one's life for a noble cause. Did Abbu send him on a suicidal mission? And for what noble cause? His profound faith in

Abbu's love, that he could never push him into any trouble, refused to accept it, but then there was that look of deep sadness in his eyes as he bade Anwar farewell! Did he knowingly send him with the backpack that he was sure now carried a parcel not of drugs but explosives?

The thought crawled pertinaciously inside him like a snake, and raised its head as many times as he tried to curb it down with his unflinching trust in Abbu. But it got more and more difficult, to fight the envenoming thought off. It was a horrifying experience, and there was no escape from it. He was now extremely frightened to reveal the truth of his accidental survival. Abbu and his associates must have by now believed, he thought bitterly, that he had succumbed to the deadly blast. He dropped the plan of sending a message to his father through someone that he was alive and fine. He must keep his survival a secret and run away to some other place using a false name and identity, out of the reach of Abbu, he decided. It would be easy, he hoped, since the luggage of the passengers in the bus, including his own wallet and mobile phone now lie unidentifiably charred in a mound of black ash with almost no chance of recovery. He could convince the police and the authorities to provide him with a new I-card and he could also pretend he was still in a state of shock and was not able to think coherently. He could say he was parentless and had arrived newly in the town seeking a job. There could be so many alternatives.

His thoughts now revolved around the girl. Where was she? Was she alive? He looked at the beds in the big ward, desperately hoping to discover her. All the beds were occupied with the victims of the blast. Many were lying in threadbare mattresses in the corridor outside. The mass of wounded and mangled humanity crying in excruciating pain was a terrible sight to bear. Their howling and agonized groans of pain rent the air around. Two nurses in white uniforms hurried in followed by a couple of ward boys who wheeled in a stretcher on which lay a heavily bandaged person. The ward boys spread out a not-too-clean mattress on an iron cot along the wall at the far end of the hall and transferred the motionless patient to it. One of the nurses wandered to the bed where Anwar lay. She adjusted the bottle of glucose hanging from the slender stand and cast a casual glance at him. 'You are fine, no internal injuries, only some burn- wounds and scratches at places. You will be discharged today.' She said in a perfunctory manner that is common in nurses and in other medical personnel.

'There was a girl with me in the bus. She is my close relative. We were travelling together. Where is she?'

'There are about twenty or more blast-victims admitted here.' The nurse said looking sympathetic. 'Some of them are young girls. How did she look like? What is her name? Can you tell us of any identifying mark?'

Anwar fumbled. He had no idea what the name of the girl was. 'She is between seventeen and eighteen. She has a gold chain with an oval pendant around her neck and wears a purple scarf.' He answered trying to bypass the question about the girl's name.

'There is also a girl of the same age here in the last bed. She had a grievous face injury. A good looking girl, but a shard of glass that caught the right side of her face had damaged it badly. Luckily there is no burn injury.'

'Can I take a look at her?' Anwar asked anxiously.

'You can, but do not go very near her. She has not yet recovered from the trauma.' The nurse moved away to another bed.

Anwar swung his feet down the bed and stood up. A wave of dizziness swept over him and a sharp pang of pain shot through his right arm. He stood still for a while to let the pain subside. It was an effort to walk steadily but he managed after a few steps, and reached the last bed where a girl lay, the right side of her face heavily swathed in bandage.

He looked at the girl closely. She was in a hospital gown. A white sheet was drawn up that covered the lower part of her body. She was perhaps under the impact of some strong sedative and slept heavily. There was no movement in her. The bandage hid about three-fourth of her face and it was not possible to identify her from the part of her face that was visible.

Then his eyes fell on it.

It was the gold chain with the oval pendant. It was still there, looping awkwardly around her slender throat.

***

The right side of her face felt as if someone had poured a full bottle of molten metal on it. A maddening, corroding pain ate into the flesh. Then someone pricked a needle into her arm and the gushing waves of pain calmed down. The pains now came at long intervals. She relapsed into the relaxing arms of slumber, her mind vaguely pondering over the incidents immediately preceding the terrible blast. She remembered she stood by the exit gate of the bus that was dropping its speed. It was about to stop at the Globe Supermarket area. Another bunch of passengers stood close behind her waiting to get down. The handsome young man too stood before her, his back pressed to the handbag she held clutched to her chest. Everything looked so normal, so ordinary!! Nothing out of place! Nothing unusual! The young man rummaged in his back pocket and took out his phone. That reminded Apoorva that she must inform her mother that she had reached her destination. She unzipped her handbag and picked out her phone, and at that same moment, the young man in her front clicked the call icon on his phone screen and the bus exploded into a volcano of red and orange flames. The last thing she remembered that she and the young man were thrown out of the bus, flying in the smouldering emptiness for a fractured second before hurtling down to the concrete road. She remembered nothing after that. The singeing pain in her right cheek made her wince. The power of painkiller they administered to her was wearing out. She moaned a little and turned to her right and lay face up.

'You seem to be in a lot of pain.' A gentle voice came from very close. She tried to open her eyes to see who spoke. She suddenly realized that her right eye was bandaged. She tried to open her left eye but the lid felt unusually heavy.

'Can you hear me?' It said again. A gentle, soothing voice. Apoorva opened her left eye with a great effort and squinted at the face that was bending over her.

It was the young man who had offered her his seat and who had stood by the exit door. Her eye now opened a little wide in recognition, and a relief that he too was alive. She remembered his intense gaze that kind of bored into her, melting her with a warmth she never knew before, not even when Bipul had kissed her throat.

'Can you hear me?' the same soft, caressing voice. She nodded her head. It was a painful effort and she winced. And he also looked blurred. She waited for a while before speaking.

'Will you help me?' she asked, her voice barely above a whisper.

'Of course,' Anwar said trustfully. He was not feeling very confident and was not sure his body could take the strain if the girl asked him to go to some place. But he tried to sound assuring.

'Apoorva, that is my name,' the girl said again, her voice a bit stronger than before. 'I will give you a number. My father's. Would you please call him?'

'Why not? There is however a small problem. My cellphone is gone. But I can go down to the lobby or borrow a phone from some well-wishing fellow to pass on the news.'

Anwar said wondering why she did not ask the hospital people to call her parents. That was her choice, he thought, glad that she trusted him. But he could not hold back the curiosity. 'Why don't you ask the hospital people to do that?'

'No!' The voice was feeble but the denial was very strong, very determined. 'I don't want everyone to know that I am alive. My face is badly damaged. I do not want people to pity me. I just want to go back to my parents and live in seclusion.'

'But your well-wishers would flock in to your house to pay either a courtesy visit or in genuine concern. How are you going to avoid that?'

'My father will take care of that. Just pass the message to him and ask him not to disclose to anyone that I am here.'

Apoorva said the number of her father. Anwar was amazed that she could remember the numerals correctly even while she was passing through a trauma.

'Do not worry. I will call your father and ask him not to reveal your whereabouts to anyone.' Anwar assured. 'Won't it be better if you give me your home address too?' He added as an afterthought.

'May I know your name?' Apoorva asked in a feeble voice.

'Anoop,' Anwar said unthinkingly, as if the name was lying dormant in some hidden recess of his heart, as if he had always wished to be recognized by that name.

Apoorva squinted at the young man who called himself Anoop, doubtfully. He looked handsome even in his disheveled state. She could not reason out why but she was beginning to trust him, as if he was the only person she could rely upon in any given time of distress. She shrank away from the thought of showing herself to Bipul in her present plight, dubious if the marriage would materialize at all, but surprisingly enough she was not ashamed to open up to this handsome boy leaning over her, a shadow of consternation in his eyes. Her lips curled slightly in a thankful smile. She gave him the address.

***

Anwar climbed up the steps painfully that led to the floor where Apoorva was. He was still limping a little. It had been a week since he was discharged from the hospital. He had met the parents of Apoorva and it was an overwhelming experience, to watch the joy and relief flowing down in the copious tears they shed and the look of gratitude in their eyes. He had introduced himself to them as Anoop, a parentless young man arriving in the town in search of a job. Her father took him in his arms, and blabbered his thanks. And the poor, weeping mother showered her blessings on him. It was an embarrassing experience too, to bask in the pure, unalloyed love of caring parents. He thought about his foster father whom he had always worshipped as if he was a godsend who had lifted him out of ignominy and gave him his name. Did Abbu love him at all? The appalling realization of how he was used to wreck a mayhem filled him with a repulsive bitterness. He was consumed by a self-loathing. Apoorva would be discharged today. He wanted to meet her for one last time before she went away with her parents. He was visiting the hospital regularly for the last few days inquiring after Apoorva's condition. The doctors had declared her clinically fit to go home and resume her daily activities. The right side of her face was disfigured unrecognizably and needed a series of plastic surgeries to be brought back to shape. It would be a prolonged and expensive treatment, they had made clear. Her parents were eager to take their daughter back home, relieved beyond measure that she had survived the fatal blast. At that point of time, they had not yet made up their mind about the plastic surgery and the future treatments coming in tandem. Anwar could sense the misery of Apoorva even if she tried to conceal it with a brave veneer. He was amazed at the girl's resilience. Any other girl of her age and at her place would have been mortified by the tragedy inflicted upon her, but

Apoorva was different. Not to be curbed, not to be broken so easily.

Anwar's eyes fell on a man standing at the far end of the corridor where the elevator was, his back turned to him. He was looking closely at the persons stepping in and out of the elevator, as if he was searching someone. The man, even from the back side looked somehow familiar. Suddenly he remembered seeing him a week before, the day on which he was discharged from the hospital. He had not taken much notice then, thinking that he must be here to attend some patient here. And he was standing at the very same spot where he was now, he thought uneasily. He was a bit surprised to find him there again, watching the elevator.

A coincidence?

He had an instinctive feeling that he was being followed, he was not sure by whom. But there was that frisson of fear that kept haunting him.

***

She knew her dreams of a future with Bipul were now in ruins. Surprisingly she did not seem to regret it much. The brief meetings with Anoop, when he came to inquire after her health was like a cluster of sparkling stars in her dark sky that seemed to be expanding unendingly. She kept waiting for that brief span of time when he would be there by her bed, talking to her, solacing her. Anoop was like a stream of fresh cool water in the burning desert she treaded every moment. She was haunted by the moment her eyes had met his in the misfortunate bus. And her earth had stopped still on its axis. The moment had remained frozen in her time like an infinity.

She had no idea when she would be meeting him again once she returned home with her parents. She had also no idea if she would at all be able to live the life of a normal human being. But she did not reveal any of those disheartening thoughts to her parents. But she knew, rather intuitively that Anoop knew all about it, her misery, how devastated she was; he could look deep within her, feel every beat of her pulse in his own. Strange!! But true!!

She wished her stay in the hospital to continue forever, to spend her evenings in the company of Anoop, forgetting how the blast had plagued her existence. But like every mundane thing lapsing into nonexistence in course of time, that too had come to its end. She was heartbroken, and was not sure what was more painful, to live through the agony of being irreparably disfigured, or to live away from someone who cared so deeply about her.

***

Anwar was still thinking of the man by the elevator as he entered the ward where Apoorva was. He dismissed the uneasiness from his mind and walked up to the bed. Apoorva's mother and sister stood by the bed. Her father was downstairs settling the bills at the reception counter and filling up other formalities relating to the patient's discharge.

Her mother waited for the advices from the

doctor who was in charge of Apoorva's treatment. He would soon be taking his morning rounds.

Anwar looked at Apoorva. She seemed to be well disposed but there was a deep-set pathos in her left eye. The right eye was still hidden under a thin bandage.

'I will miss you,' her voice was moist and her eye heavy. Anwar moved closer to her bed. 'I too will miss you,' he said in a strangled whisper. Much more than you will!' He wanted to take her in his arms, to run his hand on her head and comfort her.

Tears trickled down Apoorva's free eye and wetted the pillow. Anwar moved away from the bed.

'She is still very weak.' Apoorva's mother said. 'We have arranged for a nurse to come and dress her wound on alternative days.' She looked at Anwar affectionately. We will always be in your debt son,' she touched his head. 'Please keep visiting our house whenever you find time.'

'Of course, aunty.' Anwar promised. Apoorva's father too had comeback and Anwar bade him farewell. Before leaving he cast a last lingering look at Apoorva. Her unwavering gaze was fixed on him. Anwar smiled. A ghost of a smile. Then strode out of the ward, not looking back for once.

He looked up and down the corridor, expecting to see the man in the long kurta and baggy trousers. He was not there. Visitors were entering and exiting out of the elevator. He saw nothing unusual to rouse his suspicion. He entered the elevator. His heart gave a lurch. The man was standing at one corner of the big cage, scanning the screen of his mobile phone. Anwar swung back, turning his face to the door of the elevator. He was sure now the man was one of Abbu's associates. He also knew that he was searching for Anwar. Why?? To ensure that he was safe, or……. ? He cringed away from the thought, 'he was not alive?' They knew now that Anwar knew about the mission and his roaming free would be dangerous. What would they do in this circumstance? Anwar could make a guess, and it sent a chill down his spine.

The one silver line was he had now grown a dense beard and moustaches. He had not visited a hairdressing saloon after getting discharged from the hospital. It was his good luck that the blast had not dislodged the gold bracelet around his wrist, (it was a gift from Abbu on his nineteenth birth day) and a gold ring (yet another token of Abbu's generosity). He had pawned them in a modest local jewelry shop. The money collected thus, he thought hopefully, might last him near about a month. He was sharing a room with another young man, a fellow who worked in a biscuit factory eight hours a day, in the suburb area. He had planned to leave the town for good once the appropriate authorities issued him a fresh I-Card. Each passing day the feeling that his life was in danger here, grew stronger.

***

The elevator landed on the first floor with a

gentle thump. Anwar blended himself in the group of visitors making their exit and strode quickly out to the safety of a big hall where out-patients sat waiting on benches. He sat by the door, watching the man who too had come out of the elevator. Another man donned in a similar outfit, the length of his greyish brown matted hair reaching up to his shoulder, ambled casually up to him. They spoke to each other for a moment and walking abreast approached the desks of the receptionists at the far end of the wide corridor. Anwar got off the bench and walked up to a wash room. He inspected the reflection in the mirror carefully. The stubbles were now grown to long beard and hid the lower part of his face. He adjusted the cloth cap to cover most part of his forehead. The big sunglasses and the newly grown moustache gave him a look he himself could not recognize. Feeling confident that the two men could not recognize him in his present get up he came out of the waiting hall and looked around for them. He saw them standing at the counter behind which a young woman sat, her eyes glued to the monitoring screen of the computer in front of her, browsing, he guessed, the particulars of the patients. One of the men was holding out his mobile phone showing her something. Anwar edged forward guardedly. He stopped when he was within earshot and pretended to read the newspaper which he had bought, his ears pricked to listen.

'His name is Anwar,' the taller of the two

said. 'He is my nephew. He was there in the bus, but we have not found him till today. We have been searching the hospitals in the town and its vicinity. Someone told us that most of the blast-victims are in this hospital. Please take a good look at the photo and say if you happened to have seen him here. The receptionist, a sympathetic young girl in her twenties scanned the photo and shook her head. So many patients come here every day. It is not possible to identify every one of them. What is his name you said, by the way?'

'Anwar. Anwar Hussain.' The other one answered promptly.

'Most of the blast victims have lost their I-Cards and other identifying documents. We ask the less injured ones, who are in a stable state to answer our queries like their names and their address and relations. But let me check once again.' The girl said and returned her eyes to the computer screen. After a careful scrutiny, she made it clear that no one by that name was admitted in the hospital.'

The two men stood looking at each other for a while, perplexed and frustrated at losing their quarry. Anwar could capture snatches of their conversation. 'We have checked the small hotels and lodges. He is not there. Neither is he in the hospitals. Where has he holed up?'

Anwar's heartbeat quickened. They have been trawling the lodges and the hospitals in the town. It was by sheer good luck they have not been able to reach him. He knew he could not escape their keen search for long. He must leave the town as soon as possible.

***

He sat by the window and looked out at the buzzing, bustling platform. He had boarded a north bound train, thinking hopefully that his pursuers would not be expecting him there. He slid back the zip of his small handbag that contained his personal possessions and took out the new I-card issued to him. His name was Anoop Sahay, son of Aniruddh Sahay, Deoria, UP. He had booked the train ticked by that name. The coach was crowded with strangers and he felt safe amidst them. No one was looking at him suspiciously. A family of five had occupied the rest of the berths and were chattering nonstop. The train blew the last horn and began to slither out of the platform. It gathered momentum a few minutes later and headed towards a destination unknown to Anoop.

***

'Life is a train', Anoop reflected philosophically, moving along a chartered course, in its propulsive rhythm towards its destination. But there is a difference, the train has a specified place to reach while life, at least *his* life had no such fixed destination. Unlike the train that rolled across the idyllic, picturesque landscapes that looked like flitting pages from some fairytale as they flashed enthrallingly for a fraction of a moment and rushed back as if an impatient, invisible hand had turned the pages quickly, his life moved in a dark tunnel, and there was nothing to tell him what awaited him at the tunnel's end. He remembered Apoorva. The picture of her clambering into the bus in a hurry, the anxiety in her eyes as they wandered about the bus searching a vacant seat, the sweat beads on her forehead and chin, and the oval pendant dangling from a chain around her delicate throat flashed vividly before him. He also remembered her lying in the hospital bed moaning in pain, the heavy swathing across the right side of her face, her trauma and the look in her one free eye as he bade her goodbye, the wistful, longing, lingering look which was a voice, imploring him not to leave. He knew Apoorva was a distant dream, luring and beautiful but like most dreams, unreal!! The train like his life, was moving away farther and farther from Apoorva, to some obscure, unexpected and never-dreamt-of destination. He would be henceforward living a false life, wearing a fake identity. But then, he reflected wryly, what was his true identity? Was he Anwar? It was a name given to him by Abbu, a man whom he had loved with all his heart but was betrayed by in the weirdest possible way. It mattered a little whether he was Anwar or Anoop, except for that he could not use the certificate of his academic qualification. As such the certificate was at home. Home? He smiled sourly. There would not be a home where he would be safe from now on. The fear would track him down, haunt his days and nights unstoppably. Because the man who he thought had made his home was now a stranger, hounding after his blood.

And, Anwar thought grimly, he cared not much for the certificate now. He wanted to have a life of resigned unobtrusiveness, out of the mainstream, as a nonentity.

His eyes moistened without his knowledge.

***

Apoorva touched the right side of her face gingerly. The strip of bandage, though thinner now, was still there covering half of the cheek. She had been discharged from the hospital and returned home a week ago, after the second cosmetic surgery. The doctors sounded very positive about the result of the procedure. It had been nearly two years since the fatal explosion had turned her life upside down. She had somehow managed to appear in the final examination and completed her graduation. It was a terrible effort to meet the friends and teachers, some genuinely pained at the mishap that befell her, and some ostentatiously sympathetic at her misfortune. But she, with sheer will power had managed to preserve equanimity amidst the crowd of curious classmates who could not take their eyes off the bruises and wound marks. It was a relief when the papers were finally over.

***

The experience of watching her reflection in the washroom mirror after the preliminary treatments in the City Hospital was one like straight from a Kafkaesque nightmare. She had tiptoed into the washroom around midnight after ensuring that her parents were fast asleep, and turned on the light. Then she lifted the drape off the mirror. The drape was always there since the day she had come home from the hospital. She had never dared to lift it. But the anxiety to see her face was irrepressible. Slowly, carefully she rolled the bandage of her right cheek and eye and looked, and a thin scream escaped her. The two-inch wide scar, that was now a livid red and brown ran from her right temple down to the chin. The skin around was reddishly patchy and repulsive like that of a diseased reptile and the right eye slightly bulged out adding to the grotesqueness. She pressed her hand over her mouth to force another scream down. And almost at the same instant, synchronous with the screams, the tears came down in scalding torrents. She staggered out of the washroom and reaching her bed, flopped down, hard, desperate sobs racking her frail body. The scream had awakened her mother who ran to her bedroom, petrified.

Then started the prolonged procedures of cosmetic surgery, the shuttling between home to hospitals. The doctors, the ordeal, the pain, the torment. Through changing seasons, month after month, through hopes and despair, month after month. Living and dying alternately in each passing moment!

***

Bipul and his parents had made a formal visit during the gap between the two surgeries. It would not have made a big difference, Apoorva thought indifferently, if they would not have. In fact, they were the last amongst all who made the courtesy visits, or more appropriately, sympathy-visits. But she knew how badly her parents had hoped for this visit, as if their daughter's future hung from the fine thread of a commitment they made in some distant past. The effusive joy and excitement with which her father received Bipul's parents wounded her self-esteem. And the noncommittal replies they made when father asked anxiously when they were planning to solemnize the marriage scraped the wound to draw out blood. The fine thread of hope snapped.

She wondered what was her father expecting from these callous people who did not care to make a phone call to inquire about her health, let alone making a visit to the hospital or at least to her home, on learning that she had returned home.

Apoorva had no qualms in accepting the truth. She was depressed only because her parents still believed the lie of Bipul's parents.

'You do not have to lie to me,' she said to Bipul and smiled. It was not a faked, artificial smile, but simple and genuine. 'I know the truth, both yours and mine, and I know neither you nor I could accept each other's truth. Every body's truth is different, or should I say that everybody, at one time or other has to build up his private truth out of a lie. I know how difficult it is for you to reconcile to your truth and how delicate to forge a lie out of it to manipulate that truth to impress me. Trust me, I do not blame you nor shall I ever. Whatever something was between us is now a thing of past. You do not have to put your future at stake on account of that. I cannot forgive myself for the rest of my life if you, coerced by any incongruous code of morality resign yourself to a self-designed inevitability.'

Bipul did not say anything. Nor did he let his facial contour reveal the conflict, if at all there was one, within. There was a vague look in his eyes, indecipherable and distant. Was he unhappy? Guilty? Relieved? Apoorva could not decide.

'I need some more time to come to a decision Apoorva,' he said after a pensive pause. 'I do not want you to guess that the unfortunate accident had changed my feelings for you. I would just ask you to wait till the second surgery is done. It will, I am sure, repair your face and bring back the original look.'

'The scar will remain, Bipul,' Apoorva said, as if making a final statement. 'Not just on my face, on my life, on my destiny and yours too if you marry me! Would you prefer to live a scarred life?' Bipul could trace the mild sarcasm underlying the question. He did not counter it.

'I would always prefer a life with you, Apoorva, scarred or polished. You need not doubt *that* truth. But my parents might be having their predilections regarding this alliance, and I do not want to be harsh on them. That is the reason I request you to give me some time, to wait till the second cosmetic surgery is done.'

'I hold nothing against your parents or you,' Apoorva said. 'And I am not sure if I would go for a second surgery. I will *make* other plans for the future. You know marriage is not the only option one is left with in life.' She laughed a little to take the edge off her remark.

The discussion was dropped at that. Bipul left with his parents.

'Do not be so upset, Baba,' Apoorva solaced her grief-stricken father. 'God might be having better plans. Bipul was not the last man left on earth for me.' Suddenly, even as she was speaking to her father, a face, young, handsome and innocent, flashed before her eyes. *Anoop! Anoop Sahaya!* That was the name of the young man who had saved her life. He was the one who stood by her bed infusing strength to her sinking mind. A person she had trusted through her trauma and turmoil. And who never failed her!!

She wondered where he was. Apoorva doubted if he was there in the town. He would surely have come to inquire after her condition. She had heard him once saying to her mother that he was an orphan and was reared up by his foster father. Apoorva had no idea who his foster father was or where he lived. Anoop did not leave any contact number or address and had gone out of her life as abruptly and as unexpectedly as he came. She could not place it why exactly but she experienced a sudden and terrible urge to speak to him, to lay her heart open before him. He *had* her phone number,

He knew where she lived, too. But, would he ever contact her? Apoorva wondered wistfully.

She looked vaguely out of the window of her room at the street. Her father was closing the gate after Bipul and his parents had driven away. He looked pale and older. Two people, in shabby long kurtas and baggy trousers rode by her house on a motorbike. They cast a flitting glance at the house as they passed it. A few minutes later she again heard the sound of a motorbike. They were the same men, the same riders, returning. Once again, they looked at her house as they rode by. She could vaguely remember seeing them before, on the street in front of her house, but could not recollect exactly whether they were the same men or not. Apoorva wondered briefly who they could be, but soon she dismissed the curiosity as the gloomy look on her father's face filled her with a deep sorrow.

***

The vehicles ahead of him crawled to a halt as the traffic signal changed to red. He dropped the speed of the cab and let it roll to a stop keeping the engine running and looked out the window to his left. The space to his left was crammed by two and three wheelers. His eyes caught sight of a pair on a motorbike a little ahead to his left. Both of them were having their helmets on and were laughing over some joke or something. The girl had a purple scarf loosely wound round her neck. Anoop's heartbeat quickened. Who was the girl? Apoorva?? He remembered the moment he had seen her for the first time in the bus and the two objects that remained permanently etched in his mind, the oval shaped pendant dangling from the gold chain she wore around her throat and the purple scarf sprawled on her shoulder.

When was that? How many moments ago? How many lifetimes ago?

Is Apoorva here, in this city? His wishful gaze was fixed on the end of the purple scarf draped over the girl's shoulder. As if she could sense it, the girl turned her face to look. And a sigh of despair heaved out of Anwar.

She was a total stranger!!

The signal changed and the vehicles beeped and honked and revved loudly to make quick gateways across the traffic. The bike too wheeled forward, as Anwar let the cab worm through the throng of the automobiles.

***

The city seemed like a vast sea of buffeting, anonymous humanity when Anwar got down from the train, two years ago and entered it, a tiny boat without a rowing paddle, propelled defenseless into its turbulent waters. But he had managed to ride over the waves and had sailed into the calmer patches. He did not have the certificate of his academic qualification with him to apply for a job. The certificate, however, would not have been of any use to him since it was in the name of Anwar Hussain. He had to struggle hard through days of fasting and restless, scary nights on the railway platforms and the open porches of shops and the benches in public parks before finally by a stroke of luck he was hired by a private cab company. He was contented with the remuneration the company paid, and had no objection in doing long hours or travelling long distances. The boss was satisfied too and had made a raise in the wage. In short, life was slowly getting back to normal once again. He had found a comfortable and neat one room-kitchen unit in a chawl and had settled there, apparently peacefully. But the memory of Apoorva had never stopped haunting him in the lone, long nights he was off-duty, and slept in his rooming house. He felt torn by remorse and guilt. The longing, urging look in Apoorva's eye goaded him, tormented him. He should have inquired how was she and if she underwent the cosmetic surgeries. He wondered if she had recovered from the trauma and married the person she had been engaged to. But he was afraid to make contact with her. He was afraid that the men hunting him, Abbu's men, in the meanwhile, might have discovered through their efficient network and informers that he was there in the same hospital where Apoorva was, and was close to her family. He was apprehensive about Apoorva and her family's safety and decided it would be good if he kept himself away from her. He hoped to God no harm was brought to Apoorva or her family.

He wondered why, after such a long time he felt an overwhelming desire to see Apoorva, to know how was she.

The purple scarf!!

The memory that lay buried in the dark recess of his heart sprang back to life at the sight of the purple scarf. Should he make a call to Apoorva from some landline? From a shop or an office? His pursuers might track him down to this city through that call. It was a big city, he assured himself and it would not be easy for them to find him. But Anwar could guess how tenacious and how persistent they could be when it came to hunting down the prime witness to an organized crime.

***

The night was silent except for the soft whirr of the ceiling fan. Apoorva turned on her side again and checked the time on her mobile phone. Twenty minutes after eleven. She was experiencing a strange restlessness. It was nearly a half-year since the second surgery was done. There was a remarkable improvement in her looks after it. The ugly cutmarks on the right side of her face had almost disappeared, leaving only a faint, hairline scar that ran from the right corner of her eye to the chin. Her right eye too had returned to its normal shape. Apoorva could not believe her eyes when the plump, motherly nurse showed her the mirror after the bandages were removed. She was seeing her own reflection for the first time in months and what she saw was enough to boost up her sunken confidence. Her face had repaired excellently except for some small reddish patches which the doctors assured would fade away in course of time. Apoorva was not sure if she was happy at the developments. It was, however, a relief to get rid of that horrible cutmarks that gave her face a grotesque look.

Bipul had called to inquire how the surgery went a month after she came home. She asked him not to bother and disconnected the call. She did not want to chase a future that held no promises for her. She had made it clear to her parents too, who seemed too eager to start the negotiation afresh with Bipul's parents with a renewed hope. She had decided to join a nursing college. The long, exhausting months she had spent moving from one hospital to another, the seemingly unending, morbid nights of unbearable physical pain and mental turmoil and the hopes the nurses and the doctors tried to infuse into patients through encouraging words had motivated her to devote her life to serving the suffering mankind, to soothe and solace them in whichever possible way she could.

Her thoughts returned to the strangers on the motorbike whom she had seen again by the front gate of her house. Her life was so full of troubles and turmoil that she had failed to take note of a good many things happening around her. She could now recollect that a week or so after she was discharged from the City Hospital, she had noticed two men wearing baggy trousers and knee-length kurtas loitering outside her house. It was odd since they seemed not to be passing by but walked a few meters ahead and then meandered back, flicking furtive, quick glimpses at the house as they moved away.

They were seen almost regularly every afternoon and then after a couple of weeks or so and just as Apoorva began feeling wary about their unusual presence in the neighbourhood, they had abruptly stopped their dubious visits. Apoorva thought no more of them.

Turning on her side again on the bed, through the mysterious, sleepless night Apoorva tried to remember when was that she saw the men last. Suddenly it came to her, like a flash of lightning. On the afternoon when her father was bidding farewell to Bipul and his parents by the front gate. She stood at the window of her room upstairs and watched them. Then he saw the men. The same baggy trousers, shabby kurta, frizzy, shoulder-length hair and long beard. They were on a motorbike this time, crawling past the house. The bike took a U-turn, returned with increased speed and crossed past the house. And this time neither of the men looked at the house.

She had not seen either of them till today.

But there was absolutely no difficulty in recognizing them. They were the same two men who had been keeping an eye on her house, or her? It was the first time in all these days she felt oddly alert, like a deer scenting danger in the wind.

She decided to tell mother about the strangers next morning. And as she thought about it she remembered mother mentioning Anoop in the evening. It was for the first time in months she mentioned him. 'Do you know where Anoop is these days?' she asked Apoorva.

'No, why?'

'Just that I happened to remember him. He was a responsible boy. Courteous and decent.'

It was shortly after the faceoff with Bipul that Apoorva had experienced an irrepressible longing to see Anoop, but the ordeal of the long treatments and surgery, and the apprehension and uncertainty involving the consequences had cast an ominous shadow over her mind to block all thoughts of him.

She wondered if it was her mother's mention of Anoop had triggered the memory, or it was there lying dormant inside her all the time waiting to surface, and the realization of how genuine he was compared to Bipul, had brought him back to her mind with such fervency and intensity. She knew it was not easy to find out where he was unless he made the first move himself. But will he? Apoorva was skeptical about it. Anoop had never made a call, never tried to contact her in all these days. Why then she missed him so badly now? The memory of meeting Anoop first time in the bus returned to her in all its vividity. The tall, handsome young man looking at her fixedly and shyly averting his eyes as she turned to look back, offering her his own seat and pulling her out of the bus putting his own life at stake and then the fierce, volcanic explosion flinging them together on the sidewalk of the road. And in the hospital, his concern, the deep love lurking in his sad eyes as he held her hand and whispered encouraging, consoling words to her. Even her parents were greatly impressed by the sincere efforts he made to intimate them about their daughter.

Before she finally drifted into sleep that night her last thoughts revolved around Anoop. There was an irresistible desire to meet him, an intense urge that had turned into, she admitted reluctantly, to some kind of an obsession.

***

Anwar was in two minds. He stood at the counter table of an average looking garment store watching the fat man, who he guessed was the owner of the establishment, reclining in a cushioned chair behind it, his eyes half closed. A land-line phone stood nonchalantly on the glass topped counter table. Anwar had bought a purple scarf from the store, an expensive affair when it came to the modest wages of a speed-cab driver. He tried to put up a casual, indifferent look to douse any suspicion in the man's mind when he requested for his permission to use his land-line phone. The man opened his eyes and looked questioningly at Anwar. 'What is it young man? Haven't you paid the bill at the billing section?'

'I did sir. Could I use your land-phone, sir? I have an urgent call to make and the battery of my cellphone has drained out.'

'Go ahead,' the fat man said agreeably.

Anwar took out a tiny notebook from his pocket and consulted it. He turned to the page that contained the number of Apoorva's father. It was Apoorva who had given him that number while she was in the City Hospital. He was not sure if her father still used the number. Saying a silent prayer he dialed the number, his hands clammy, his stomach fluttering.

***

'Hello. Who is it?' A male voice answered.

'This is Anoop sir,' he said politely into the receiver. 'Hope you haven't forgotten me. I had been to your house, when Apoorva was in the City Hospital.'

Apoorva's father was effusive in his greetings at the other end of the line. Anoop carefully avoided giving him the details of his whereabouts except making a passing information that he was outside the state. He learnt about Apoorva's successful surgery and also about her joining a nursing college in the same town. Presumably she had not got married. But Anoop did not ask about that.

'Would you be coming here one of these days?' Apoorva's father asked.

Anoop did not have any specifics to offer to that. Instead, he asked something else. 'Apoorva must be feeling more confident now,' he said instead.

'By God's grace she is almost normal now.'

Anoop, hovered between an urging to ask if he could have Apoorva's number, and an apprehension that he might take it amiss. But the urge was too much to put aside.

'Would you like to speak to her?' Apoorva's father asked as if he could interpret the long pause Anoop took.

'If you permit, sir,' Anoop fumbled for words but could not think of anything else to say.

'Why shouldn't I son?' he returned fondly. 'Had it not been for you God knows when we could have found our daughter.'

It was as simple as that. Apoorva's father gave him her number and once again requested Anoop to visit his house.

***

Anoop looked out of the window as the train thundered ahead on the track of time back to a destination he had left far behind. He smiled wryly at the paradox. An enchanting panorama of landscape kept opening up unendingly as the fields and farmlands, and hills and jungles rushed behind like a montage of films sliding slickly back. He closed his eyes and tried to remember his conversation with Apoorva a couple of days back.

***

The kindly looking man behind the counter did not refuse when Anoop sought his permission to make another phone call. A nervous tingling flitted through his finger as he pressed the digits on the phone. He clutched the receiver tightly fearing it would slip off his sweaty grip and pressed it to his ear, his heart beating unusually fast as he listened to the burring at the other end. Then there was a soft click and then Apoorva's delicate voice, 'Hello!' Anoop's tongue felt stiff. 'Hello! Is that you, Anoop?' Apoorva asked as Anoop was still fumbling for words.

'Yes,' It was just above a whisper. 'Where are you? Why did you not contact me earlier?' Anoop was beginning to feel a bit easier now. 'How are you?' he asked after a brief pause.

And then she narrated the tale of her trauma. She began speaking slowly at first, then words gushed out, a snowball of pain gathering speed and bulk as she hurtled through the whole, awful story of her suffering, her ordeal, her misery. Then suddenly the snowball exploded, and flowed out in racking sobs. Tears streamed down Anoop's eyes as he heard her, experiencing a complex emotion, part sorrow, part guilt and part anger. The tears were for her and for himself, for the cruel betrayal of trust, for the violent, twisted world that allowed this sort of horror to happen to innocent men. To beautiful girls like Apoorva. His hands closed over the packet that contained the purple scarf.

***

Apoorva sang a song as she sprinted along the narrow stream that cut through a lush valley. He did not understand the words of the song but his heart swayed to the melody. Her luscious hair billowed in the wind and the purple scarf swung across her back as she glided on, flashing luminously through the thickets hemming the foothills. Every time he leaped forward to catch hold of the scarf and pull Apoorva towards him, she slipped out of his reach and laughed, a sweet, tinkling laughter that mingled with the ripples of the stream. He hummed to the tune of the song, and laughed as he chased Apoorva. She was now running alongside the foot of a rocky hill, turning back from time to time to flick a teasing, 'catch me if you can' glance at him. She did not see the boulder that was rolling downhill. Nor did Anwar. She turned and stood by the hill waving at him, beckoning him to join her. And the boulder sped down unbelievably fast and Anwar dashed forward, shouting warnings, his heart in his mouth. It was too late, and the boulder hurtled down the foot of the hill hitting Apoorva with great force, pushing her down and crushing her. Anwar could see nothing of Apoorva except a part of the purple scarf and the patches of fresh blood on it.

He was still screaming when he sprang up on the bed, bathed in sweat.

He decided to leave for Bharatpur the next day, and called Apoorva from the landline phone in a grocery shop. He had made up his mind to reveal his truth to Apoorva and leave it to her to decide if she still believed him and, he thought dubiously, *loved* him!

***

Apoorva noticed them just by a sheer chance when the ola cab she was travelling in dropped speed at the traffic signal.

Bharatpur was not a very big town and the broad roads proved not enough always to accommodate the crowd of vehicles that seemed to be in a perpetual hurry to get past one another. Traffic jam is a common scenario on these roads mostly during the early hours of the morning when people travelled to their offices and in the late afternoons when they returned home. She cast a cursory glance at her wristwatch. Wearing wristwatches has somehow been an outdated choice. But Apoorva had always preferred to have one around her wrist. It showed twenty after five. The sun hovered across the western skyline, oozing crimson before taking the final plunge. She had to reach the Café Venus, one of the few posh snack-joints the town could boast. Anoop would be waiting there for her. A wave of electric thrill swept through her as she tried to imagine the meeting with Anoop.

She looked out of the window. A motorbike, two men astride on it, had crawled to a stop alongside the cab, so close that she could have touched it. She thought little of it and looked impatiently at her watch once again, and hoped she would not be late.

She turned her gaze back to the bike by the cab, prompted more by instinct than interest. One of the men looked slightly familiar and then she remembered where she had seen him.

They were the same seedy looking men she had seen outside the house the day before, and on the day Bipul and his parents visited her house, in the same grimy outfit, a pair of baggy trousers and a long, loosely fitted kurta.

A mild, spidery fear, crept through her nerves at the sight of the men.

A coincidence? Too much of a coincidence if it was one!!

But none of the two cared to cast even a glance at her. The one that was driving the vehicle looked straight ahead, a stiff, impassive look on his face, and the other, on the pillion seat, the man who was seen in the company of the first one outside her house more than once, wore a look of absolute indifference. And they looked so uncannily normal!

The cab moved ahead and she drove the odd apprehensions out of her mind.

***

They sat on the narrow wooden bench in the Vivekanand Garden, sensing the intense intimacy that needed no words to evince itself. Anoop was waiting at the outside of Café Venus as she got down from the ola cab. They had coffee there. But the place was too crowded to give them a private space. So they had strolled into the relatively less peopled Vivekanand Garden, a few meters ahead of the café.

The sun had set but it was still light in the garden. They sat on a bench in a solitary corner. A soft breeze blowing from the south ruffled Apoorva's hair. He twined an arm around her waist and pulled her closer to him. 'I have brought something for you,' he said, savouring the smell of her as she leaned harder on him.

'Show me!' Apoorva said, shifting back a little, a fond smile lighting up her face. Anwar unzipped the sling bag, took out the packet, and unwrapped it. He held out the scarf to her. 'Wow!' Apoorva exclaimed, 'What a lovely scarf. How do you know purple is my favourite colour?'

'I know many things about you which you do not know yourself,' Anwar mocked and touched Apoorva's cheek. Her face had regained its earlier look after the two cosmetic surgeries and the thin hairline scar was almost invisible. 'You had a purple scarf on when I saw you for the first time in that bus and lost my heart to you instantly.'

Apoorva blushed.

He draped the scarf over her shoulder and took her in his arms.

Apoorva looked at him lovingly. The intense passion in Anwar's eyes numbed her nerves. A wave of ecstasy rushed through her as his hot breath fanned her neck. 'I remember a few lines of a famous poet…' Anwar whispered. 'They so exactly describe my feelings…would you like me to quote them?

'Yes,… please, yes!' She mumbled huskily.

'hazaroon khwahise aisi ke har khwahis pe dum nikle

Bahut nikle mere aarman lekin phir bhi kum nikle..'

Apoorva closed her eyes, sipping in the intoxicating passion in the words and Anwar lowered his face over hers, enjoying the gossamer caress of her swirling curls on his face.

She was not sure if it was an intuition cr instinct but she could sense the danger very close. She stiffened and darted her gaze around. 'What is it?' Anwar asked, astonished at the sudden change that had come over her. 'Let us get away from here,' Apoorva urged, the fear in her voice turning to a demand. Anwar looked at her questioningly, feeling a bit tense himself but not knowing the reason. Apoorva decided to tell him about the two suspicious looking characters as they travelled back home. Let's go. She said urgently, half rising from the bench.

Anwar did not want the divine moment to end. 'Wait a moment. What are you so wary about?' He asked without making any move to get up. Apoorva looked helplessly at him.

The sharp, searing pain was almost synchronous with the sound of the soft crack. And then the frantic cry of Anoop as he tried to gather her in his arms before she fell off the bench. Then another simultaneous crack and an agonizing scream from Anoop. She saw Anoop toppling off the bench, but everything was beginning to look so bleary. She heard Anoop's frenzied scream and felt the grip of his arms around her slackening. He struggled to lift her off the ground but failed as many times he tried. Desperate, he grabbed at the purple scarf smeared with blood, he was not sure whose, his or Apoorva's. 'Apoorva', he croaked, making a super human effort to drag both of them under the bench, to escape further assault. But the move made him slide away from her. He tried to prop himself up on his elbow but it was too much of an effort. He lay back on his side, his breath coming out in halting, scratchy gasps. The glazed look in his eyes, locked in Apoorva's glassy gaze were eloquent with his love. Apoorva could read the lines he had recited minutes ago in his sinking gaze... ......
hazaroon khwahise aisi ke har khwahish pe dum nikle... before they turned into slits. She stretched a feeble

hand at him as her lips twisted in a painful smile and her last breath escaped her in a soft hiss.

The smile was still pasted to her lips when they found them after hours. The young man who lay by her, still clutched the bloodstained purple scarf that draped over her still body, in a desperate, tight grip.

THE GHOST STORY

Monsters are real, ghosts are too. They live inside us, and sometimes they win...

Stephen King

'This time the potatoes and cauliflowers have come out nicely. Robust and large.' Govind said, satisfaction ringing in his voice.

'Mine too. Had not hoped for such heavy yield.' Madhu showed a row of off-white teeth in a broad grin. 'Nature has been very kind to us this year. They would fetch good profit.' He added.

'Yes, but not in the local market. We have to sell them in the market place at the village of Nilapur. That is a large market and many people from neighbouring villages come there to buy vegetables.'

'You have a point there. The local buyers are not ready to pay more.' Govind agreed.

This was the conversation between two farmers who had grown potatoes and cauliflowers in their lands. The mid-winter harvesting was on and the two farmer friends were working hard, digging out the potatoes. The potatoes had grown in abundance and looked quite healthy. To watch the potatoes piled up on the ridges along the lands was an exciting experience.

This is a tale of older times when people had no idea about travelling in motorbikes or other motor -run vehicles and communicating on mobile phones. Villages did not have electricity and people used kerosene lamps and lanterns for lighting their homes. A large segment of the population in the villages were peasants and earned their living from farming of land. There were others who depended on other vocations like livestock farming, weaving or pottery.

Govind and Madhu were good friends and were neighbours living in the village Shrutipur. They did not own large patches of lands to grow paddy and other grains. They depended mostly on growing potatoes and seasonal vegetables. Each had a cow tethered in the cowshed that fulfilled the need of milk of the family. Govind's father, though grown old, shouldered the responsibility of looking after and milking the cow. Govind had grown cauliflowers in a small patch and potatoes in a relatively larger patch of land. Potatoes sold at more or less uniform prices all through the year with slight variations in the rate now and then. But the land where they had grown cauliflowers had yielded a good harvest. They decided to carry the potatoes and the cauliflowers to the weekly-market in the village of Nilapur where, both of them knew, they would be sold at a higher rate. Selling them in the local market would not bring good profit.

And so, one misty morning of mid-winter the friends set out to the market place of village of Nilapur that was some seven to eight kilometers away, their bicycles loaded with the farm produces. Each bicycles had a couple of canvas bags stuffed with cauliflowers hanging from its handles and a large sack of potatoes tied to its passenger-carrier seat behind. It was early morning and there was still some time for the sun to come up. A cold wind was blowing from the north and Govind and Madhu pulled their thin blankets tightly around them. The birds had started their morning chatters in the trees that grew scatteringly along the road. The bicycles, sagging under the combined load of the vegetables and the rider rolled sluggishly along the uneven, bumpy path. They reached the narrow wooden bridge that passed over a stream and led into a dense mango grove at the other side in about half an hour. The village Nilapur was at another few kilometers away from the other end of the big mango grove. A thin film of mist hung low over the stream. Splashed randomly with the light from the sun that was lazily climbing up the east it created an illusion of a mystique mantle of luminous blue stretching out over the still drowsy earth. The bicycle riding, though a little strenuous, was a pleasant experience. A few minutes later they crossed the bridge and entered the thick orchard of mango. It was winter time and the boughs, looking dusty and pale hung darkly from the big, dispassionate trees. The patch was so thickly crowded with the mango trees that the feeble light of the morning sun hardly found a way into the grove. Even in the morning the grove wore a gloomy, heavy look as if some deep secret lay hidden inside it. The ride through the mango grove was a slightly discomforting experience for both the friends and they felt relaxed when they were out of it in the lighted road at the other side. They joined a couple of farmers who were travelling to the market and covered the rest part of the journey in light hearted chatting, and discussing and exchanging ideas on farming.

Govind and Madhu took out their tiffin carriages from their bags and sat down to eat under a big banyan tree in the slanted sunlight of the winter noon. Other traders who had arrived at the village market of Nilapur to sell their farm produces too ate their lunch sitting in small groups. All of them looked relaxed after doing a satisfactory business.

Madhu put a ball of soaked rice in his mouth and smiled at Govind. 'A lucky day for me. All my cauliflowers are sold away at good rate. Only some ten kilos of potato are left. They too will be sold away by afternoon if luck favours.'

'Same here friend,' Govind said taking a bite from the onion. 'I have only five cauliflowers and seven or eight kilos of potato left. God willing the afternoon buyers will take them.'

The crowd in the market had thinned out. People in scanty numbers, mostly from the village

Nilapur and the neighbouring ones, while returning after the morning shift at the farmlands, stopped by to buy vegetables. The traders stretched themselves under the trees for a while.

Business was not so encouraging in the afternoon for Govind and Madhu. The cauliflowers were sold away but not the potatoes. The number of buyers did not increase as Govind and Madhu had expected and there was a slight, unexpected drizzle which turned the weather bleak and chilly. Most traders left while it was still light. Govind and Madhu waited till it was evening. They had expected to sell away all the products they had brought. The return journey could have been easy and quick without the load of the vegetables. A load of about ten kilos of potatoes was not however a big obstruction but it would have made them happier had all the potatoes been sold away. They did not want to carry back the potatoes and decided to keep it in the custody of some reliable person of the village for a few days till the next sale-day of the week, and go back. They sat on the steps of the temple of Goddess Durga at one end of the market place, pondering over the problem. The compound of the temple was wide and spacious. As they sat discussing the priest came in to perform the evening worships. It began to get chillier as the evening advanced. When the priest came out after completing the worship the two friends approached him with a request to permit them to keep the sacks of potatoes in the temple premises for a couple of nights.

But the priest refused. 'It is not possible young men,' he said apologetically. I understand your problem. But I will have to answer the trustees of the temple, and I don't think they would approve of it. You better ask in the shop over there that sells snacks and sweetmeats. The shop owner is a good man. He might help you,' the priest suggested before leaving.

'We are strangers here. Do you think the shop owner will agree to help us?' Govind looked at Madhu.

'No harm in trying. What will happen in the worst case? We will have to carry them back to our village. That is not so big an issue. Come, let us ask the man.'

The shop owner was frying fitters in a big pan. He raised his eyes from the pan to look at Madhu and Govind as they approached.

'Would you like some fritters? They have just come off the pan. Hot and crispy.'

'Yes. They look tempting.' Madhu agreed and smiled. 'However, we have come with a request,' he added uncertainly.

'What is it?' The shop owner cast a questioning glance at them.

Govind narrated about how they were left with some ten kilos of potatoes each which they did not want to take back to their village and again carry them back here in the next sale-day of the week. He requested the man to keep the sacks safe for a couple of days somewhere inside the shop.

The man nodded his head understandingly. 'It is not a big problem. You could keep the sacks here for a couple of days. However, I would not have taken the risk of returning to the village in the night had I been in your place. It is not wise.'

'But we must. We have not intimated our families that we would be staying here overnight. They would worry themselves to death if we do not get back tonight.' Govind expressed his concern.

'Why do you say it would not be wise to take the risk of returning to the village in the night? What risk?' Madhu inquired.

'Have some fritters and tea first. I would tell you about it.' The man said and mopped a small, rickety wooden table with a greasy piece of cloth. 'Sit here, please.' He pointed to a wooden bench. The two friends looked at each other. 'I don't think we could have anything to eat before we reach home. Better eat something here.' Govind suggested.

'That is really thoughtful of you,' the shop owner smiled amicably. 'Hey, Raghu, bring two plates of fritters here and put the tea-kettle on the stove.' He called out. A skinny boy who looked barely over ten years brought water in a couple of metal glasses and put them on the table. Then he ran back and brought two plates of fritters.

'You enjoy the fritters. Tea will be ready in a minute.'

Both the friends were hungry and the fritters tasted really good. They finished the fritters and drank some water. The shop owner came carrying the tea in two glasses.

'What were you telling about a risk? Would you please tell us in detail?' Govind asked the man.

' I would not want to frighten you, but it is not wise to travel across that big mango grove in night.'

'Why?' Madhu asked, his voice a bit apprehensive.

'They say there are spirits in the trees. They come down the trees in the deep nights and trouble the one who confronts them.'

'Has anyone seen them?' Madhu asked again. 'I do not believe in ghosts,' he tried to sound bold and convincing. But his voice lacked confidence.

'Many had seen large shadows swinging from the thick boughs and heard the loud sounds of stones pelting and branches breaking. Some had fainted or fallen terribly sick after the gruesome experience. Most people avoid moving through the mango grove in the night. I would advise you to spend the night either here or in the shed at the corner of the market-place and return in the morning.'

Govind and Madhu looked again at each other, and Govind shook his head. 'We must return tonight, and we would rather take the sacks back home. It is not a big load, after all. What do you say, Madhu?'

Madhu nodded his assent. 'Yes. We should take them back. We are not sure if we will be able to come back on the next sale-day of the week.'

'Whatever suits you,' the man in the shop said

wondering what made them change their minds. 'But I would still say it would be wise to spend the night here instead of venturing into that notorious grove.'

'Do not you worry. We would be riding bicycles which are made of iron. I know ghosts keep away from iron. Nothing will happen.' Govind said.

'You are right about the iron in the bicycle. Ghosts do not come near you if you have iron with you. But, be very careful. It is after seven in the evening. It will take about half an hour to reach the grove if you start now. Do you have a battery-run torch light or a kerosene lantern with you?'

'No.' Madhu shook his head.

The shop owner gave them a matchbox. 'Keep it with you. You can burn a match stick now and then to get some light.'

'That is so kind of you.' Madhu and Govind said in one voice and took leave of him.

***

The drizzle had stopped by the time they reached at the fringe of the mango grove, but the darkness had thickened. The air had a wetness in it that made them shiver. A chilly wind whistled softly through the dense boughs of the massive trees. Standing at the outer edge of the grove the two friends cast an uneasy glance inside. The grove wore a deserted look. There was something oddly unwelcoming about it. Shadows hung in thick ribbons of black from the dense boughs of the trees that stood like tall and quirky figures straight out of some horror tale.

Madhu felt a frisson of fear, and touched Govind's hand. 'Should we go back and spend the night in that snack shop?' He sounded dubious. 'That would mean going back nearly two kilometers. There is nothing to worry. The tale of ghosts could be just a hearsay. There is no such thing as ghost. And even if there at all is, we are well protected against it because of our bicycles. The iron-made bicycles will keep the evil spirits, if there is any, at bay. Be brave and come along. Govind tried to infuse confidence into his voice even though he was not feeling very confident inside. They rode cautiously into the grove, moving abreast and talking loudly to override the nagging discomfort.

The sound of a loud splat close by, as if some heavy thing had dropped from above, startled them.

What could it be?

A mango? But that was not possible. Mangoes do not grow in winter.

What was it then?

Potatoes falling from the sack?

But they had tied the mouth of the sacks tightly. May be a stone that had got stuck in the foliage dropped down. Then there was another splatting sound which was followed by still another. Govind and Madhu dismounted their cycles and stood close together gripping each other's hand.

'Do not fear. Let me light a matchstick.' Govind said encouragingly and taking out a matchstick rubbed it against the side of the matchbox. In the sepulchral silence that cloaked the grove the soft scratch sounded like the burst of a firecracker. The burning matchstick formed a tiny, stirring pool of light on the ground. They looked around to find out the objects that had supposedly fallen from above in such quick succession. There was nothing of the sort. As they lifted their heads to look up the light went out and darkness pounced upon them like a huge, diaphanous animal. A light scream escaped Madhu. 'You are such a nervy fellow,' Govind admonished him in mock anger. 'There is nothing to panic about. Let us move on. Pedal faster and harder. We will be soon out of the grove. There will be nothing to worry about once we reach the wooden bridge.' And they pedaled faster, letting the bicycles roll smoothly on the comparatively even floor of the grove.

'Hey, Govind! Look at that.' Madhu whispered, pointing at something ahead, breathing wildly.

Govind let his gaze move in the direction Madhu pointed at.

His heart missed a beat, and then began to race. A luminous object that looked like a flickering flame was moving ahead of them. Govind gaped at it, his mouth hung open in shock, goosebumps breaking out on his skin. The flame that was swaying erratically seemed to be rising up from a big half-circle of dense blackness that tapered down to a long, hanging shadow. As they stared unblinkingly ahead at it, the floating column of black ambled forward, the flame of light swinging on its top. Madhu screamed and let go of the bicycle. It hit the ground with a loud metallic sound and the sack of potato thudded to the ground. The string that was tied to its mouth had come loose God knew how. And the potatoes, released from their long confinement in the sack went rolling merrily across the grove. Govind, terrified out of his wits, grabbed at Madhu wildly. His feet fell on the potatoes as his body nudged forward. Losing his balance, he careened to the ground pulling Madhu along with him. They screamed loudly for a while and then stopped abruptly. They could hear now the low ringing of a bell approaching them. Govind and Madhu, their blood frozen in their veins, waited breathlessly. They could hear clearly now. It was the ringing of a cycle bell, as if someone was moving towards them from the opposite direction riding a bicycle. They tried to get up and even as they got to their feet something that looked like a black boat came rushing towards from behind and hit them with full force. A loud scream that followed it immediately sounded like the cry of some aboriginal animal. They howled crazily and another howl from the boat like thing joined theirs.

'Who is that?' Govind, trying to regain his composure asked, his voice quivering in fear.

'I am Mangu,' a farmer from Malikanthpur,' a frightened, breathless voice replied. 'I had come to sell dried fish in the weekly market of Nilapur with my friend. But he left early leaving me alone. I had no alternative other than taking the risk of travelling alone in this darned night.'

Govind let out a deep sigh of relief. He struck another match and in the feeble light looked at the man who called himself Mangu. He struck more matches and helped Madhu to get up. The three of them stood in the grove, their legs still trembling slightly but feeling much less agitated now.

'We thought you to be a ghost,' Govind said and smiled uneasily. 'I also thought the same,' Mangu laughed. 'But I am worried about my friend Sinu. Had he crossed this grove and reached home safely? He should have waited for me.'

'He must have reached home by this time. There is no point in waiting for him in this place. The sooner we cross it the better.'

'But what is that swinging light? Madhu asked. 'It is certainly a ghost. It is moving ahead of us. How can we step past it?'

Mangu stared ahead. 'Let us wait till it disappears. It will not attack us unless we disturb it.'

'I have another idea.' Govind said. 'We three will sound the bells of our bicycles as loudly as possible. the sound may prompt the thing, ghost or whatever, make way for us and we will ride past it quickly.'

'Let us chant loudly the forty-liner prayer of Lord Hanuman and move on,' Madhu suggested. Joining their palms in reverence to Lord Hanuman, the god who is believed to have the power to destroy the ghosts and other such evil souls, the trio set out on the tricky journey.

The swinging flame over the moving column of black seemed to have been moving now slowly and hesitantly. As they looked on the light stopped by a big tree. A long, branchy shape that drooped from the tree and touched the upper point of the flame, looked like a headgear of a sentry of some dark netherworld. 'Now', Govind cried and together the three of them began pressing the bells with all the force they could use. In that still, desolate grove the sound of the three bells ringing in unison created a big, earsplitting noise. Suddenly the swinging light was seen climbing down the black column. It seemed to have been flung down by some invisible power and at the same time the three of them heard a loud scream, 'O Mother Goddess, save me! O' Mother Goddess Save me!!'

'It sounds like Sinu's voice,' Mangu exclaimed in surprise.

'Hey, Sinu!' He called out loudly. The black column lurched down to where they stood and grabbed blindly at them. 'Brother Mangu!' It croaked. 'Are you Brother Mangu?'

Mangu moved forward and put his arms round the man. 'Where had you been brother Sinu? I had looked for you everywhere in the market but did not find you. I thought you had left.'

'I remembered some urgent work at home and decided to return early. I searched for you, but you were perhaps at the far end of the market place. As such, all my dried fish were sold away before it began to drizzle. I assumed it would be late by the time you wrapped up your business and left. I am so sorry, brother.' Sinu was at the verge of weeping.

'You need not be sorry brother Sinu. I was just worried about you.' Mangu patted the back of his friend.

'I did not know this grove is thronged with spirits,' Sinu whined. 'They are swinging from the branches, jumping here and there hissing and whistling, and pelting stones at me.' He added.

Madhu cast a glance at the flame that had now climbed down to the ground. To his utter amazement he discovered that it was a lantern in a big round shaped basket. It was the basket in which Sinu had brought the dried fish to sell. In the flame of the lantern that was raised, perhaps to get more light, the outline of the basket formed a ring of shadow. The flame rising from looked like a flicking tongue of fire protruding out of the hideous mouth of some phantom.

'Hey, Govind! He touched Govind's shoulder, grinning broadly. 'We were fooled by the light of the lantern in the basket.' 'Seems so.' Govind smiled skeptically.

The four of them moved across the grove, now feeling more confident and well protected in one another's company, against any possible assault from the invisible or imagined creatures. In another half hour they were safely out of the grove and at the wooden bridge.

The weather had cleared and they rode back to their villages, Mangu and Sinu on one cycle, and Govind and Madhu each riding his own. They chatted loudly about the day's experience at the market place and the profit they earned from the selling. But somewhere deep within each of them carried a doubt, each mulled over the experiences in the mango grove, trying to judge them with his power of reasoning.

'Were those things my imagination? Some weird fantasy?' Govind thought. 'What were those sounds of something heavy falling from the trees? Was it the wind that hissed through the boughs, and not the panting of a thousand invisible beings?'

'What were those grotesque shadows that seemed to be hanging from the branches?' Mangu thought. 'Just optical illusions? Or….?'

'There is nothing there in the grove. All that we happened to experience there were conjured up by our imagination, and a preconceived notion.' Sinu tried to convince himself.

'It was because of the big flame of the lantern. The spooky shadows that seemed to be swinging around were actually made by the flickering light from the lantern. Were they really…?'

Madhu wiped his forehead where sweat beads had formed despite the chill in the air.

But each one of them had made a decision, without revealing it to the other.

Even if the selling of the firm produces did not fetch good money in the local market, like it did in the weekly market of Nilapur, it would be wise not to venture into that mysterious grove again.

INFIDEL

There is no suspense in inevitability...
Damon Lindeloff

Trisha sat on the steps of the temple of Radha-Krishna nursing the weal on her arm where the leather belt had slashed her. The mark looked purple and ugly and livid and the singe ate into her flesh. She winced as her fingers touched it. But she did not shed tears. Perhaps the hot block of sorrow inside her had drained her eyes dry. It had not happened for the first time though, Chandrakant hitting her at the slightest pretext. She had no idea as such why her husband flew into a rage so easily at the small slips she made. She had learnt he was a habitual drinker while the negotiations for her marriage with him were going on. Her mother was warned against the alliance by some kindly neighbours and well-wishing kins. But Chandrakant was rich, owned a stationary shop and being an orphan, had not much familial responsibilities to shoulder. 'What else do you need in a husband? Which young man does not drink these days? He will slowly come out of the habit when a baby comes to your life.' Her mother explained persuasively. Trisha knew how her mother had struggled to run the household, to rear her and her brother up after her father's untimely death. She decided to believe what her mother predicted would come true in course of time. And she had given her consent.

But what her mother had presaged never became a reality. After three years of marriage there was no baby, and no brake to Chandrakant's drinking spree. And, to add to it Chandrakant had begun hitting her. He appeared to derive a savage pleasure out of that, as if he was avenging the frustration of his childlessness. He would keep arguing over trifles and his anger would flare up at the small mistakes she made in managing the household chores.

Most nights he would return late, sloshed to the tip of his hair and flop into bed without eating his dinner. It is only in those nights when he was urged on by his sub-human libido, he would come closer to her, and after a loathsome and repulsive session of lovemaking that made her flesh creep, would roll away to the edge of the bed. Trisha would get up and stagger to the washroom, hating her body, hating her lack of courage to protest, hating her for allowing herself to be molested by his animal passion. She would sit under the water tap for hours letting the running water wash down the dirt, the defilement, and the despondency.

A nightbird hooted, interrupting the flow of the bitter reminiscence. The temple premises was deserted. A pale moon hanging from the woolly clouds shed a feeble light on a patch below the steps and the shadow of the tall coconut tree that sprawled across that pool of light looked like a giant umbrella gone into shreds. She experienced a throbbing pain where the weal was and her head also began to ache.

She glanced at the closed portals of the inner section of the temple. 'What is my fault, Krishna? Why have you been subjecting me to such terrible misery? Is this the reward for the unwavering faith I had put on you all these years?' She mumbled accusingly.

***

It was not new on the part of Chandrakant to hit her, to hurl abuses at her. But tonight, the savagery had reached its optimum level. And the cause that had fanned the embers of Chandrakant's anger to raging flames was so ridiculously paltry that Trisha's lips twisted in a crooked, sardonic smile when she recollected it.

The cause was Bikash, Chandrakant's friend. It was election time and different political parties were paying people money to join their respective rallies. Bikash was an active worker for a regional political party. Chandrakant, Bikash and others joined the rallies organized by the party and treaded across the sun scorched streets of a furious summer. Most days Chandrakant would keep his shop closed in the post- lunch hours to join the rally, and then spend the evenings in the liquor sheds.

That day Chandrakant returned early, around three in the afternoon. He was not alone.

'Meet Bikash,' Chandrakant introduced him to Trisha. 'One of the party workers.' Bikash flicked a polite smile at Trisha. He was handsome in a gentle, agreeable way, and the smile had an arresting quality about it. Trisha could not restrain herself from smiling back at him.

'Give us something to eat. We are famished. The fellows made us walk ten kilometers on the sun-blazed streets, without giving us even a bottle of water and handed us just seven hundred rupees each for all the trouble taken.'

'Will I be eating your share of food, Bhabi?' Bikash asked looking into Trisha's eyes. 'No issue there,' Trisha returned amiably. 'There is enough for all three of us.'

'Will you please stop exchanging the pleasantries and serve food?' Chandrakant snapped, a hard glint in his eyes.

Bikash thanked Trisha profusely as they left after having their belated lunch. 'You have magic in your hand Bhabi. The food was just divine.' Trisha laughed. 'Come again,' she said trying to sound formal for the benefit of Chandrakant. Chandrakant cast a sharp, biting look at Trisha as he followed Bikash out of the door.

'You love to chat with other men, don't you?' Chandrakant's voice was harsh and rude like the crack of a whiplash. Trisha could not see his face clearly in the darkness. 'Why do you say such things?" She protested, feeling hurt. 'Do not play that innocent act with me. I know women like you. They like to get close to every other man except for their husbands. Whores!' The hatred with which he spat the word out made Trisha cringe. That was the night Chandrakant had begun hitting her with the belt. She turned her face away and squeezed her eyes shut.

But the hatred and suspicion that smouldered inside Chandrakant erupted in a volcanic explosion the afternoon he discovered Bikash sitting in a basket chair in the front veranda of his house and sipping tea. Trisha stood by him, smiling perhaps at some joke Bikash had said.

'I came here looking for you, buddy, when I did not find you at the shop' Bikash explained. 'Yes, I had gone out to collect some items for the shop from the wholesale store.' Chandrakant replied tersely.

And they left, but not before Bikash offered his effusive thanks to Trisha for the tea.

That night was the culminating point of her agony. A night of showdown, for both Trisha and Chandrakant. The last straw of forbearance she had clutched desperately at, was swept away by the surging, storming currents of Chandrakant's unfounded suspicion and wrath. That night he turned to, for Trisha, a monster.

'You sinning slut!' He hissed at her. 'You like to have it off with outsiders, don't you?' He snarled, swinging the belt. The contempt in his words was more searing than the whipping from the belt.

After Chandrakant slept, venting out his anger and frustration, she sneaked out of the house and reached the temple of Radha Krishna.

***

She sat on the steps leading up to the front hall and gazed behind. A solitary low powered bulb scattered a dim light across the terrace. She was now breathing hard as the solid, hot block of pain began to melt, and tears that had started to drip in trickles, soon morphed into scalding, salty rivulets and streamed down her eyes.

'Tell me Krishna! Am I a sinner?' She stammered through her sobs. 'Chandrakant calls me one. He calls me infidel. Am I an infidel? Yes, I admit that I had felt slightly drawn towards Bikash. He was way apart from Chandrakant, a misfit in the aggressive political scenario. An out and out gentleman. The endless days and nights of suffering, of humiliation, of unjust accusations, of ruthless physical assaults had taken their toll on the steadfastness of sincerity. May be there was a small slip. But would that justify Chandrakant's action? The way he disparages me? Stigmatizes me as a sinner!'

'O Krishna, you stand there great and glorious with goddess Radha. She is not your wedded wife. Is she? Does that make her a sinner? An infidel? I have never deviated from the path of loyalty to my husband. Why then am I punished? Why the label of sinner is pasted on me?'

'If I have ever trusted you, worshipped you with all my heart Krishna, take me back to you. I cannot take it anymore. Do not let me go back to that monster!'

Hard, dry sobs racked her frail body and she leaned against the pillar to steady the trembling inside her.' Suddenly the lights went out. The street was plunged into darkness, so was the temple. Only the faint glimmer of the moon that peeped through the cotton wool clouds cast a feeble glow across the steps and the ground below. Suddenly from nowhere an enchanting, subdued tune of a flute floated in to the spot where Trisha sat slumped on the step. And she sensed a presence of someone very close to her, so close that the warm, fragrant breath of that someone fanned her face. She felt a tingle of fear. She tried to spring up to her feet, but a strange lassitude had crept into her.

'Radha!'

She heard a soft, melodious voice very close to her, barely above a whisper. She turned her frantic gaze around. Was someone calling her? But she was Trisha, not Radha. Still, she knew intuitively that the voice called her, though she had no idea why it addressed her as Radha.

She squinted hard and could make out the outlines of a wispy, bluish shadow, like a transparent, intangible shape. She felt a hand on her shoulder, a very gentle, tender hand and she slowly got to her feet. 'Come, Radha' she heard the voice again and saw the transparent shadow like figure moving ahead of her. Kind of sailing slightly above the ground, and as if she was held under some sort of hypnosis Trisha trudged behind it. She followed the shadow to the back of the temple, an unfrequented spot which she guessed she had never been to. The spot was almost hidden by dense growths of thickets and vines. The shadow pushed aside the vines and creepers and moved on, and stopped by what looked like a small, rough-surfaced block of wood. She wondered that during her so many visits to the temple she had never discovered this bowery spot. 'Come,' she heard the enchanting whisper again. 'Sit here by me. I will make you forget all your pain.' The diaphanous figure with the bluish outline sat down on the block of wood. Like she was under the impact of some magical spell Trisha sat down, close to the figure inhaling thirstily the exotic fragrance that seemed to be seeping out from it. The weal made by the lash of Chandrakant's belt no longer hurt, nor did her body and head ache. A wave of calm swept over her tormented soul and she closed her eyes, drinking in the tranquil joy.

***

Chandrakant came out slowly of the drunken stupor at the touch of the warm sunlight streaming in through the window bars. He opened his eyes and made a feeble effort to shake off last night's hangover. His head felt unusually light as if it was stuffed with cotton wools and he felt queasy. He needed a glass of lemon water badly. 'Trisha,' he called. 'Get me a glass of lemon water, quick.' There was no reply. He called again; this time louder. There was no answer. Nor did Trisha come into the room carrying the glass of lemon water as she often did. Chandrakant tried to listen. He could not hear the familiar hiss of the pressure cooker and the clatter of cookware from the kitchen. He sat up rubbing his droopy eyelids. The house seemed to be wrapped in a blanket of a mysterious silence. Where was Trisha? Slowly, like images sliding out of a montage the events of last night crept into his mind. His returning home early, and finding Bikash in his house having tea with Trisha. How he had gone high with alcohol to drown his suspicion and frustration and how he had hit Trisha with his belt. He had flopped into the cot in the outer hall after venting out his wrath. He did not remember what had happened after that.

He got off the bed and stood up. He waited for a moment to steady himself and then wobbled towards the room of worship. Usually by this time Trisha had completed the morning worship and the scent of the incense sticks diffused across the house. He pushed the door gently and peeped in. He could not smell the incense sticks. The figurines and idols of gods and goddesses appeared dull and lusterless since Trisha had not bathed them and put the sandalwood paste and fresh flowers on. The image of Krishna and Radha too looked pale and unsmiling inside the glass framing. The flower-garland Trisha had put on it was withered. It was odd, Chandrakant thought, apprehension and unease crowding into his still unsober mind. Trisha never left the previous day's flower garland of Lord Krishna and Radha unchanged. He racked his brain trying to figure out what could have made Trisha skip the routine worship.

He tried to fight off the foreboding that lurked at the back of his mind.

Soon the fear was replaced by bitterness and anger. The first thing that came into his mind was Bikash.

The bitch must have gone away with Bikash, that dirty, unscrupulous betrayer.

He strode back to the bedroom and swallowed a large swig from the bottle of country liquor. And without bothering to take a wash he stormed out of the house, anxious to track Bikash and Trisha down before they escape his reach. He knew Bikash would not be there at his house. But still he was sure he could gather some helpful information from the neighbourhood. He scrambled and stumbled along the street leading towards Bikash's house, squinting his eyes against the dazzling summer sun.

And he stopped short.

Bikash was walking towards him, a broad grin on his friendly face. 'You are early, buddy,' he said. 'The rally starts at two in the afternoon.' Chandrakant remembered the election rally they had to join that day. And the sudden and unexpected meeting with Bikash had fazed him. 'How could Bikash be here?' He was caught in a confounding mishmash of speculations. 'He had to be with Trisha somewhere far away from the town. How come is he still here?' He thought dubiously. 'May be, he has kept her hidden somewhere and comes to me pretending innocence. The despicable hypocrite!'

Bikash put a hand on his shoulder. 'You been drinking in the morning! What happened?' he asked in genuine concern. Chandrakant was not so sure now of Bikash's involvement in Trisha's disappearance. He guessed she had perhaps gone to some relative or may be to her mother, disheartened by his rude behaviour. She would comeback once she gets over her anger and resentment. Despite the reasonings he was crushed under a mixed feeling of shame and guilt. Probably, he thought reluctantly, he had misconstrued the relationship between her and Bikash. May be, he had been extra sensitive. Something hard and hot seemed to have stuck inside him and he knew he would choke unless it is released. 'Trisha has gone away,' he stammered, his voice breaking into a sob. Bikash looked at him in surprise. 'Gone away? Where? Why?'

And Chandrakant came out with the episode of last night's fight with Trisha. He hedged at first to admit his inhuman treatment of Trisha but Bikash could easily guess how men like Chandrakant turn to animals under the influence of alcohol. But he solaced his friend and assured him that Trisha would return when she gets over her emotional upheaval. They got back to Chandrakant's house.

Trisha had not returned and Chandrakant called her on her mobile. They could hear the rings inside the house. It was coming from the room of worship. 'Is Trisha in there? Worshipping?' They ran in to see. Trisha's mobile phone was on the wall-shelf, and the strident ringing filled the room. The two men looked at each other, surprised and helpless.

'Do not worry. She will be back by the time you return from the rally.' He said, trying to sound convincing, but not feeling very sure. He was not very clear what exactly transpired between Trisha and Chandrakant but he could guess that it was much more serious than what Chandrakant had told him. What if Trisha did not return by the evening, he thought, disturbed at this sudden turn of events in his friend's life. Chandrakant, after looking into the closets and drawers declared that Trisha had not taken any clothes with her, nor even her handbag. Where could a woman go without her handbag without money, and most shockingly without her mobile? He was worried but he did not reveal it to Chandrakant. He had developed a certain liking for Trisha during his brief acquaintance with her. She was beautiful in a serene way, but Bikash could read unmistakably the deep sadness in her eyes despite her efforts to hide it under a cheerful veneer. There were moments when he wanted to know her more closely, to know about the sorrow she hides under her smile, but desisted from making an intimate conversation with her. Was it because she could not be a mother after long years of marriage? Three years is not too long a time to feel that way, he reasoned. Was it Chandrakant? His drinking spree? He remembered slightly guiltily the forbidden thoughts that had sneaked into his unguarded moments, to take Trisha in his arms and solace her, and shrank away from them. But he had never laid his heart open to her though he could guess that Trisha wanted to share her sorrow with someone close, someone who would understand her. Trisha's sudden and unexpected disappearance had thrown him off balance, too. And he was sure Chandrakant was responsible.

'Did you hit her?' He asked guardedly after a short wavering.

Chandrakant looked sharply at him. But lowered his eyes the next moment. Bikash did not pursue the matter. He knew now why Trisha left. He was filled with resentment for his friend but did not say it aloud. And he knew it was not an uncomplicated, normal row between a husband and wife. But there was no time to ponder over it. With some effort he managed to persuade Chandrakant to come with him in the rally.

The election rally was the first priority for Bikash at that time. He was a petty but active party worker and was entrusted with the charge of drawing more and more people to join the rally. 'I am sure she would come back before evening.' He said trying to allay Chandrakant's fear.

***

The house was in darkness when Chandrakant

returned in the evening, exhausted and bone-weary after the long walk in the sun scorched streets. His throat parched and his body felt hot and burning. Trisha had not come back. Bikash had gone to the party office to sort out the details of the next day's program. 'I will be back in half an hour,' he had said. 'We will decide what to do if she had not returned by that time. Wait for me and do not do anything rash.'

Chandrakant needed a drink badly to calm down his jittery nerves. He turned and walked up to the liquor shop. He was somehow afraid to face Bikash's questioning glance. Perhaps Bikash had guessed what Chandrakant had accused Trisha of. It was around eight when he finally came out of the shed, after drinking a lot more than his usual quota, feeling a bit high but no longer perturbed and desperate. The alcohol had taken effect. He walked back home in unsteady steps humming the tune of a Hindi song.

He was at about a hundred meters away from his house when he saw it. A shadowy, slender figure, possibly of a woman, since it was clad in a yellow sari. It came out of the front gate and walked briskly straight on, in the direction of the Radha-Krishna temple. Chandrakant stopped abruptly. His heart skipped a beat and then began to pound erratically.

Who is the woman? Trisha?

Without thinking he followed the figure of the woman. He quickened his pace and drew closer.

Now he could have a better glimpse of the back of the woman. The figure was heading towards the temple. It was just when the figure was almost within the reach of Chandrakant a large group of *Kirtan* singers emerged from the temple gate. It was a practice that the *kirtan* singers sang devotional songs in praise of Lord Krishna and Radha in the temple every evening. The yellow clad figure moved faster weaving its way through the crowd of the singers and disappeared out of sight. Chandrakant broke into a shambling run and tried to squeeze his way through the singing crowd, his eyes desperately searching the woman in yellow.

She was gone!

Chandrakant barged into the temple premises and darted across the small open space leading to the steps. The temple premises was almost empty except for the two priests who were now preparing to leave after performing the evening rituals. Chandrakant ran up the steps gasping hard, flicking a frantic look around. The two priests eyed him curiously, surprised at his dishevelled look and the insane anxiety in his eyes. 'Have you seen a woman here a short while ago,' he asked one of the priests impatiently. 'She was clad in a yellow sari.' He added. 'There were a number of women here clad in yellow, my son,' the priest said. 'They come here every evening to sing the glory of Lord Krishna. Which was the one you are looking for?' He asked, puzzled. The other priest was closing the door of the inner section where the idols of the deities were installed. Chandrakant's eyes caught a brief glimpse of the deities, Krishna and Radha. His mouth hung open. His eyes opened wide, and his tongue went dry. The idol of Radha that stood clinging to Krishna looked so familiar!! He rubbed his eyes and looked again.

It was Trisha, the same face, the same eyes and lips. She was clad in yellow silk. But her hair was done in a different style, and she wore a small tiara across her forehead. As Chandrakant stared through an alcoholic haze her lips twisted in a derisive smile and she looking like an airy, transparent shadow of yellow came leaping out of the statue and ran out of the door at the very same instant the priest drew forward the panels and pushed the bolt into the socket. Then she glided down the steps, her feet floating in the air and moved behind the temple.

Chandrakant followed the fast-moving shadowy figure. He quickened his pace not to lose sight of it but suddenly felt a sharp sting just below the ankle and a faint 'oh' escaped him. As a reflex movement his eyes turned towards the ground but nothing was visible. Must be an insect, he thought and ignoring the stinging pain in his heel ran forward, frightened that he would miss the darting figure if he stopped to examine his heel. Now he was sure it was Trisha but his alcohol- soaked brain was not able to think of a reason why she played such a nasty game of hide and sick with him. 'Trisha,' he called out at the top of his voice but the sound came echoing back from the dense trees and the temple walls. The wound in his heel was now beginning to ache burningly. He wanted to sit down somewhere to rest his legs for a while. He could make out the wooden block in a vine covered patch in that far corner of the temple compound, lit up dimly by a cloud-wrapped moon. He flopped onto the wooden block, breathing hard, all soaked in sweat. He did not know why but his whole body was beginning to burn and his tongue that had gone dry and stiff, stuck to the roof of his mouth. He found it difficult to sit and stretched his exhausted body out on the block. From somewhere inside the bowery growths came an enchanting, soothing smell. He shut his tired eyes peacefully.

The woman came out from behind a thicket and stood by the block watching the outstretched figure of Chandrakant. She touched his forehead tenderly, waited for a moment and then moved back into the dense hedges.

***

Bikash was worried. There was no sign of Chandrakant. He was neither in the house nor in the liquor shop he frequented. He had gone straight to Chandrakant's house on returning from the party office. Later he came to know that he had been to the liquor shop. He waited up for him all through the night at his house. Chandrakant did not return. Around noon he filed a missing complaint of both Chandrakant and Trisha in the local police station. It was election time and Bikash was an active party worker. The police came promptly to action. It was only in the evening when they questioned the priests of the Radha-Krishna temple the police came to know that those were the two people who had seen Chandrakant last. The police organized a thorough search in and around the temple.

They found him after about half-an hour, sleeping quietly on a wooden block amidst the thick growths of vines and creepers. He was carried to the hospital where he was declared dead on arrival. The wound on his heel was discovered during the post mortem. The doctors presumed snakebite but there were not any telltale symptoms of snake poisoning in his body. 'It could be a heat stroke. The long walk in the rally and excessive drinking of alcohol could have caused a heart failure,' another group of doctors pronounced. The police registered it as a UD case in the office record and closed the file.

The police carried out an extensive search for Trisha, Chandrakant's missing wife.

She was never found!!

TRUST ME!

I will look for you in every lifetime and love you there...
Kamand Kojouri

Arnab drifted slowly out of sleep at the dull thud, thud on the wooden staircase. Arma was climbing down the flight of stairs, laboriously, putting down her healthy right leg first and her left prosthetic foot repeating the act, producing a lazy, dragging but a series of rhythmic thumping. He could also guess the obvious presence of Subha, his wife, behind her, guarding her steps, always ready to support her daughter if she made a wrong move. But Arma had till now, never needed her mother's help to get down the wooden steps of the staircase. He waited listening to the sound, growing louder as she came down the last few steps, cringing within. After a while it trailed away and stopped finally, as Arma sat down by the dining table to eat her breakfast. He raised himself off the bed, a wave of gloomy lethargy, as always, swept over him dampening his early-morning spirit. It was the daily routine, except for holidays. Subha would get Arma ready, help her put on her school uniform, comb her hair while Arma put the books and copies in her big school bag. Then Subha would serve her breakfast of sandwiches or toasts and a glass of milk. And he would then come down, ready to drop Arma at her school. They had always desisted from using the conveyance the school provided, afraid that Arma might take a wrong step and fall and hurt herself. Later perhaps, when she grew up, they might afford to be more confident.

Of late, Arnab had been noticing a change in Arma. Especially after her eighth birth day. Her face had acquired a mature look and an awkward smile flickered at the corners of her lips when Arnab looked at her. It was not the innocent, sprightly smile of the earlier Arma who hurried towards him, all giggles, struggling though on her prosthetic foot, approximating its movement to the speed of the good one, her eyes sparkling in joy. That broad, bright smile that used to lit up her angelic face and lifted his spirit was lately replaced by an incongruous, indecipherable smile that made her look like a different person. She got back to her normal self as the smile slipped off her face a little later. Arnab flinched away from that smile involuntarily, as if it was a living fright. He did not know why but it gave him a spooky feeling. He had not disclosed it to his wife, who was already reeling under the agony of having a daughter with a deformity. He would not add to her worries by discussing with her about such trifles, he decided. Besides, that awful little smile came to Arma's face usually when she was alone with him, when Subha was getting her lunchbox ready in the kitchen and Arma sat across from him at the dining table, sipping from the glass of milk. She would look over the rim of the glass at him, a fixed gaze in her eyes, with that quirky, little smile on her face which transformed her to a stranger.

Arnab came down the stairs to the hall hoping he would not have to encounter that queer little smile on his daughter's face, and went round gingerly to the chair where Arma sat, rummaging through her school bag anxiously, a disturbed look in her big eyes. 'Where is my marker pen, mama?' she called out to Subha. 'It must be in your school bag, darling,' Subha answered from the kitchen. 'It is not there. I have kept it in the bag last evening after completing my homework. Where did it go?' Arma sounded desperate. 'You might have put it somewhere else, try to remember.' Subha said as she scuttled out of the kitchen, carrying Arma's lunchbox in one hand and the water bottle in the other.' 'Your mama is right. You must have forgotten it at some other place. I will get it. Do not worry.' Arnab said trying to comfort the agitated Arma. 'I have not forgotten it anywhere, Papa. I have kept it in this bag only.' She gave a long stare to Arnab. 'Trust me!' She said looking straight into his eyes.

His heart gave a wild lurch. It was a different voice, certainly not Arma's, but a voice from the distant past, a voice he knew so well, a voice lost in oblivion!

***

They waited outside the operation theatre gazing anxiously at the red light to go off, indicating that the surgery was over. Arnab, his parents and Subha's parents.

After an hour, that seemed like a century, a nurse in white uniform, came out of the closed, heavy portals wearing a smile that nurses keep reserved for the anxious relatives of the patient, and walked over to the grill- partition in the corridor that separated the restricted area from the space meant for the patient's companions. 'It is a baby girl,' she announced and walked back into the observation room adjacent to the operation theatre. The gynecologist emerged from the operation theatre followed by another doctor, and two more nurses. 'You can take a look at the baby now,' she said and slid open the collapsible grill-partition. 'Mr. Arnab,' the senior doctor said stopping him as Arnab moved quickly, edging past the team. Arnab looked questioningly at him. 'Come with me,' the doctor said walking Arnab down the corridor out of the earshot of the other family members. The other doctor and the nurses had made their exit from the scene. 'What is it doctor?' Arnab asked, his voice quivering. He had intuitively guessed that there was something wrong with the baby. 'The baby has a slight issue in its left foot.' 'What issue?" Arnab's breath was coming in scratchy rasps as his heart hammered in apprehension. 'Nothing much that could not be handled. You just have to be a little patient. Take a look at your baby first.' They walked into the cabin where Subha lay in bed, her eyes half closed. A bassinet stood by the side of the bed where the baby was laid.

Arnab glanced at the tiny creature that lay in the bassinet swathed up in white. He moved forward and looked closely. The pinkish white face, with eyes large and liquid, and lips like a rose bud, framed in a thick mop of dark, curly hair, looked almost divine. The little hands were held out in tiny fists as if the baby, on its entry to this world, had tried to grab some of its bleak emptiness for itself. Blood in Arnab's veins raced wildly as his eyes travelled down to the legs. The right one looked healthy and normal but in the place of the left foot there was a tiny lump of flesh, that looked like an ugly appendage stemming out from an otherwise well-shaped ankle. Arnab wanted to scream out, to release the pain that was choking him but it proved to be a vain effort. He glanced at his wife. The deep agony she was trying to cloak in a false, pale smile that failed to reach up to her eyes was like a slash at his heart from the serrated blade of a knife.

He felt the gentle hand of the doctor on his shoulder, who stood by him, waiting, giving him time to absorb the initial shock. 'This is not a big issue. It can be fixed easily. You will just have to be a little patient, as I told. She could walk like any normal child with the prosthetic foot. But the procedure could only be done when the baby is within the stage between crawling to standing.'

'*Not a big issue!!* How easily the pediatrist could speak those words!' Arnab thought bitterly, 'when his world was crumbling apart!'

The next few months were of extensive research and exploring the easy and effective ways of getting their child accommodated to move with an artificial limb, in serious consultation with the doctors in the department of Prosthetics and Orthotics. The long sleepless nights of despair fading into bleak cheerless dawns of fragile hopes. Subha shedding tears on his shoulder and he consoling her, comforting her with words he secretly admitted to himself were false and empty.

With the sincere help and effort of the concerned doctors Arma finally could manage to manipulate her movements almost to a degree of perfection. She was just two and the doctors were surprised at the developments she showed. 'She is a brave girl,' the doctor said excited at the performance of Arma. Usually, the kids take some time to adapt to the maneuvering of their artificial limbs, but not Arma. At eight, her walk was almost equally easy and supple as the normal kids of her age except for a slight limp in the left foot. Arnab and Subha made efforts to accept life as it was given to them without a lot of complaints. Arma happened to have an unusual attachment with her father and would hover about him all the time he was at home. 'You ungrateful kid!' Subha would say in mock anger. I slog day and night to fulfil your demands and you shower all your love on your father!' Arnab laughed happily and picked up Arma to his lap and she would entwine his neck with her delicate arms and rub her cheek to his face. 'My cuddly kitten,' Arnab would hug Arma and kiss her.

Things were beginning to fall in line as the days slid into months and then into years.

It was a rainy evening and Arnab returned early. He sat sipping from a steaming cup of tea watching the splatters of rain as they made patterns on the outer side of the frosted window glass. Subha was busy preparing dinner. He heard the soft but thwacking footfalls as Arma walked over to him. She was holding something in her left hand.

Arnab smiled pleasantly at his daughter. 'Come.' He lifted her and made her sit on the table. 'Look what I have made,' she said excitement dripping from her voice. Arnab laughed. 'Really? Show me!'

Arma produced a drawing sheet from her left hand and stretched it flat on the table. It was a picture of something that looked like a row of broken houses and abraded rocks. An orange sun was about to take a dip behind a zigzag mountain ridge and the sky was touched with blue and red. Two figures with hands and legs of straight lines drawn with a pencil, and with heads of the alphabet O stood on one flat rock.

Arnab looked at the picture closely. It was a

child's drawing but all the same a matured concept for a kid between eight and nine. The rocks and the dilapidated structures had a familiar look about them but he could not figure out what they were actually. 'It is beautiful, kiddo. I love it and I love you.' He smiled. 'I love you too. more than you love me. Trust me!' The way Arma said it had a staggering effect on Arnab. He looked sharply at the girl. And for the first time he noticed that awful, little smile that flickered at the corners of her lips. Was it a smile? A jeer?

Trust me!

Two words spoken steeped in love! When? How many centuries ago? In which far gone age?

***

They sat on a rock in a relatively isolated spot in the ruins of the ancient Jain caves. It was their choicest hangout. Tourists who visited these caves usually do not show interest in this secluded part that was screened partly by broken, drooping walls and patches of bushy undergrowth that stretched thickly out to the woods down beyond the caves. She looked at the sun that was making its way to the west, casting shapeless, eerie shadows of the dilapidated pillars and other structures which were once testaments of architectural excellence but were now in ruins, around. His eyes riveted on her face that caught the reflection of the setting sun and flushed a light crimson. There was a thoughtful, distant look in her eyes. 'What is it? Why are you so glum?' He touched her hand lightly.

She turned her face towards him and smiled. 'Nothing. Soon it will be evening. I have to leave.'

'Stay a little while more.' He urged. 'Let us watch the moon coming up. There will be a full moon tonight. These ruins will be enchanting in the moonlight.'

She laughed. 'You sound like the hero of that Hindi movie who sings a passionate song persuading his beloved to stay back for some more time.

'That was Dev Anand, the legendary hero and the song was a musical marvel. *Abhi na jao chhod kar ke dil abhi bhara nahin…*'

'I have heard that there are spirits in these caves, spirits of ancient Jain monks who incant mantras in the still of the night.'

'But I have heard something else,' he said smiling naughtily. 'I have heard that apsaras from heaven alight here in the full moon nights. They sing and dance.' He nudged closer to her and put his arms around her.

'Liar!!' She laughed and pushed him gently away.

'I do not have any fascination for the apsaras. I just want to see my apsara dazzling in the moonlit night.' He tightened his arms around her. She trembled a little.

A few minutes passed. The light was fading. The crowd was thinning out, too. She pressed her right hand on the rock floor and stood up with a little effort. Her defective left foot had got a cramp that hurt when she tried to stand up. She grimaced a little. The cramp went away in a few moments and she relaxed. She was born with a slightly abnormally shaped left foot. In the beginning she found it difficult to cope with the deformity but later as she became able to manipulate its movement to her convenience, she got over the demeaning complex that used to overwhelm her and became easy and agreeable in her disposition.

She had met him in her second year in the college. He was tall, handsome and jovial and she was instantly drawn towards him. The attraction was mutual, as it happens in case of most young boys and girls, beginning with exchange small talks, with a belief in the self-deceiving notion that it was just a 'friendship', which seems to be a very convenient and accommodative term, and steadily growing more intimate to reach far beyond that.

They began to meet in the college library in the beginning, and later selected less frequented areas of the town for their clandestine meetings. But such blissful seclusions were a rarity in a town bustling with activities. They had, finally discovered the dilapidated caves at the end of the town that seemed to be a safe and ideal spot. The 'rendezvous in the ruins' as they used to call it was hardly ever disturbed by unwanted presences.

***

'It is getting late. I must reach home before it gets dark. I would have to think of a plausible explanation to convince my father.'

'What about my wish to see my apsara in the full moon night?' He asked, faking a frustrated tone.

She laughed aloud. The ring of her laughter came echoing back from the emptiness behind the crumbling pillars. He pulled her again into his arms and kissed her on the lips. It was a gentle kiss at first that grew more demanding as she leaned hard on him to release the pressure on her left foot, her hand curling around his neck. They remained like that for a long time. A gust of wind blew from the woods in the ravine below the edge of the rocky plain and rippled through the hollow of the deserted caves in an uncanny rustle. She disengaged herself from his arms and walked, limping slightly, to the more frequented parts. He followed her down the steps to the narrow road below that led to the highway. 'Will you meet me here tomorrow?' he asked anxiously, unwilling to part from her. She gazed into his eyes. They were heavy with a deep longing. She gave a short nod.

'Promise?' He urged.

'Yes.'

'I know you will not.' He sounded desperate.

'Trust me!!' Her voice was thick with emotion. He grabbed her hand, held it for a moment then let go.

***

It was a mesmeric, bewitching night. The full moon hanging over the dense growth of trees surrounding the rocky floor which appeared to be the foyer of an ancient structure that perhaps was huge and imposing once, but stood precariously tilted now, supported by only a cluster of drooping columns of sandstone, cast a light around that was a translucent green. Strips of clouds capturing the moonlight that diffused from the dense foliage around floated down to hang in awnings of flimsy green around the foyer. The lonely, noiseless night, wrapped in a fluttering mantle of shimmering green lay sprawled over the ruins. He sat on a broken step at the front exit of what looked like a derelict hall. A couple of decaying stone elephants, on either side of its exit stood silhouetted against the shadow of dead time looking melancholically morbid, waiting to crumble down any moment. He looked up at the moon which now appeared to have slid further down and was hovering close above the foyer where he sat.

The night was unusually still, and silence echoed through the dark emptiness around the dilapidated edifices that bore testimony to the rich architectural heritage of an ancient civilization.

From somewhere inside the depth of darkness drifted out a ripple of music, as if someone strummed the strings of a sitar with delicate fingers, caressing a melody out of it, sending a magic vibration through the thick silence. It was soon followed by a rhythmic thwacking like deft hands beating a tabla to the tune of the sitar music. As he tried to listen hard, bewildered but enchanted, a low tintinnabulation, faint as fairy bells, as if the jingle of the anklets around the feet of some ethereal damsel rang through the darkness. And slowly, but steadily the sound floated out to the open, to the foyer and filled the ruins with a delicate symphony. Even the scent-waves that rolled through the air carried a rapturous melody in them. The moonlight now was limpid, looming across the rock floor like a glimmering and flowy screen of transparent, enigmatic green.

He saw her then. Her face half hidden in a dazzling drape of green, the floor length ghagra billowing in the wind. She stepped out of a stone pillar. The jingle of her anklets filled the night as she waltzed about the rocks, and vibrated through the hushed solitude in a merry rhythm to the beat of the tabla and the music of the sitar that had grown louder. His curious gaze riveted on the figure of the woman. She looked exactly like Madhu from that distance. He narrowed his eyes to get a clearer look at her face, and the figure sailed towards the stone step he sat on like some ethereal being, her feet floating above the ground, her drape slid off her head. And she smiled at him! It was Madhu alright! He was amazed, and shocked. How could Madhu move like that, so effortlessly, with her defective foot? She moved closer to him, so close that he could smell her warmth, could hear the erotic swish in her breathing. 'Didn't I tell you to trust me? That I will come to you in the moonlit night?' She whispered. He took her in his arms and lowered his lips to her delicate face. 'O' Madhu, my precious! How I love you!!' He panted as the ecstasy of holding her so close to him became too much to bear. 'Tell me you love me!' He whispered into her ear. 'Yes. Yes.' She sobbed out the words. 'I love you Arnab, more than my life. Trust me!' And Arnab lifted her in his arms and carried her into the cave. The moon hid itself behind the massive, drooping walls. And a thin film of darkness enveloped the ruins.

***

They sat by the far end section of the caves, by a stone wall at the edge of the rocky foyer that inclined in a precarious gradient over the deep ravine below. There was no sun in the sky that day, only a thick mass of slate gray clouds that lent it a scowling look. The gloom in the sky had descended to settle on the face of Madhu. Arnab looked up at the sky and sighed. 'I know how hard it is for you to accept it, darling,' he said, his voice faltering in a deep remorse, 'but you must also try to understand the dilemma I am caught in. Try to put yourself in my position. What would have you done in a similar circumstance? My father has had a recent a cardiac issue. He is not to be put under any kind of stress. You know how conventional he is and how tough it will be on him. What all I ask of you to wait for some more time till he gets a bit stronger to accept our relationship.' He moved closer to Madhu and gripped her hand, 'Please Madhu, try to understand.' He urged.

She stared at him for a long, uninterrupted moment and slowly disengaged her hand from his hold.

'I understand.' She said grimly after a thoughtful pause. 'But will the society understand? Will it be liberal enough to accept an unwed mother?'

She waited, listening to the foreboding hiss of the wind blowing through the trees in the ravine and the ruins above it.

He did not say a word.

And he held his head down, lacing and unlacing his fingers helplessly. His eyelids drooped in discomfort.

She did not ask him again and rose to her feet. Her left foot was aching slightly and she grimaced. She limped towards the central segment of the huge foyer. There were not many visitors and tourists in the caves that day. Arnab followed her, quickening his pace, calling after her. But she did not look back. He caught up with her as she climbed down the steps with effort. He tried to support her but she pushed his hand away.

'Do not be upset,' she said gently as she stood on the sidewalk waiting for an autorickshaw. 'I will not trouble you nor will force you into any dilemma.'

'Please do not say that. Understand my situation please! And understand that I will wait for you till the end.'

Her face creased in a rueful, bitter smile.

'Yes. And I will come back to you in the end. Trust me!'

She got into an autorickshaw that stopped by, and waved at him as the vehicle moved off. He stood there for a long time, looking in the direction the autorickshaw rolled away, till it disappeared from the sight. Rain had begun to fall in large, warm drops like the tears of a sky that seemed to be mourning an irrevocable loss.

***

Madhu did not return his calls. Nor did she come to the college. After a lot of dithering, he finally decided to take a chance and approached Lila, one of Madhu's close friends.

'Madhu has left here. She is now living with her maternal aunt somewhere in western Odisha. She has joined a college there. Didn't she tell you?' Lila looked surprised.

***

Arnab was not sure how should he react to this unexpected development. He had other plans for both of them, but Madhu did not give him a chance even to discuss it. He wondered how her parents and the relatives with whom she lived would accept the situation. He tried several more times to reach her through phone in the following days but now it said that the number was not in service. He was desperate and his desperateness was now slowly changing into misery and then, to anger.

A feeble flame of hope still flickered in him. He went to the caves and sat on the steps by the crumbling stone elephant hoping that Madhu would meet him there someday. But she didn't.

Seasons followed one another and the calendars changed.

He stopped visiting the ruins.

***

Then Subha came to his life. Subha was his father's choice, the daughter of his friend. Arnab had no reason to refuse to the alliance. It had been more than five years since Madhu had made her exit from his life. He was now an auditor associate in a reputed law firm and his father was eager to get him settled in life. His marriage to Subha was a marvel of an experience. For both he and Subha the next one year was one of those rare, idyllic periods when everything went right, a magic time of slipping from one blissful day to the next, with not the faintest cloud on the horizon.

And then one summer evening a bashful Subha announced that she was pregnant. Life had offered him more than he believed he deserved, Arnab thought thankfully and taking Subha in a fond embrace kissed her. Each passing day was a day of joy and hope, a waiting for the new arrival in their lives. His parents were euphoric. They were more eager to welcome the baby than he and Subha were. Subha had no significant pre-natal health issues and everything went on smoothly till Subha was led into the operation theater on the stretcher.

And then, time played the cruelest prank on him, blessing him with a baby daughter with a face like an angel, pink lotus-stalk like fingers, a shapely, healthy body and a lump of flesh in place of the left foot!!

A corroding strip of pain ate into him as Arnab stared at the beautiful creature in the crib, eyes half closed, its tiny petal-like lips parted slightly in a cryptic smile!!

***

'We should try this one,' Subha said pointing her finger up at the luminous sign board that flashed the name 'Blessed Babies'. The storefront signage by the entrance displayed the picture of chubby babies amidst accessories like diapers, baby clothing, baby beds, baby creams and powders and things like that. Subha was in the seventh month of her pregnancy. She was heavy and gross at her middle and walked clumsily. But she was in a great spirit. She followed Arnab to the clothing section. An elated Subha busied herself in selecting from the dresses for a baby girl. 'Why shouldn't we choose a boy's clothing?' Arnab asked, amused at the excitement of his wife. 'Because I know it will be a girl,' Subha said like she was making a pronouncement.

'Arnab?' A voice called from behind. A female voice. Arnab swung on his heels. A woman, stood by the shelves crammed with towels and diaper packets and looked at him. She looked familiar and then he remembered her. It was Lila, his classmate in the college and Madhu's close friend. She smiled at him. 'Why, Lila! What a pleasant surprise.' Arnab introduced her to Subha. After a brief exchange of pleasantries Subha returned to her act of selecting clothes and other baby articles.

Lila moved towards another counter and Arnab followed her there, pretending to select some other items for the baby. 'Do you know what happened to Madhu?' Lila asked in a low voice when they were out of the earshot of Subha. The unexpected meeting with Lila had let memories of Madhu that lay dormant inside him for the last many years, surface all of a sudden. He shook his head lamely, the feeling of guilt that was kept at bay for a long time now taking hold of him. 'How is she?' He asked slowly, his voice quivering. 'Haven't you heard? She died of a miscarriage. The foetus was about twenty weeks old. They say it was a botched surgery.'

Lila cast a long glance at him and Arnab winced away from the accusing look in her eyes.

'She went for an abortion when it was too late to have it. Her parents pestered her to get rid of the illicit pregnancy. She had no alternative. But she had not revealed the name of her offender till the last.' She looked again at him, blaming him, derogating him for his cowardice with her steady, steely gaze.

'Take a look at this,' Subha called and Arnab stammering out an indistinct 'excuse me' to Lila, walked over to the counter where a confused Subha was trying to select clothes from the scattered piles an over enthusiastic salesgirl had placed before her.

After a while he stole a look behind. Lila had left. Heaving a deep sigh out, he returned his thoughts to the present.

***

He sat on the same broken step by the half-damaged statue of the stone elephant at the entrance of the big, dark cave. That night there was not a full moon in the sky. A crescent moon cradled in its ghostly outline played hide and seek with the clouds that kept morphing themselves into absurd shapes. The derelict edifices looked like pathetic pictures of decadence in the pale, shifting moonlight. As he looked on, the crescent moon took a slow, downward sweep and he now could see the figure reclining on it. The moon came down finally and settled on the outside edge of the large foyer, just above the ravines. And the figure, it was a woman in a dancer's costume of a wispy white, put out one of her legs. The silver tiara on her head scintillated in the dim light of the moon as she stepped gracefully down. She stood there uncertainly for a while as he watched and waited holding on to his breath. Then she took a step forward and faltered. She tried again and limped painfully to the steps where he sat, transfixed.

'Madhu!' he screamed, and his voice came bouncing back from the hollow of the cave and rang through the silent night. The faraway figure quickened its space, outstretching its hands to balance its steps across the stony floor. It seemed to be moving very slowly, laboriously ahead. He sprang up to his feet and rushed forward to lend her support. As he moved ahead the figure seemed to be shrinking in size. He looked closely, bewildered by this sudden change in it, and stopped. The figure stood still as if waiting for him to approach it. Once again he started walking towards it and as he neared it the figure grew even smaller. Now he was within a range where he could get a better look at its face. In the obscure light the face looked a little like Madhu's but the woman was not the Madhu he knew. The face was one of an immature childlike face of a girl much younger in age, carrying a shadowy resemblance of Madhu. He had reached the verge of the flat surface of rocky floor and the girl began to back away, moving clumsily as if she had a problem in her foot. 'Don't move back any further' he cried out *hysterically, aware that she would straight go down in to the deep pit below the uneven edge of the foyer if she took a single step back. But the girl did not stop and her foot slipped. Thoroughly panicked, he rushed forward to grab her hand she held up. But at the very same moment the ghostly moon rolled off the edge and hit the bottom of the pit in an earsplitting crash. In the next instant clouds of black smoke rose mushrooming out of the ravine and enveloped the ruins. He gasped for breath and tried to run away from the place to a clearer area but the smoke filled his lungs and choked him. He tried to fight away the clouds of smoke frantically beating out his hands, wheezing and screaming.*

He felt a hand shaking him. 'What is it? Why are you coughing like that?' Arnab opened his eyes and looked blankly at his wife's face that was contorted with fear and worry. He felt around himself. His whole body was bathed in sweat. Arnab sat up throwing the counterpane off. 'It was sort of a nightmare,' he said, gathering up himself. 'Do not worry. Go to sleep.' he soothed his fear-stricken wife.

'Oh God! What a fright you gave me!' Subha exclaimed, now easy and relaxed.

Arnab poured out a glass of water from the jug and drank in large swallows. He lay back on the bed, mulling over the terrible dream. What could the dream imply? The remorse at the news of Madhu's abnormal death? The guilt that was lying in hibernation for years suddenly coming to surface to haunt his conscience?

He spent a long part of the night tossing and turning on the bed before drifting into an uneasy sleep.

***

'I will be late for the school, Papa,' Arma called from the front door, jerking him back to the present. 'You are always keeping her waiting.' Subha joined her daughter, flicking a fond smile at little Arma. But Arma looked the other way, her face expressionless. Arnab looked at his wife, as she walked to the front door. 'Finish your lunch,' Subha said to Arma, not fazed by the lack of response from her daughter. 'Yes.' Arma said indifferently. The rude undertone in that single word was not lost either on Arnab or Subha. The smile froze on Subha's face. Arma moved forward, hobbling slightly on her artificial foot without waiting to see if Arnab was following her or not. Arnab pressed Subha's shoulder in a gesture of consolation and walked to the car. This was another change he had been noticing in Arma recently. Her total apathy to Subha. She seemed to be nurturing a silent hostility towards her mother, not letting any opportunity to hurt her sentiments, slip. And on the other hand, Arma was growing more and more close to her father, spending most of her time with him when he was at home, getting agitated if Subha came in to interrupt them. If Arnab was worried at this reaction from his daughter, he did not express it. He hoped that it will go in appropriate time, when Arma grew a bit older and sensible. But it did not happen that way.

A few months passed but there was no change in Arma's behaviour, either in her unusual inclination towards her father, or the harsh indifference with which she interacted with Subha.

Then things began disappearing from the house.

At first it was the wedding album. The album was kept in a closet along with some diaries and folders containing important official papers. It was a habit with Subha to take out the album now and then and look at the throwback pictures of her wedding ceremony, refreshing the fond memories. On one bright Sunday noon, after a sumptuous and delicious lunch, as they relaxed in the bed, she got up to get the album. Arma was asleep in her bedroom.

'Where is the album?' Subha asked turning her face to her husband, her hands on the wooden panels of the closet. 'Why ask me? It must be where you have kept it.'

'It is not there,' Subha sounded perturbed. 'I am sure I had kept it here. I am not in the habit of shifting things from their right places.'

'You might have forgotten. Try to remember when you had seen it last. And do not get so worked up. It will be somewhere in the house.' Subha came back to sit by him. 'I tell you I have not forgotten it at some other place.' She looked disturbed. A faint shadow of worry hung over her lovely face.

'It will be found,' Arnab said consolingly and turned his gaze to the pages of the newspaper.

But the wedding album was never found.

And a gold bracelet which Subha had gifted to Arnab on his birthday went missing.

Then there was the episode of Subha's expensive silk sari, one she valued a lot since it was a present from Arnab in their fifth wedding anniversary. Arnab could recall the incident vividly since it was a recent happening. They were about to visit the house of one of Arnab's colleagues on the occasion of the birthday of his son. Subha had decided to wear that sari and had taken it out. As she was at the ironing board pressing it, the doorbell chimed and Subha switched off the ironing machine and went out to answer the bell. She was away for only about a couple of minutes when she smelt the smoke. She ran into the house to check. The ironing machine which she had kept standing had toppled on the sari and the burning-hot plate of the machine had eaten into the sari causing a tear of the size of the machine's outline. She was petrified at the terrible sight in her front. She examined the switch of the ironing machine. It was off. How could the flat of the machine get so hot when it was switched off? Arnab was in the living room watching the news, and Arma was upstairs. The cook was in the kitchen preparing the midday meal. Had the machine got automatically switched on? She dismissed the idea as soon as it occurred her. It was recently bought and quite safe. How then...? Even Arnab was puzzled this time. Was it the cook? The maid? Both of them were quite reliable and innocent characters.

Tears of utter helplessness streamed down Subha's eyes. She, though with much reluctance and doubt, reasoned that she must have gone out leaving the ironing machine on the sari in her hurry to answer the bell. Since the machine was too hot even if it was switched off it had corroded the delicate fabric of the sari.

'How was the party, Arma?' Arnab asked Arma who was ensconced comfortably in the backseat of the car, her eyes glued to the screen of Arnab's mobile phone. 'It was great Papa. I enjoyed it immensely.' She returned effusively. 'But your mama did not enjoy much. Her favourite sari has been damaged.' 'Yes. I know. Sad for mama!' she said sympathetically. Arnab glanced at the reflection of Arma's face in the rearview mirror. Even though the inside of the car was partially dark he could clearly make out that small, lopsided smile on her face. It sent a tingle through his nerves.

***

He could sense her presence before he felt the cool touch of her small hand on his face. His eyes snapped open. It was a rainy night and they had gone to bed early. Subha had a bad headache and she now slept soundly after taking a painkiller pill. He saw Arma standing by him. There was a look of deep sadness in her big, innocent eyes. 'What are you doing here my dear? Why aren't you sleeping in your room?' He asked, trying to focus his groggy eyes on his daughter's face. 'What is there to be so surprised? Didn't I tell you to trust me, that I will come back to you? Or have you forgotten?' Arnab's heart was pounding wildly as he listened to the familiar voice, it was not Arma's voice. It was a voice from the past, a voice he would never forget!! It gave him the creeps.

'Arma! You are not my Arma!! Who are you?' his voice was a croak. Arma giggled. 'As if you do not know!!' She cast an intense look at him and backed away toward the door. Then she turned and went out, moving effortlessly and closed the door behind her, leaving Arnab sitting stupefied on the bed.

***

'What are your plans for the anniversary?' Subha asked over the evening coffee. They sat across from each other at the dining table. Arma was in the living room watching a cartoon show.

'Like always we will visit some small town with idyllic landscapes.' Arnab smiled. They always travel to different places, at times on sightseeing tours, and on other times taking trips to places away from the hustle and bustle of the city, 'far from the madding crowd' as a novelist might have described it.

'Why not a hill station? I love the long drives along the mountain roads, and the solitude of the place.'

'Hadn't we been to one the year before last?'

'So what? What is the harm in a 'second time visit'? Subha urged.

O.K, O.K,' Arnab laughed. 'I will ask my assistant to contact a travel agent and get a family suite booked in a resort in one hill station of your choice.'

'Hey Arma, come here,' Arnab called out.

'Yes, Papa!' She shuffled out of the living room and stood leaning on Arnab, twining her hand around his neck.

'How would you like a trip to the mountains?'

'Mountains, Papa? Oh!! I'd love it!' her eyes sparkled in excitement. Arnab loved her a lot when she sounded like that, like any normal kid of her age! It was only when she smiled that bitter, twisted smile at him, he felt uneasy. Subha laughed. 'Most children do not find mountains interesting but our baby is different,' She came over to Arma and kissed her forehead. Arma hid her face in her mother's middle and mumbled happily. The usual absurd and angry indifference was not there in her behaviour. Arnab smiled, relaxed at the change in Arma. She was just like how a girl of her age would be.

*****

Arnab discovered Valley View in the internet. It was a calm and peaceful resort in the small township of KK Nagar, nestled in a hilly terrain, surrounded by lush green woodlands and slim meandering streams that gave an ethereal charm to the landscape.

Arnab had hired a car and a driver for a three days' stay at the resort. Next week, on a fine sunny morning the three of them set out to the hill station some five hundred kilometers away. The journey along the zigzag mountain road of shifting elevations, though tricky and adventurous, was a memory to be cherished lifelong. The driver, well acquainted with the road expertly negotiated the challenges of the varying gradients and the sharp, treacherous bends. The journey was an experience out of a dream. Rows of hills, high and low, green and bald, bordered the narrow road on one side, and on the other side there was the deep valley of lush green, elusively enchanting but dangerous. At certain parts there were vines that sprawled along the steep mountainsides in wild abandon. They grew big, blue wheel-shaped flowers. At places the thick growth of hedge plants and entangled length of the vines reached out to the road. Some times as they drove along the edge of the valley below, the fragrance of strange flowers drifted above and filled the inside of the car with an enchanting smell. In the beginning of the journey, they had encountered flocks of wild monkeys who roamed in the road without a care for the vehicles passing at long intervals. They saw tourists offering them food. The monkeys, like humans, took the biscuits and other food items from the hands of people. Others stretched out their hands asking for more. Arma was excited at the sight and wanted to feed the monkeys. They stopped the car and some monkeys waddled towards it. One of them, relatively smaller than its companions, extended a hand and took the loaf of bread Arma held out at it. Arma squealed in joy.

'Look Papa, look Mama,' she shrilled from

the front seat, 'How the little monkey ate from my hand!'

'It is because the monkey liked you. You too are a little girl.' Subha said, enjoying her daughter's excitement. 'Where are its father and mother?' Arma asked again. 'Must be somewhere near by'.

'But it is not afraid to wander about in the mountain-roads alone. Little ones should always keep close their parents.'

'Yes darling.' Arnab laughed. 'Like you are.' Another big monkey approached their car and this time Arma threw the loaf of bread at the creature daring not to stretch out her hand.

They saw various species of birds who chirped and chattered cheerily, and the air throbbed with a musical mélange . Arma seemed to be enjoying the journey a lot. They drove up and up the roads that snaked precariously about the mountains and occasional precipices. There were no monkeys or other creatures and not even the birds up there at that altitude. The air grew cooler and moist. The road too was deserted. Not a single vehicle was in sight.

'Look Papa,' Arma screamed suddenly, her eyes wide open in wild excitement. 'Look at the clouds. They are coming down to touch us.' Arnab and Subha turned to look in the direction she pointed at. It was a sight straight out of a dream. Fluffy strips of clouds came cascading down the cliffs in wispy waves of white to the road, cloaking it in a muslin mist. In the next instant their car was enveloped in that mist. For a few moments it appeared as if they were floating through a sea of diaphanous whiteness and then the clouds drifted away and the road cleared.

'I love you Papa and Mama,' she exclaimed happily turning to look back at them. 'We love you too darling!' Subha said and laughed. She and Arnab exchanged glances. It was a different Arma, just like her earlier self, a sweet little angelic thing! The odd glint in her eyes, and the awful little smile at the corner of her lips were gone. Arnab felt relaxed.

'We have reached sir, 'the driver announced politely. Arnab looked out. Valley View was a white two storied structure nestled in the hilly terrain, and spread out on about an acre of rocky plains with several scattered patches of tall trees and wild undergrowth. The resort offered a panoramic view of the surrounding landscape.

The manager greeted them warmly and escorted them to their rooms. They had booked two rooms, since Arma preferred to sleep in her own bed.

'What would you suggest we should visit here?' Arnab asked the manager as they sat in the lounge relaxing after a sumptuous and delicious lunch.

'There is a beautiful park sir,' he said, 'children love it. Then there is the fort, though dilapidated now, but had once been a massive and formidable structure. It bears testimony to the British architectural excellence. There is also a small mountain lake where you can boat. But the spot which the tourists preferred above all these is the Cloud Point.'

'What is so special about it?' Subha was curious.

'It is an old wooden platform on a plateau amidst the mountains. If you stand on it you feel as if you are suspended between the earth and the sky wrapped in the embrace of the clouds.' Arnab laughed at the way the manager put it, trying to make it sound like poetry. 'We should rather avoid visiting there. It sounds scary.' Subha said.

'We have to have some adventure to narrate to our friends and make them envious,' Arnab put his hand on Subha's arm and pressed it a little. In that post lunch hour, the lounge was empty since most of the tourists were either resting or gone out exploring the place. Arma was playing on the swings in the game area beyond the lawn with some other kids whose parents too were staying in the resort. Subha shifted closer to Arnab to rest her head on his shoulder. Arma pushed the big glass door of the mezzanine open and stepped in at the same moment Arnab's hand encircled Subha's back. She gave them a queer look that disturbed Arnab. She seemed to have once again slipped into her weird, mysterious other persona. There was a strange glint in her eyes that could have been deciphered as displeasure, or accusation or even indignation. He quickly took his hand off Subha. Subha turned and saw Arma. She smiled at her daughter. But Arma did not smile back and limped away towards their suite.

***

They were in a small motorboat sailing in the narrow, mountain lake. It was a moonlit night and the crystal-clear water shimmered languidly in that soft luminescence. The lurid lights at the bank receded as the boat sailed further away from it. The wild, entangling growth of marshy vines and vegetations bordering the lake on both sides that looked a greenish black in the pale, ghostly light was like an enigma. The moon seemed to be floating just above them as they sailed on. A waft of chilly wind swept in and Subha shivered a little. She nudged closer to Arnab who pulled her to him and put his arms around her. Arma sat on the metal bench a little away from them looking at the reflection of the moon on the water that danced and stirred out of shape and then returned to normal form as the boat moved forward furrowing the water surface. Arnab cast a thoughtful glance at her. There was a pensive look in her eyes which he found oddly disturbing.

***

'I have been speaking to Mr. Nanda and Mr. Sukla in the afternoon,' Arnab said. 'They have come all the way to visit the Cloud Point. It is an experience not to be missed, they say. I think tomorrow we will give it a try.'

'I too have been discussing with Mrs. Mishra. She says you have to climb steep steps to reach the wooden platform. How is Arma going to climb them? Ever thought about that?'

'I will carry her. She will be delighted. Didn't you see how excited was she when clouds rolled into the road as we drove along?' Arnab said encouragingly.

After arguing back and forth Arnab and Subha finally decided that they would climb up to the Cloud Point next day. They would go during the day time to avoid possible difficulties arising from lack of enough light.

Arnab wandered over to the bench Arma sat on. He sat beside her and lifted her to his lap. 'How would you like to walk through the clouds?' He asked, touching her cheek. Arma's eyes sparkled. 'Oh I would love to, Papa.' She blurted out excitedly.

'Tomorrow we are going to the Cloud Point and we will sail through the clouds.' Arnab said, patting her back. Arma giggled and cast a furtive glance at Subha. 'My Mama will also be there.' She said, her voice a low whisper.

'Of course.' Arnab exclaimed wondering a bit why Arma said that. He dismissed the thought soon and looked ahead. The boat was now heading back towards the lakefront and he could see the lights there gleaming brighter.

***

The sun was shining bright when they started to climb the mountains. A couple, newly married perhaps, had joined them as they had started from the resort but parted company at the foothills.

Arnab wondered which way they had gone. They should have climbed up this face of the mountain to reach the steps that led to the plateau at the top if they intended to visit Cloud Point. May be, they would first explore some other parts before coming up, he thought.

It was an easy climb in the beginning. But the progress was slow for Arnab since he carried Arma in his arms. Sudha straggled behind him. As they hobbled up the steep gradient, the air seemed to get thinner and breathing became difficult. Arnab wondered for the second time if it would have been wiser not to refuse the guide who had insisted to accompany them.

After an hour or so they discovered the steps leading to the plateau. Arnab decided to rest a while before starting on the steps that looked not too welcoming.

The sun had come up high by the time they began climbing the steps. Arnab and Subha struggled on, shifting the load of Arma alternately between themselves.

'Put me down, Papa,' Arma said midway through the journey up the steps. 'I can climb on my own.'

'Are you sure?' Arnab asked skeptically. He knew Arma would take a lot of time to climb up the rest of the steps with her artificial foot. But he was feeling breathless from the rising altitude and from the added weight of Arma on him. 'Better put her down. We will climb slowly.' Subha suggested.

She too was slightly panting. Surprisingly enough, Arma hopped up the uneven steps without floundering much, as if she was prodded on by an overwhelming urge. Arnab and Subha exchanged glances, and strove up behind her. Abruptly the steps ended and they discovered themselves on a large plateau. They slumped on the rocky floor to get their breathing back to normal, and looked down. The peaceful idyllic town that lay below looked like a painting in multiple colours. The few white stucco buildings scattered across the town, and even the Valley View resort looked like toy houses. It was very cool up there and Subha shivered. There was no one in sight. The couple they had met on their way was not seen anywhere. They seemed to be the only three people stuck in the folds of the rolling mountains.

'We will take a brief rest and then move on.' Arnab said, looking up at the sky that seemed to be hanging just above their heads like a canopy of luminous blue. The sun was bright at one end of it but they did not feel much of the heat.

He stood up after a few minutes and inspected the place, looking for the Cloud Point. The manager of the resort had told that they would find the observation platform at Cloud Point without any trouble. But there was nothing around to match the description he had given them. Arnab looked about searchingly for a signboard to guide them to the Cloud Point. There was none. After a short walk towards the west, they discovered a small bridge with rope handholds on either side. The planks looked rotten and Arnab was in two minds whether to risk the crossing or not. And again, surprising both of them Arma moved ahead and put her prosthetic foot on the first wooden plank of the bridge. She caught hold of the rope handhold and looked behind at Arnab and Subha. And smiled that awful little smile that seemed to flicker at the corners of her lips. 'Come Papa, Mama is waiting.' Subha who stood behind Arnab watching Arma fearfully, her heart at her throat, gripped Arnab's hand. 'Mama is here, darling. Right behind you. What are you saying?' Again, Arma looked back at them and smiled. She had now reached the second plank and as the bridge swung slightly in the wind, she looked like an angel floating in the cool emptiness between the earth and the sky.

'Come back Arma. We will not cross that bridge.' Arnab called out to her. But Arma moved on, not turning to look back. She was walking effortlessly on her prosthetic foot, as if there was nothing wrong with that foot. She had reached the middle of the small bridge. Arnab hurried forward to catch up with her, Subha scrambling behind him. But the planks proved to be strong enough, so also the rope handholds on either side of the bridge. Miraculously, they reached another small plateau across it without any problem. There, on the flat face of a boulder was written Coud Point in bold white letters. A wooden observation platform was set up on the plateau. An old railing bordered the arched edge from which there was a spectacular view of the dizzying panorama below. Some hundred meters away Subha could see the flight of steps leading down to the other side of the mountains. Another flight of steps? They looked different. The steps were not the ones they had climbed. She could see some tourists going down the steps too. She watched them with a horrifying realization that they had travelled up here the wrong way. Other tourists who had come to the Cloud Point had taken a different path, easier and safer, and haven't had to cross the bridge that was hanging perilously over the large crevice. They would have approached Cloud Point from the right direction had the guide been there with him, she thought.

'Look,' suddenly Arma squealed in excitement. Both Arnab and Subha swung around to see. A puffy white cloud was drifting towards them pushed along by the brisk mountain breeze. In a few seconds Arma was enveloped in the swirling gray-white mist. 'Papa, I am feeling like I am in the sky! No, in heaven!' She cried out from inside the fluffy mass of the cloud. Arnab and Subha made a scrambling rush to where Arma was, now lost under a quilt of cloud patches. 'It feels like soft rain, Papa.'

They heard her voice but could not see her. Soon the cloud mass drifted forward and took Arnab and Subha in its billowing folds. 'Arnab, where are you?' Subha screamed groping blindly for him. Arnab was by her side instantly, grabbing her arm. 'Easy, easy!' he said comforting his wife. And the cloud floated away leaving them standing on the wooden platform, shaking all over, a few meters away from the railing. 'Where is Arma?' Subha cried, still unable to shake off the impact of the experience. They looked frantically around, panic gripping them. 'She was standing just here,' Arnab stammered, where could she disappear like this?' 'Arma,' he cried out, in a frenzy of fear. And another mass of cloud rolled in, blocking his vision. They stood there, trembling, clinging to each other. Slowly the cloud rolled away and they could see Arma, moving slowly towards the arched railing of the wooden platform. She was almost there when suddenly a slender strip of cloud floated in and stopped a little away from Arma. As they looked the cloud took a shape, hazy and wraith like, but it was the shape of a human being, a woman in all probability and moved closer to Arma. They gaped at the wispy, translucent figure unbelievingly, blood freezing in their veins, their reflexes numb. They saw Arma moving towards the woman, who had gone now, God knows how, to the other side of the railing and stood leaning on it, one foot on the edge of the plateau, and the other in the emptiness ahead of it, smiling at her. 'Arma, Come back, baby,' Arnab and Subha shrieked, blind fear taking hold of them and just at that moment the hazy figure of the woman raised her eyes to look straight at them. There was something in the eyes that made

Arnab catch his breath sharply. He stood rooted, bewildered, and shocked out of his wits.

The woman who looked like she was shaped out from the clouds was an exact replica of Madhu!! And she smiled at him, the same enigmatic, enchanting smile Arnab had always loved.

'Mama!' Arma cried out in joy and darted towards the woman. 'Don't Arma!' Arnab cried out, stretching out his hand to stop Arma. The woman gave a short laugh. Arma was now very close to the woman.

'I have always loved you,' Madhu said, her voice a hollow rasp, 'And will always come back to you. *Trust me!!*'

Slowly, as if he was in a trance, Arnab moved forward towards the railing at the edge of the platform, ignoring the hysterical screams of Subha that rang through the hollow heights, his eyes fixed on the wraithlike figure of Madhu. Arma beckoned him. Madhu smiled once more and turned her back to him. Arnab, in one quick, rushing movement was by the side of Arma who had now climbed over the last of the horizontal rungs of the railing and was leaning down. He reached out to pull her back but at the very instant Madhu gripped Arma's hand. She let herself go off the rail, gripping Arma's hand in hers. Her frail, smoky frame seemed to be floating in the vast emptiness before taking a plunge into the dizzying abyss below. Arnab grabbed at Arma's other hand which she waved at him, still smiling her mysterious smile, but his foot slipped and he went flying into the air, then taking a sharp dive to the dark oblivion. As his body dropped, he felt strangely light, as if a load which he had been carrying within had suddenly lifted off him. A calm, peaceful smile lit up his face as his body hit the rocky floor thousands of feet down.

At any given moment, you have the power to say: this is not how the story is going to end...

Christine Masson Miller

ANOTHER FAIRY TALE

*But someday you will be old enough
to start reading fairytales again.*
                                   C.S .Lewis

Rashmika snuggled into her mother's arms and urged, 'Ma, tell me a story.'

Sabri was feeling exhausted after the day's slogging at different houses, doing the household chores and cooking. Her head ached badly. 'I am tired baby,' she ran her hand affectionately on her daughter's back. 'Tomorrow, I will surely tell you one'. But Rashmika would not give up. 'Just a short story,' she held out the thumb and index finger of her small hand, spacing them slightly apart to suggest the length of the story. Sabri had not had the heart to refuse now. 'Okay. Okay.' She laughed, 'I will tell you a true story of a fairy.'

'Wow!' Rashmika nestled more cozily in her mother's arms.

'There was a poor woman who lived by doing odd jobs in peoples' houses like cleaning used up plates and cooking pots, washing clothes, and mopping floors. She cooked in some houses too. Her husband had abandoned her to live with another woman.

One day a fairy alighted from heaven in the poor woman's one room- kitchen house. The fairy was such a tiny thing that wings have not yet grown on her back. But when she came the house of the poor woman was illumined with a brilliant light. The poor woman fed her whatever little she could make through her meagre earning and the fairy-baby grew up to be a cute, charming little girl. But still the wings have not grown on her back.'

'Will not the wings ever grow on the baby-fairy's back, Ma?' Rashmika asked eagerly.

'Why not? Of course they will grow, one day at the appropriate time.'

'When?' Rashmika was insistent.

'When it becomes old and intelligent enough to understand the world around her.'

Rashmika yawned. 'You must tell me tomorrow more about the fairy.' She mumbled sleepily.

Sabri stared at the dark asbestos ceiling for a long time after her daughter fell asleep. 'You are my fairy, darling! I will see that you get your wings even if my hands and legs wear away in making them grow.' She promised to herself and smiled dolefully into the greyish darkness.

***

Everybody in the slum and the masters and

mistresses of the households where she worked had advised her against putting her daughter in the high profile English medium school but she did not listen to anyone's advice. Her heart swelled in joy when little Rashmika climbed into the school van in her smart school uniform, looking like a little fairy. Sabri had taken up two more household jobs and was working all through the days and afternoons only with a short break at lunch time. She did neither have any regret or complaint. She wanted to earn more and more to provide her daughter all comforts and all privileges other students of the school enjoyed.

***

'Some of my friends would be visiting our house on my birthday this time. You must make some of your special dishes for the occasion.' Rashmika announced that afternoon, returning from school. She was now in class eighth and had grown up to a lovely young girl. Sabri had planned something else for her daughter's birthday. The usual things like visiting a temple in the morning, a modest cake cutting event along with some of her friends in the neighbourhood and a not-so-lavish dinner in a moderate restaurant. She looked askance at her daughter. 'How could you invite your school friends to the slum? Why make yourself a laughing stock?' She reproached.

'I did not invite them. They want to come here. Don't I go to their homes?' Rashmika shot back, her eyes heavy with tears of despair.

'Alright dear, do not be so upset. I will ask Agarwal sir to let us use the community hall of their apartment for one evening. He is the society secretary and no one would ask him a question.

The party went well. A birthday cake that cost one thousand, snacks, ballons, confetti and other decorations and the fashionable outfit sliced a sizable strip off Sabri's savings. Rashmika's friends had a great time, and Sabri had to work extra hours to pay back the advance amount she had borrowed from a couple of generous bosses. She did not mind it. The happy spark in Rashmika's large eyes were compensation enough.

***

Whether you want it or not Time has a way of its own to carry you along its sweep. And Rashmika was soon in her final year at school.

'This is my last year at school, Ma,' she began in her usual compelling style. Sabri smiled and waited for her daughter to pronounce her new demand. 'I would like to celebrate my birthday in the Euphoria Mall this time.'

'Euphoria mall!!' Sabri uttered in disbelief. 'You know dear we cannot afford that. That is for the rich people, far too expensive.' She tried to explain without hurting her daughter's sentiments.

'I am not asking you for money this time Ma. So be least bothered.' Rashmika cut in, her face glowing in a triumphant smile.

'Who is going to arrange it then? Your friends?' Sabri asked, her tone one of lighthearted mockery.

'No, not my friends! *My father*!!' Rashmika answered, her voice excited at the thought of a special birth day party sponsored by her financially well-off father.

'Father?? '

Sabri's eyes opened wide in shocked surprise. 'When did you speak to your father? How did you get his contact number?'

'You wouldn't understand all that Ma. So, as I said don't bother. If you really want to know, I found him on the face book and wrote in the comment box. That's how.' Rashmika looked at her mother, waiting to find a glow of joy at her daughter's competence in the latter's eyes. There was none. Instead, a shadow of a dull pain clouded them.

She had requested one of her employers to get a smart phone for her because Rashmika needed one to keep in touch with her school teachers and friends. Sabri had no idea about face book, or WhatsApp or any such application. She hardly ever called anyone. Just received the calls and most of them were from the houses where she worked as a maid. And look at this girl! She thought desperately, 'contacting the man from whom Sabri had always tried to keep her away! And had given away all her years to see that Rashmika was reared up with the affordable comfort!' Solid tears choked her heart.

'What have you planned for your birth day this time?' Sabri asked, because she did not want to douse the spark of Rashmika's enthusiasm with any depressing remark.

'Father will speak to you one of these days. I have asked him to get me a fairy costume of white because you always call me your fairy.' Rashmika's voice was placating. 'Does she know I am hurt by her irresponsible behaviour, and is trying to mollify me?' Sabri asked herself, but did not say anything aloud.

Rashmika gazed at her mother unblinkingly for a moment. 'I will not let you toil once I become a doctor,' she said. We will have a house of our own, as big as the one Maya madam has, and a four wheeler too. We will have a chauffeur to drive the car and he will hold open the door when you get down.' There was something so intense in her voice that Sabri was startled. 'I have no such big dreams my dear,' she interrupted. 'I just want you to live a comfortable life and do not have to struggle like I had to.'

'I know Ma, but you must trust this fairy of yours. Once she becomes a doctor, she will own that magic wand that can make all the doors to the lavish world rich people live in, open.' She promised.

'And Ma, father said that he had no other children except me. He assured me that he will finance my studies once I get through my school finals.'

This was news! Her husband who worked as a peon in a government office at Visakhapatnam and earned well, had deserted her for another woman, but the other woman could not beget him a child. That must be the reason why her husband was so keen on the idea of financing Rashmika's education.

Sabri let out a deep sigh. She was neither happy nor sad. It was all so intriguing. She had never wished him to be unhappy, strangely though. But at the same time, she had never wanted him to trespass on her daughter's life. She had been economically independent all these years. She felt no qualms or embarrassment working as a cook cum housemaid in people's houses. She had always lived with the satisfaction that she had never needed her husband's support to survive. But the big dream of Rashmika was going to upset everything, and the cruelest irony was she herself had been feeding her daughter with the ideas of climbing to the top, to grow wings and soar above the world of poverty and dirt and obscurity.

Sabri spent a sleepless night pondering over the ways to find a way out of the terrible dilemma she was caught in. There seemed to be none.

***

The parcel arrived in courier two days before Rashmika's sixteenth birth day. She ran out to the door and almost snatched the packet from the courier boy's hand.

'How much?' Sabri asked.

Rashmika was already at the packet cutting the cello tapes with a pair of scissors. Sabri watched her daughter, horrified. What a shame it would be if she hadn't the amount with her.

'Wait!' She snapped at Rashmika. 'Let me make the payment.'

'It has already been paid for,' the courier boy said and departed.

'Look!' Rashmika cried out in delight. She had cut open the wrappers and taken out the dress. 'Isn't it just divine?' She asked Sabri. It was a beautiful outfit, a three- piece ensemble of a floor length tulle gown with silvery floral designs stitched into its lace-hemming, a wide waistband looking like a belt of silver, and a lace applique veil. 'My daughter would look like a fairy in this dress,' Sabri thought happy and miserable at the same time.

That afternoon, while she was coming out of the Agarwal house after completing cooking, she saw Rashmika running towards the apartment building. It was a surprise. Her daughter never came to the houses where her mother worked.

'What is the matter?' She asked, a look in her eyes that was a blend of surprise and apprehension.

'Father wants to speak to you. The call is on hold.' She held out the phone.

'Father?' Sabri fumbled.

'Speak, please. He is on the line.' Rashmika said urgently.

Sabri took the phone in unsteady hands and moved out of Rashmika's earshot.

'Hello,' She spoke into the screen guardedly. 'Hello Sabri. Nice to hear your voice after such a long time. I will not make the conversation lengthy and come straight to the point. Rashmika must have told you that I and my wife have no issues. Rashmika is my only child. I must thank you for taking care of her and putting her in a good school. I think I too have some responsibility towards *my* daughter.' The stress he put on 'my' was not lost on Sabri. She wanted to ask him where had his sense of responsibility gone all these years when she managed a milk-suckling baby and a maid's job at four households singlehanded, alone. Instead, she said, 'I can take care of my daughter's future.'

'How?' He scoffed. 'With your job of a housemaid?'

Sabri pursed her lips hard. She did not want to pick up a fight with her *responsible* husband. Rashmika was watching her closely though Sabri knew she could not hear what she was saying.

'What do you want me to do, then?' She asked trying to sound indifferent.

'Just allow me to take care of the expenses of her education. She wants to become a doctor and you know you cannot afford to meet the heavy expenses from the meagre amount you earn. Just think reasonably, keeping aside your ego for a while.'

Sabri thought reasonably, sensibly and decided that Rashmika's father was right, in a way. If she wanted her daughter's ambition fulfilled, she must have to shun her ego and act sensibly. What is the harm if the father wants to extend financial support for his daughter's education? She tried to reason with herself.

'I will think about it.' She said taking a short pause.

'There is nothing to think,' her ex-husband said persuasively. She will be appearing in the school finals in a month. She will have to take admission in a junior college that offers coaching for the medical and engineering entrance examination. I know many good colleges here at Visakhapatnam. I can get her admitted to one of those. The expenses are high, around five lakhs for a two-year course. You cannot afford it. Do not allow your petty ego destroy your daughter's future.' Her ex-husband's tone was solicitous.

'Still, I will think about it.' Sabri disconnected the call.

'What did you say to him? Did you make him angry?' The eager urgency in Rashmika's voice was like a needle prick at her heart. She glanced at her daughter for a long moment slowly letting the feeling sink into her that Rashmika now had grown up. Her fairy had grown wings and is ready to fly, chasing her ambition. Sabri could no longer keep her chained to the earth by her love.

'No. You will study at Vishakhapatnam after your final board examination is over.'

Rashmika hugged Sabri tightly. 'You are the best mother of the world!' She declared happily and taking back the mobile phone ran away towards her home.

***

Rashmika's sixteenth birth day party at the

Euphoria Mall was a memory to be cherished for a lifetime. Sabri felt she had strayed into the pages of a fairytale. In the beginning She did not want to join the youngsters. 'I will be a misfit there,' she protested but Rashmika would not listen. And in the end Sabri had to borrow a silk sari and imitation jewelries to go with it from one of her closest friends. She examined her reflection in the small mirror, and felt satisfied that she would not look too out of place in the gathering. She shrank away from Rashmika's keen, appraising eyes, who after a thorough and meticulous scrutiny passed her getup as 'not bad' and smiled.

The evening was something straight out of a dream for Rashmika. She knew she looked extraordinarily beautiful in the white tulle floor-length gown and the lace applique veil, almost ethereal. Her mother had always called her a fairy, and that evening, donned in the fairy-costume, she felt that she actually was one. Her friends were vociferous in their admiration. She could sense the gaze of the people in the mall had remained glued to her.

Sabri stood aloof, away from the crowd of the blooming youth, at one end of the hall, feeling oddly embarrassed. But she was happy seeing how Rashmika enjoyed the evening. For a brief while, she even appreciated her ex-husband's efforts to make her daughter happy. But it was a relief when the party was finally over around ten in the night.

***

It was a mysterious, unknown land fringed by a range of indigo mountains on one side and a blue ribbon of a rippling river on the other. The vast glen shimmered a purplish green under a big, full moon. A woman stood in the middle of the glen, her back to Sabri. She was clad in spotless white and the tiny sequins of silver on her mantle caught the light of the moon and dazzled. She wore a small crown on her head. Prompted by an irresistible curiosity Sabri moved guardedly towards the slender figure, and stopped abruptly at a few feet behind her. She could now see clearly the back of the woman. Extending from the back of her white flouncy gown were a pair of elegant, lacy wings spun in sparkling silver threads that fluttered gently in the wafts of the wind. As if she sensed Sabri's presence behind her, the woman swung behind, and Sabri had had a full view of her face. She stared at the face, spellbound, mesmerized.

It was the face of Rashmika!!

The fairy that wore Rashmika's face flashed her an enigmatic smile. Then she flapped her fairy wings and let her feet lift off the ground. Slowly she ascended into the air. As Sabri stared, openmouthed but wordless at her, Rashmika went up and up, became a tiny silver spec and disappeared out of sight. She cried out 'Rashmika, my baby!' wildly, and suddenly the moon vanished from the sky. From nowhere huge masses of heavy, rain-swollen clouds sailed into the sky and spread out like blankets of black. The mountain ranges looking like angry monsters emerging out of the netherworld, advanced towards Sabri with a vengeful determination. The wind now had become a raging storm and the sky burst forth into torrents of spiky liquid. Sabri ran, wallowing across the waterlogged glen, pressing her hands to her ears to shut out the loud cracks of thunderclaps, blinded by the lashing spatters of rain. As she ran clumsily across the glen, she stumbled against something like the stump of a dead tree and went crashing down, coughing and screaming wildly.

Someone was rocking her hard. 'What happened Ma? Why are you screaming like this?'

Rashmika's voice. Sabri sprang up on the bed and glared at Rashmika. Then the look in her eyes softened and she stroked her daughter's head fondly. 'Not to worry, dear. It was just a dream, a terrible dream!'

'Dream? You frightened me out of my wits.' Rashmika flopped back into the bed.

Sabri remained awake the rest of the night, her mind cluttered with strange premonitions.

***

'Who had been you talking to?' Sabri asked. She was having a nasty headache and had returned home early that evening. She saw Rashmika speaking into the phone. She disconnected the call abruptly when Sabri approached.

'Who had you been speaking to?' Sabri repeated. 'My Father', Rashmika answered putting extra stress on 'my'.

'Why?'

'What do you mean by 'why'?' Rashmika snapped at her mother. 'The result of my final board examination is due by the end of this month. Father had got me enlisted for admission in the Sai

Chaitanya International school there by paying an amount of one lakh. I will have to join there after the results came out. I must speak to him and let him know my plannings.'

'He had paid one lakh? And you never cared to tell me?' Sabri's voice choked. What kind of a conspiracy father and daughter are hatching without her knowledge?

Perhaps her daughter could sense the tremor in her voice and looked curiously at Sabri.

'You need not feel so bad about it. Not many students get this opportunity to study in such reputed schools. You should thank your stars that your daughter has found entry there.'

'Yes, I must thank my stars!' Sabri thought bitterly. Her husband had belittled her before her daughter in the crudest possible way. But she could not defy that! And her daughter says she must thank her stars!!'

She heaved out a deep sigh and walked away.

***

Sabri lay awake, turning restlessly on her sides. It was May and there was no respite from the heat even in the nights. Rashmika was sleeping peacefully in front of the small cooler. Sabri squinted at her daughter's face. There was the semblance of a smile there. She is perhaps dreaming about her new school, Sabri thought, her heart heavy with pent up sorrows. Why could not have she studied here? Why was she so keen on becoming a doctor? Sabri thought and in the next instant fought the thought off her mind. She was becoming selfish! Sabri had always dreamed her fairy to soar to great heights. She should rather be happy. But the tears did not accept her logic and flowed obstinately down her sleepless eyes.

***

The result of Rashmika's school finals came. As expected, she had secured good percentage, more than enough needed for getting a seat confirmed in the Sai Chaitanya International School at Visakhapatnam. Her father had called to express his joy at his daughter's success. Rashmika had kept the phone on the speaker for Sabri to listen. 'I am so proud of you, my dear child,' he said. 'Soon you will be coming here, to study in one of the finest schools.'

It was an effort to restrain herself from lashing out at the vainglorious man. It was Sabri who had been taking all the pains to sustain both herself and Rashmika in a world riddled in apathy. And look at the audacity of the man! He speaks as if he owns all the credit! What a joke!!'

'Aren't you happy Ma?' Rashmika asked.

'Of course, my fairy!! Could there be any doubt about it?" She took her daughter in her arms.

'I will be leaving here soon.' Rashmika shifted closer to her mother as they retired for the night. 'A few years later I will return as somebody and then you will no longer have to cook at other people's houses.' She said, her voice was a blend of promise and solace.

The words hit her like a knife stab. She had always tried to keep the frightening truth of getting separated from her daughter at bay. But now it was there in her front, naked and ugly, staring at her with a boldness that made her cower. She could not sleep that night, nor could she shed tears. She wondered where all her tears had gone. May be sucked into the sands of a blazing desert of grief.

***

Like sometimes it happens in a horror tale, the hands of the clock moved in a nightmarish speed shrinking the days into hours and hours into minutes and soon it was the day of Rashmika's departure. Sabri's ex -husband had called Sabri just once to let her know that he would be sending the flight ticket for Rashmika. 'It was just forty-five minutes by air,' he said. 'Just ask your nephew to drop her at the airport. I have explained Rashmika what she will have to do. You do not have to worry.'

You do not have to worry!!

How easily he said that! Rashmika was Sabri's flesh and blood. She was everything Sabri had lived for. Sabri knew her world will be nothing but a vast, unending emptiness with Rashmika gone. But he would not understand that, nor would Rashmika. But she could not stop the fairy from taking a flight above. The fairy did not belong here, in this dreary, squalid slum. She did not belong to Sabri, the petty, base woman who had accidentally come into her life.

***

She stood outside the airport for a long time after her daughter disappeared into the lounge of the airport. 'Let us go home, aunty,' her nephew said. 'Rashmika's flight has taken off.'

Sabri looked at her nephew. And then up at the sky. Aircrafts were taking off and swooping down every five or ten minutes. Rashmika might be in one such aircraft soaring above. She could see the red and blue and yellow lights blinking and then melting into the vast darkness of the evening sky. Her Rashmika, her baby fairy has finally grown wings and is flying far above to explore a skyful of dreams.

Women like Sabri could never grow wings to fly. They have their feet chained to their earthbound existence. Sometimes, by some lucky chance a fairy finds a way to their world, and illumines it for a short while. But a fairy has to take a flight back to her sky, plunging the houses of the 'Sabri's into an impenetrable darkness.

'Yes, let us go back home.' She heaved out a sigh and followed her nephew out of the airport.

KEEP IT SECRET

'A person often meets his destiny on the road he took to avoid it'

Jean de La Fontaine

She sat ensconced in the fluffy upholstery of the backseat of the big, luxurious car, beside her husband. Sandhya Kiran, shortened as Kiran, her husband's personal secretary sat in the passenger's seat by the uniformed chauffer. The car sped along the mountain road in a silky rustle. Strips of clouds that caught the light of a big moon that lurked above the proud heads of the mountains looked like streamers of spun-silver. The road ahead was deserted. Kalyan Kumar said something and Kiran giggled from the front seat. Karisma smiled absent mindedly, her gaze fixed on the rushing stretch of road that was captured in the range of the car's headlights. The car increased speed and raced along the winding road, and Karisma cried out, 'Slow down,' and Sandhya Kiram smiled amusedly. 'You are such a skittish girl!' Kalyan Kumar laughed. Out of nowhere another car, that shone blue in the moonlight raced past them, blaring its horns.

Their car swerved a little and the driver struggled at the wheel trying to steady it, cursing the blue car under his breath. In the next instant they saw the blue car making a U turn and rushing at them in an unbelievable speed. In that fractured moment before it smashed into their car sending it flying over the guardrail into the deep valley below, she caught a glimpse of the car and the driver. It was the same car, and the driver was the same too, the lower part of his face covered in a handkerchief, eyes hidden behind greenish sunglasses. She screamed as the car leaped over the rail, and another woman screamed too. it was not Sandhya Kiran. It was a woman in the blue car, sitting by the driver, her face partially hidden by his bulk. There was an earsplitting grinding sound of huge sheets of metals hitting one another and total silence in the next moment. Karisma lay face down on the stony edge of the road, her mind frozen, her body not registering any pain. Someone gripped her hand and lifted her up. She saw a figure of a woman clad in white, was trying to raise her. The woman's face was hidden by the shadows from the thick growth of bushes and creepers along the foothills. But she emitted a familiar smell, a blend of a scented hair-oil, a popular face cream and spices and vanilla custard. 'Ma!!' Karisma sprang to her feet to see the woman's face but no one was there. The figure had simply disappeared into an empty nowhere.

***

Karisma stood in the sea-view terrace of her posh bungalow gazing at the shore, the flouncy, flowy pleats of her sea-blue full-length gown fluttering in the early morning breeze that came wafting from the sea, her slender hands folded across her chest, a distant and indecipherably mysterious look in her eyes. The trawlers her husband's fishing company owned were moored in the sea in a majestic row of glossy red and white and silver. It had been nearly a month since the accident when her husband's car had made a fatal swerve on the mountain road crashed into the guardrail and lunged into the deep ravine below and exploded. The fire was so terrible that almost nothing except the charred, mangled bodies of the passengers could be recovered after the rescue crew's relentless efforts since dawn to evening the next day. A sharp tingle rode across her nerves and her eyes squeezed shut at the thought. The police said that the other body was of Kiran, her husband's personal secretary but nothing much was left to identify her except a semi molten bracelet that had her name monogrammed on it. All everything was devoured by the monstrous fire. A deep sigh heaved out of her and a few drops of tears trickled down her eyes.

She heard the faint rustle of cautious footsteps approaching her and wiped her eyes. The woman who now stood holding her head down, her face a picture of grief was Aruna aunty, the head of the housekeeping staff, a middle-aged woman who despite her dowdy outfit still looked her plump, motherly self.

'Should I send your tea here madam?' she asked in a voice so empathically affectionate that it almost palpitated with a desire to wrap her mistress in her plump arms. May be, it sounded more so because now the house staff had realized that she was the sole owner of the company shares and the house, the widow of a business king. She sighed again and gave a short nod. The sun, that was now coming out from the vast turquoise expanse at the distant skyline looked like a huge fireball. It was a new morning, a fresh morning that announced the beginning of a new life. She was now a queen. Or would it be more appropriate if she phrased it this way, 'a princess turned queen'. Her lips twisted slightly... not in a smile. There was something obscurely cryptic in that. She turned and lowered herself to the luxurious, leather padded chair watching another maid approaching pushing a sophisticated trolley-cart of tea and breakfast.

***

It was her father who had made her wander the roseate dreamworlds since she was a child and had nothing else to believe other than what he made her believe.

She was born to be a princess, he had said. She was laid in a white bassinet with a lace canopy, decorated with pink ribbons, rotating starlight musicals hanging from it, soft stuffed toys and shiny rattles. She was made to believe that if she opened her mouth someone would hurry in to hold her, to fulfil her demand. She, by some divine magic, was made to alight in the tenement house in a port-town where her father worked for a fishing factory. He had to spend a large segment of time in the sea in fishing trawlers and when he was home, he worked as a part time mechanic in a motor garage. For her father, and it was what his father announced boastfully to his neighbours and friends not once but several times, her birth in his narrow tenement house was no less than a miracle.

And so, he named her Karisma.

She loved the sea, its unendingness, the force with which the waves crashed on the shore, and the ships and the fleet of trawlers moored along the coastline.

They said her looks bore no resemblance to either of her parents, her father a tall, sturdy, muscular, brown skinned man and her mother a quaint, slim, fair and delicate featured woman who hailed from a mediocre family of farmers. She had, however, completed her schooling before marrying her father. The neighbours looked at Karisma in astonished admiration, wondering secretly wherefrom she got the aristocratic looks, the mass of thick curly hair framing her golden face, the big black eyes and the rosy lips, the artistic arch of the dense eyebrows, the sharp aquiline nose and long delicate fingers with the pinkish nails. Every feature as though, proudly announced a royal descendance. 'She is my princess,' her father would boast, cradling her in his big, muscular arms and would flick a strange smile at her mother. Karisma was too young to understand the look in her mother's eyes, that was an odd blend of fear and relief. Friends and relations guessed that she was afraid for the arresting beauty of her daughter, worried for her safety.

'She must be a throwback to some aristocratic blood in our family, must be one of our great, great grandmothers or grandfathers had owned this gorgeous look.' Karisma's father would declare even more aggressively to his co-workers and friends, as he traded leisurely the sandy shore on Sunday afternoons, his daughter perched comfortably on his shoulders.

'My princess,' he would lift her above his head and show her the rows of trawlers bobbing at anchor in the bay. He would see the glow of delight on his daughter's face as she eyed the fishing ships. 'Do you see those big ships? One day they will be yours to command.' Her father would proclaim like a clairvoyant announcing a prophecy.

***

'I will tell you the story of a princess,' her father said, while she sat ensconced happily in his lap. 'Long, long ago a very beautiful baby daughter was born to a royal couple. She was so beautiful, just like you are, that all the subjects kept staring at her, amazed at her beauty and could not take their eyes off her. But there was an evil man who nursed a secret hostility against the king because the king had put him in prison for a crime he committed in the past. This evil man, in one dark, deep night stole the princess away from the palace and left her alone in a far-off forest. A poor woodcutter discovered the baby girl and took her to his home. His small, grimy hut was illumined with the glow of the princess. The baby princess grew up to be a little girl and everyone admired her. She radiated the aura of royalty wherever she went. Everyone craved her company, everyone wanted to gain a glance of favour from her. The princess lived in the small hut of her father through poverty and hardship. But her foster father had taught her to help and fulfil the wishes of people who needed her favour. He taught her to help those who begged her for her love. He taught her that a person with royal blood cared not for pain and suffering but finds her way out of the mire of poverty by making clever use of the love people showered on her. And, the princess obeyed her father, and made her father happy. They became rich, lived in a big palatial house. The princess grew up to be more beautiful and more attractive and pulled more love and respect for herself and her father. And one day, a king, handsome like some god, met the princess and fell in love with her. He married the princess eventually and made her his queen. The princess went away leaving the woodcutter, now old and sick, alone in the big house.' Her father paused and lifted Karisma's chin making her look up at him. 'My princess,' he said wetly, 'Will you go away leaving me alone?' and Karisma hugged him tightly. 'I would never leave you alone, father.' And her father would kiss her fondly on her forehead.

***

At seven, Karisma had realized that she not

only looked like a princess, but actually was one, every inch, and believed the story that some evil fate had made her land in that small tenement house. She adored her father when he called her a princess. She accepted every word he said as an oracle, a pronouncement made by a god. She knew instinctively that every dream he showed her would eventually come true. And she was desperately determined to please him, to fulfil his wish at whatever it might cost.

***

'You must know my princess,' his father said once, when Karishma was ten, 'You do not belong in this box of a house. But God does not always send princesses to royal families, as in the story I had told you once. He sometimes decides to send them to the houses of common people like us, and when He chooses to do so, he does it with a purpose, to make you bold enough to pave your roads to royalty on your own. To make you strong to rule your domain. You are not like the other princesses, delicate and dainty, but you are a fighter, and a winner.' A perplexed Karisma looked at her father, twining the lace border of her expensive frilly cerulean gown around her index finger. The gown was a gift from her father on her ninth birthday and she was crazy about it. She knew how her father doted on her, and she promised to herself to obey her father, to do whatever he wanted her to do.

'Won't you like to own more such outfits? Expensive and classy?' He asked and Karisma who nodded vigorously. 'And a big, comfortable house to live in?' She again nodded her assent.

'You have to help me my Princess to build you a luxurious house, to get you befitting clothes and jewelries. You have to help me to acquire resources to let you have the regalia of a real princess. Will you help me, my child?'

'Of course, father,' Karisma promised, 'Whatever you want me to do to make you happy.'

***

The motorcar slowed down the speed as it cruised towards the unobtrusive departmental store along the waterfront. Karisma, now twelve and flurrying as a newly emerged butterfly hopped off the passenger's seat as her father opened the door on her side. She looked absolutely stunning, fragile and fairy-like in a frilly scarlet gown that reached down to her feet, another gift from her besotted father. The owner of the store, Kundan Sah, a middle-aged man, with a grossly unsymmetrical physique came out from behind the countertop showing his decayed, tobacco-stained teeth in a broad welcoming grin. He took the hand of Karisma's father in a warm grip and pumped it vigorously. The unassuming looking departmental store was a front behind which Kundan Sah ran his real business of gambling and moneylending. He was passed as a sly character and a swindler by the local people but none had the courage to counter or expose him since now and then he came to their rescue, using his political connections or extending financial help to haul them out of difficulties and hardships.

Kundan Sah took Karisma in his arms and kissed her forehead. He gave her a large packet that looked attractive in a glossy wrapper. 'For you,' he said his arms tightening around her frail, soft body and kissed her again, this time on her cheek. His breath, that carried a muted smell of tobacco was hot on her cheeks. Karishma loathed the smell, but she ignored it. The snazzy look of the gift box relieved its stink in a great degree.

'I have some urgent work at the factory, dear,' her father said. 'I will get back here in a few minutes. You wait here. Uncle will give you ice cream and whatever else you want. He is a very unhappy man. You will make him happy, won't you?'

Karisma nodded a prompt 'yes', happy that here was an occasion to pay back to her adorable father who had always made her feel so special, and also to help someone who is sad, and needed her favour. After all she was a princess. She must see that people who loved her should be happy.

Kundan uncle led her into a comfortably furnished room at the back of the store. 'I will get you your butterscotch ice cream. That is your choice flavour I understand.' He scuttled out of the room and came back almost in the next instant carrying a small bowl.

'Enjoy your ice cream, I will be back in a minute.'

Karisma scooped out a generous portion from the bowl and put it in her mouth.

***

She sat in the back seat of the car. Her whole body felt bruised and her head ached. There was a mild pain between her thighs too. She could not decide why her whole body hurt so much and unknowingly a few drops of tears trailed down her eyes. She remembered her father half lifting and half walking her to the car. He drove along the wide road that arched along the shore for about half an hour and then brought the car to a stop. He lowered the window glasses and the misty sea breeze felt cool and soothing against her bruised body. She let out a small moan.

'Does it hurt a lot, my princess?' He asked, his face registering a deep sadness. 'Do not worry. I have a magic pill that will take away the pain,' he said and made her swallow a tiny pill. After a short while she felt the pain receding slowly. She looked at her father who stared vacantly out at the sea. She was afraid that her father was unhappy because she complained of the pain. 'I am okay now, father. The pain has come down. Please do not look so sad.' She implored.

Her father gathered her in his strong arms and stroked her ruffled hair. 'I am sorry my darling, but you must know that you have to take a little pain in stride to enjoy the status of a princess. This is how you will exploit the naivety of people like Kundan. There are many more like him. They could be manipulated to help you make you a real princess. You will see in less than a couple of years we will have our own palace, a car of our own and dresses and shoes and jewelries for you which your friends would envy. But you have to promise me one thing.' Her father looked at her, as if a lot depended on her making a promise. She was not angry with her father but happy that he had explained to her the easy way to become a princess. She was so overwhelmed with gratitude that she wanted to hug him tightly. 'I promise father. I will do what you say.'

'Nothing much. Just let no one know about what happened this evening. And when I say no one, I mean no one and that includes your mother. *Keep it secret.*' Karisma nodded, looking slightly puzzled. She did not understand why must she keep it secret if she had made Kundan uncle so happy that he agreed to help her father build a big house and live a life of luxury. She had seen through her bleary eyes Kundan uncle handing out a bulging envelope to her father. Money? Must be. Kundan uncle was an old man like her father or even older than him. If he wanted her to make him happy for a while and pay for it where is the harm? The old man had no one to love him after all! She felt a tinge of pity for that gross yet benign looking man.

***

'Where have both of you been?' Mother asked from the door as she got down from the car. There was an odd look in her eyes, part fear, part curiosity. Karisma turned to glance back at her father and immediately understood the meaning of his steady stare. 'Keep it secret,' she warned herself silently and smiled at her mother. Her body was a bit sore but the pain was no longer there. She was feeling euphoric and light headed. 'Guess what Ma!' She giggled. 'Father bought me this,' she spurted through her giggles as she produced the shiny packet. We had a lot of snacks and ice creams too, at the Lucky restaurant.' She walked into the house, limping slightly. 'Why are you limping? Are you hurt?' Karisma stopped abruptly. It was an effort to walk fast. Her thighs felt heavy. 'She stumbled while getting up the steps of the restaurant. There is perhaps a slight sprain in her ankle.' Karisma's father said evasively as he made her way in to the house.

Karisma took her scarlet gown off and went into the bathroom. She did not understand why, but she felt a tremendous urge to wash herself thoroughly. She sat under the tap for a long time cleansing herself. She noticed the faint red stains on the inner side of her thighs and soaped them away carefully. Her mother might see them and ask her questions. She was tired and her eyelids drooped even as she sat down to eat her dinner. She flopped herself into the bed and was fast asleep in the next few minutes.

***

She was feeling suffocated under the crushing weight of an old fat man who stank of tobacco and saliva. 'Get off me,' she opened her mouth to scream but stopped when the man dangled a frock of blue with silver stars stitched into it, that looked like a star-spangled sky and pushed a chocolate bar as white as milk and big as her geometry compass box into her mouth. She licked at the sticky drops of the chocolate and closed her eyes trying to ignore the pain in her body.

'Why are you crying baby?' A tender touch at the corner of her eyes brought her back to wakefulness. Her mother stood by her bed, looking contrite.

Karisma smiled groggily. '*Keep it secret,*' her father's voice rang through her drowsy mind.

She sat up on her bed. 'It was a bad dream, Ma!' She said, putting her arms around her mother's waist and burying her head in her lap.

***

The two of them sat on the floor eating while her mother dished out a simple meal of rice and potato curry. 'Wait for a few days,' her father said grinning at her mother. 'You will be serving us fried rice and chicken soon.' Karisma salivated at the thought of fried rice and chicken. Her mother did not say a word. Karisma did not know why these days her mother looked like a picture of remorse, as if some pain ate into her slowly, draining her earlier vivaciousness out of her and leaving her pale and sick. Karisma did not like her mother looking like that, resigned and gloomy.

It was a Sunday afternoon, two weeks after her visit to Kundan uncle's departmental store. She had made more than one visits there during the fortnight. She had ice creams and chocolates and on one occasion Kundan Uncle gifted her a gem studded bracelet. She was elated and showed it to her mother smiling from ear to ear expecting her to share her excitement. 'It is nice. But my dear, you must not accept such expensive gifts from anyone.' Mother said glumly. Karisma felt uneasy but the shine the gems radiated soon lit up that dark unease in her mind. And that Sunday afternoon as she sat doing her school homework, she heard her parents talking. It was not anything abnormal for a child though, to hear the parents conversing. Karisma too had heard often her parents talking and she had never bothered to listen. But this time, she guessed instinctively that there was something odd about the way they exchanged words, something that did not sound normal.

'Please stop doing this. It is a sin,' Her mother's voice.

'Doing what?' her father asking.

'You know what I mean,'

'No, I don't. You are making conjectures and I am not sure what exactly they are about.'

'Stop being a cynical manipulator, playing with my child's emotions to further your selfish interests.' Her mother said impatiently.

Karisma was interested. Were they discussing *her*?

'She is a princess born to us. I am trying make her a real one.'

'You know it is nothing like that,' her mother said, in a subdued voice.

'I know everything my dear,' her father said, his voice taking on a harder edge. 'I will see to it that your daughter with her aristocratic looks of a royal linage makes me feel big like a king.'

'Please do not take it out on her,' her mother begged, sobbing. 'It is a sin.'

'You are telling me that!!' Father sniggered and strode away towards the front door. Karisma had a brief glimpse of her father's face as he crossed the door of the room where she was. There was a hard glitter in his eyes and his lips parted in an ugly twist. Karisma had never seen her father looking like that.

***

She had overheard another such intriguing conversation between her parents in another occasion, a few years after. She was in the final year at school. Her board examination was round the corner and she laboured hard to secure good marks to make her father happy. Karisma never thought in terms of her own interest and happiness. She struggled to relieve the pain of others, to see people happy, most importantly, her father. After all she was born in her father's house with a purpose, to bring happiness to those who needed her love. And this act of love and kindness, her father had assured, would make her one day a real queen, who would own the fleet of ships, who would own the sea!!

'Please stop being so cruel on her,' Her mother's pleading voice.

'Have you lost your mind? She is my princess, my priceless possession. I can't even dream of being cruel to her.'

'Yes, you are! You are doing all this to torment me. She is having a problem. The doctors had said that much earlier. You are putting ideas into her mind. You are turning her a fantasist. You are using her to achieve your selfish ends. What harm had she brought on you to deserve this?' Her mother's voice broke towards the end. Karisma tiptoed to the door and peeped through the chink. They sat by the wooden table across from each other in the small veranda outside the kitchen. Her father's face was turned towards the door where she stood, holding her breath.

'She didn't.' Her father said tightly, his face slightly flushing. 'You know who did, don't you my dear?'

Her mother did not say anything. Nor could Karisma see the lines of pain and remorse that crept into her mother's face.

'God has sent her to me to recompense the misery I go through. A girl of such unusual beauty! As if she does not belong in this mundane earth, let alone this house!'

'It is not fair!' Her mother cried.

'I do not have to learn from you what is fair. Do I? So, stop moralizing.' Her father rose to his feet gave the chair a hard push. Then he walked out of the house in long, angry strides. Her mother sat there still as a statue, then she placed her folded arms on the table, buried her face into them and broke into sobbing.

Karisma walked back to her study table quietly and sat down, perturbed. It was all like a tricky puzzle, and she had no idea how to solve it. She tried to banish the disturbing thoughts out of her mind and concentrate in her studies.

***

Karisma was a sensation in the college. It was not so that she wasn't one in the school. But she stood out amongst others when she joined the college at her sweet sixteen. She smiled to herself at the thought of how the boys and even the teachers both young and old, fell over one another to earn a glance of favour from her.

Her family had shifted in the meanwhile to their two storied house in a posh locality, and her father had bought a second-hand car which looked smarter than the new ones after a thorough and careful makeover in the garage where he was now a partner.

She had not stopped visiting Kundan uncle's store in all these years and he too had not made a cutdown on his generosity, but it had become less frequent. Kundan uncle's business had flourished too and he had renovated his small store to a luxurious shopping complex. 'It is all because of you, dearie. You are my lucky charm!' He would say and take her into his loose, flaccid arms. He gifted her expensive jewelries, and dresses every time she met him, and the inevitable envelope which Karisma knew now, contained money. The envelope was for her father. A few months back Kundan uncle had ordered a smart phone for her. She had got over the shock of the initial experience of her visits to his store, and the envelopes he shoved into her hand while leaving grew thicker and bulgier each time. He no longer inveigled her to the secret love chamber behind the store that was left undemolished during the renovation, and would kiss her softly on her cheek and run a gaunt hand over her body and smile at her fondly. Astonishingly, she did not feel now any aversion towards the smell of tobacco he emitted. She was old enough to understand, had it not been for Kundan uncle she would still have been stumbling down the bumpy roads of life despite her father's unwavering faith in his princess's charismatic charm. And she loved him for that. It was not a selfish sort of love, but was sincere and genuine.

Kundan uncle was getting mellower and Karisma grew more compassionate towards him. Her father too was getting old and Karisma was feeling more inclined to keep him happy, to fulfil his wishes. She cooked his favourite dishes for him since her mother was not keeping well of late. She wondered why her mother never looked happy, even when they came to live in the new house or drove in their own car. A cloud of gloom hung over her otherwise charming face constantly and it never lifted. She had asked her more than once why was she sad but mother had cleverly evaded her questions.

*****

It rained hard that night. She had gone to bed early, her mind filled with Ronit. Ronit was one year senior to her in college. He was from another state. Karisma had heard that he had lost his parents in the epidemic and lived with his uncle. Ronit was a tall, handsome young man, his sharp jawline and attractive features pronouncing an aristocratic descent. But there was a deep-set agony in his large, expressive eyes. Karisma had hardly seen him smile. He was shy and self-effacing, not loud and aggressive like most of the other boys. 'He is trying hard to conceal his sorrow under fake smiles, but fails miserably,' Karisma thought. And the princess in her prompted her, 'He is in pain and he is in need of your help. He needs someone to paint a smile on his face! Did not father tell you that you are a princess and you must heal the sufferings of people with love?'

And that was how she felt seriously drawn to him, to assuage his pain with love, to haul him out of the pit of his woe, to make the cloud that loomed across his handsome face, dissipate. She was intuitively aware of his interest in her. She knew he waited everyday by the staircase leading to the lecture hall upstairs, to have a glimpse of her. But he never made any advance to her nor made a verbal display of his feelings.

If asked, she might not remember exactly how it began.

Perhaps in that rainy noon in July. It had been

raining hard since morning and the attendance of students in the college was thin. Karisma's father dropped her by the gate of the college. He had some urgent work and drove away in a hurry. The next moment he had driven away Karisma realized that she had forgotten the umbrella in the car. The large front-campus looked deserted except for few students and teachers who hurried into the shelter of the portico of the main building. Some of them had umbrellas and others had raincoats on. She stood under the carved wide arch supported by two onyx columns that formed the main entrance to the college looking unsurely around and then she noticed Ronit, coming towards the gate carrying an umbrella overhead. 'Come under the umbrella,' he said and it was the first time she smiled at him. Ronit did not smile back but a sparkle came to his eyes as Karisma came under the umbrella without any hesitation. And that was the beginning!

***

They met at not so conspicuous restaurants away from the main town, and on the distant patches of the seashore escaping the curious gaze of the sea bathers and tourists. There were days when Ronit and she went on long drives out of the town. There was a magnetic charm about Ronit that Karisma found difficult to resist. And the days they could not meet they chatted late into the night. And Karisma tried relentlessly to keep him happy, to make him get over the shock, the misery that gnawed at his soul.

***

'Why aren't you asleep my dear?' Her father said from the door and in a quick, frantic movement Karishma pushed the phone under the pillow. Her father stepped inside, looking concerned.

'Are you alright?'

'Yes father. Just a bit anxious about my papers.' She lied.

'Do not you worry. You are my princess! You will beat them all.'

Karisma smiled fondly at her father, loving him for the trust he had in her, feeling guilty for betraying that trust. 'Go to sleep now,' he stroked her head and went out. Karisma's anxious gaze followed him to the door. Abruptly he stopped by the door and turned back. He flicked a brief but curious glance at the pillow and then at Karisma. Karisma lowered her eyes.

'Go to sleep. Do not while away time on that phone.' He strode away from the room. Karisma sat still on the bed for a long minute staring at the disappearing back of her father. Then she got down and closed the door. She took out the mobile phone from under the pillow and carefully deleted all the chats she had had with Ronit. She lay awake for a long time, turning on her sides, feeling slightly uneasy.

***

'Do not drive so fast!' She said loudly from the pillion seat of the bike and tightened her grip around Ronit's waist. Ronit laughed naughtily.

'Would you hold me so tightly if I don't? They were driving along the deserted road that hemmed the coastline, enjoying the spray of the seas mist against their faces. Karisma rubbed her cheek against Ronit's and giggled. Her swaying, billowing mass of hair swept across Ronit's face sending an ecstatic stir through his nerves.

A blue car sped past their bike. The man that sat behind the wheel had big, greenish glasses over his eyes and had the lower part of his face covered by a scarf, as if he purposely wore a veneer of anonymity.

'Did you notice that car?'

'Which car?'

'The blue one. The driver looks .... kind of quirky.'

'Why do you say so?'

'I had seen the car last week, when we were driving along this road. It had pulled up for a brief while by that culvert. As if it waited for us to pass by. I also remember seeing it the day we were driving past the road along the lighthouse. The same driver. Big sun glasses, face covered in a scarf. Too odd to be a coincidence. Gives me a queer feeling. Like we are being shadowed!'

Karisma pressed her face against Ronit's shoulder. 'I see nothing except you when we are together.'

Ronit laughed. 'Silly girl!' He pressed the accelerator and the bike gathered more speed.

***

The front door was ajar. Karisma was a little surprised. Mother kept the door locked from inside when she was alone at home. Her father was out of town, in the sea. He was supposed to get back to the land next day or the day after. She gave a light push to the door and entered. Her father was in the living room, watching television, sipping tea from a steaming cup. Her mother stood by the door that led to the inside of the house, looking painfully frail and dull.

'Here comes my princess,' her father effused. 'Come darling, sit by me.'

Her heart beating unrhythmically, Karisma walked to the long couch and sat a little away from her father.

'You are late dear! Was there some important class or something in the college?'

'No, father.' Karisma stammered. 'I was with some of my friends.'

'It is all right dear. Nothing to look so perplexed,' his father patted her back. 'It was just that your mother gets worried when you are not back home in time. Besides you were supposed to go to Kundan uncle's' mall this afternoon. He is missing you a lot these days.'

Karisma swallowed hard. She had not been visiting Kundan uncle, in fact, she thought guiltily, she had started ignoring him after she met Ronit.

'Remember dearie, had it not been for Kundan uncle we would be still rotting in that tenement house,' her father said. His voice was gentle but the underlying accusing note was unmistakably obvious.

'I am sorry father,' Karisma muttered, her eyes lowered. 'I will meet him tomorrow without fail.'

'That's my girl!' her father kissed her forehead. 'Get her a cup of tea.' He said, turning to look at her mother who was still standing by the door. Karisma too turned. The look in her mother's eyes disturbed her. It was the same look, part resentment part fear and part sadness. She had noticed that helpless hostility in her eyes several times in the past when she visited Kundan uncle's store. Karisma was now old enough to interpret that look but she was helpless too, driven by her obsessive inclination to keep her father happy. She forced herself to think rationally, pragmatically and compromise.

Her mother coughed as she walked sluggishly towards the kitchen. It was a prolonged coughing that became a painful wheezing. Karisma ran to her mother and put her arms around her. 'You take rest, Ma,' she said. 'I will make the tea for both of us.' She walked her mother back to her bedroom. She could instinctively sense her father's intense gaze boring into her back but she did not turn to check.

***

Her mother had developed a temperature since morning and her cough too had got worse. Father was not home. Karisma had put her mother in bed after giving her some antipyretics. She cooked a simple meal for her mother and herself. She got back to her mother and took her temperature. It was normal. Karisma brought her the simple lunch she had cooked and sat by her while she ate.

'Did you go to his store last evening?' Her mother asked suddenly as she nibbled at the food. The question caught Karisma by surprise. In all these years her mother had never asked her about her visits to Kundan uncle's store. 'Yes, but...' Karisma looked at her mother. There was an odd glint in her sunken eyes. 'It is not the same any longer Ma, as you think. Kundan uncle is now too old to .....' Karisma mumbled haltingly. 'Snakes like him never grow old..' her mother said through clenched teeth. The deep disdain and antipathy in her voice sent a nervous stir through Karisma. 'Does the boy know about your visits to that evil fellow's store?' It was the second bombshell her mother had dropped in those few minutes. 'What boy?' Karisma asked pretending surprise. 'I am your mother, my dear. I know more about you than you know yourself.' 'Keep it secret from the boy. No amount of love can make one overlook such deceit.' Her mother pushed the plate away and lay back on the bed. Her eyes were closed but tears trickled down their corners. Karisma wiped the tears. 'Do not you stress yourself Ma.' She said soothingly. 'Father had promised me he would not ask me to visit Kundan uncle after I completed college. And, as I told you Kundan uncle has now stopped taking liberties with me.'

'Father!' Hmm!!'

Mother spat out the words with such venom

that Karisma cringed inwardly. She had always seen her mother as a docile, caring wife. But this was a changed woman, a woman that lived with an untold angst buried deep inside her which was now trying to find an escapeway. If she had not approved of her daughter's visit to Kundan Sah's store she had never objected to it openly. Why? Because she did not want to raise her voice against father? Why was she so intimidated by her father?

Karisma tried to think rationally. Kundan uncle was her father's friend and had played an important role in changing their lives. These days the man seemed to be happy to be just in her company. She shied away from the thoughts of the intimate moments she once shared with him in the chamber behind the store. She fought the memory off her mind. It was her father whose wish mattered most for her and she obeyed him not out of fear but out of love. She had loved her father obsessively since she was a child. She loved the way he called her 'princess' and boasted about her before his friends. She loved the way he assured her that one day she would be owning a fleet of trawlers. She believed every word of her father like an ultimate pronouncement of her destiny. She never begrudged his wish to manipulate Kundan uncle through her. The sudden and bitter display of her mother's spite and the mention of the 'boy' had caught her off guard. But she hated the tears in her mother's eyes.

***

Karisma cast a long glance at her mother who

was now sleeping soundly, and came out closing the door gently behind her. She sat by hers study table looking vaguely out of the window, seeing nothing in particular, her mind haunted by the sporadic invasions of disturbing, distracting thoughts. She forced herself to gather her erratic thoughts and focus her mind in the studies. But it proved a futile exercise.

She texted to Ronit. 'Where are you?'

'I am in the Amrit Nursing Home. Dev's mother is admitted here following a mild heart attack. I will get back to you in the evening.' He texted back.

Dev was Ronit's close friend. Karisma knew Ronit would not leave the hospital until the condition of Dev's mother improved. The Amrit Nursing Home was at the other end of the town, at about at least half an hour's drive from the college hostel where Ronit stayed. Karisma doubted if Ronit would find time to call back or message her tonight.

There was nothing to do other than wait. She decided to take a stroll to the beach to calm her agitations.

She walked leisurely down the arch shaped road that lengthened along the beach, enjoying the spray of the sea mist across her face.

She took a turn and walked along the narrow, sandy track that branched off the main beach-road and disappeared into a patch awninged by a dense growth of casuarinas, date-palms and scattered patches of stubbly shrubs, then emerged out at a distant part of the shore that was jagged and was unevenly clustered with a number of sand-dunes. She sat down on a sandy mound and glanced at the distant skyline. The sun had already gone down leaving behind trails of crimson and lavender. A brief gust of briny breeze swept past her face filling her with nostalgia. Ronit and she had spent many evenings in this secluded sandy patch, wrapped in the moist embrace of the spray mists from the sea.

She heaved a sigh and looked up. The sky hung dismal and sulking. Fluffy, foreboding mass of slate-black clouds had thronged in there announcing the advent of a storm. Karisma decided to get back home and rose to her feet. Even as she made her way through the patch of stubbly bushes the wind began to gain speed. She half ran and half walked back to her home as the storm grew fiercer. Grey, steely sheets of torrential rain shut the pale pre-evening light off and the wind howled like an angry, wounded animal.

'Where have you been? I was sick with worry.' Her mother said from the front door, her voice quivering in anxiety. 'I am fine Ma. Why are you standing here in the cold when you are supposed to be in bed? Go and take rest.' The electricity was cut off. Karisma shut the doors and windows and lit an oil lamp.

***

Ronit did not call in the evening. She too, had not expected him to call. But he could have sent her a message, she thought. It was unlike Ronit to keep out of contact from her for such a long duration. Her father had not returned by nine. Karisma gave her mother her medicine with a glass of milk and coming back to her room sat down to study. She could focus better in her studies in the silence of the night.

She yawned and looked at her mobile screen. It was twenty minutes after eleven. There was no message from Ronit. Strange. He always used to text a message to her however busy he was. The hospital was at quite a distance from the main town and the weather was stormy. Doubt and fear gnawed at her heart driving sleep away from her eyes. She turned and tossed restlessly on her sides for a long time. Her father too had not returned. She guessed he might be with Kundan uncle, drinking and gambling as he does most nights. He won't be home till the rain stopped, she thought. She checked her message box once again half expecting a message from Ronit. There was none. The power was not restored yet. She lowered the flame of the lamp and closed her eyes trying to sleep.

***

It must be long after midnight when a soft knock sounded on the front door. The sound jolted Karisma out of an uneasy sleep. She sat up on bed, her breath coming in irregular gasps. 'Must be father,' she said to herself, trying to get calmer. The knock sounded again, this time louder, demanding. 'Coming,' she said, and getting down the bed groped her way to the front door. As she was about to pull the bolt down, she remembered she was carrying the mobile phone. She switched on the torch and opened the door. It was her father. He came inside, shut the door and strode into the house. In the feeble light of the torch of her mobile phone Karisma noticed that his hair was all mussed up, and his face haggard as if he had suddenly aged ten years. The usually neatly folded sleeves of his shirt were wrinkled and there were faint muddy stains on his trousers. All this Karisma took in one quick glance, just in that same instant her father hurried inside. 'He must be in a hurry to get out of the rain-drenched clothes.' Karisma reasoned. But it struck her as awkward, her father stepping past her without a fond word of greeting. He looked different, a stranger.' She walked back to her room, raised the flame of the lamp and waited for her father to come out of his room. Five minutes passed, then another five... father did not come out. She walked up to his door and tapped softly. 'Father, should I bring you something light to eat?'

'I am not hungry. Go back to sleep.' His father said from behind the door, not caring to open it.

Karisma went back to her room, wondering what made her father behave so oddly. 'Perhaps he had drunk more than his usual,' she tried to think rationally but her heart was not ready to accept the logicizing.

***

Ronit did not call her the next day. Nor did

he send a message. Karisma left for the college early in the morning hoping to find Ronit there. His practical classes were scheduled in the morning hours. Since she did not discuss Ronit with her friends and since she knew Ronit too avoided speaking about her to his friends, with one single exception of Dev who was closest to him, it felt awkward to inquire in the laboratory if Ronit was inside. She waited for a long time in the corridor, feeling embarrassed, sensing the prick of curious glances of the staff and students, expecting him to come out of the laboratory. After what seemed a century, the practical class came to an end. Students emerged from behind the closed glass portals in solo and in groups. There was no sign of Ronit. She didn't expect Dev because his mother was in the hospital. Disappointed and wary, she dragged herself back to her own class. Her mind, torn with worry and apprehensions, refused to register any of the things the teacher said.

She did not attend the rest of the classes and walked down the long narrow road that led through the thick growth of the casuarinas and thorny bushes to the far end of the shore where she had sat last evening. The midday sun glittered on the turquoise sea and the tides like doomed souls flung themselves desperately on the vast, sandy stretch. The deserted, sunlit shore wore an ominous look. There was a foreboding in the whispering of the winds that gusted through the casuarinas and date palms. She just sat there, losing all sense of time, looking blankly at the frothy waves breaking across the sands, lamenting some primeval, irreparable loss.

The next day was a holiday. Still there was no news of Ronit. Anxiety and apprehensions were driving Karisma insane. She sat staring out of the window uttering a silent prayer. 'O' God, let nothing happen to Ronit, please!' Hot, unshed tears scalded her eyes. Mother called her to have her lunch but Karisma refused. 'I am not hungry,' she said without turning.

A hand pressed her shoulder lightly. 'What is the matter, my darling? Why do you look so somber?' it was her mother. Karisma grabbed her mother and broke to tears. The fear and pain that had been lying dormant inside her like a solid block, thawed and streamed out of her eyes in warm, stinging rivulets.

'It is Ronit, Ma. He had gone away somewhere. There is no news from him.' She stammered through her uncontrollable sobs. Her mother cradled her head in the crook of her arm. 'There might have been some emergency he had to take care of. He might not have found time to inform you. It often happens like that. Men are not as sensitive as we women are. Be patient. Wait for him to call back.' She solaced her miserable daughter. 'You take rest Ma. You are not yet fit to do hard work.' Karisma said, now a bit calmer.

Her mother ran her hand on Karisma's head, and turned to leave. She stopped at the door. 'Do you think your father had made a guess about your friendship with Ronit?' She asked, looking back, her voice mildly anxious. 'No, why?' A streak of fear crept into Karisma's eyes. 'I just asked. He must not know till you both are well settled to take care of yourselves.'

That is another way to advise 'Keep it secret', Karisma guessed, and nodded limply.

***

She had drifted into an uneasy sleep, after lunch. Her father looked concerned watching her playing with her food absentmindedly. 'What is the matter with you, darling?' he enquired. 'Are you not well?' 'No Father. A mild headache,' Karisma tried to evade. 'Take a pill or should I give you a head massage?' her father asked anxiously. 'It is just a mild ache, Father. Will go away on its own. Do not trouble yourself.' She got up and went to her room. She heard her father's heavy footfalls making an exit from the house. She turned her face to the wall and closed her eyes, feeling the liquid heat of the unshed tears in her eyes.

***

The persistent ring of the phone jerked her out of sleep. She squinted at the screen of the mobile. It was an unknown number. The screen showed ten minutes past twelve. Who could be calling her at midnight, she thought, premonitions gnawing at her heart. Could be a wrong number, she hoped and touched the red, reject symbol. But the phone rang again almost immediately. Her heart racing now, perhaps because she had intuitively felt it was for her and it was urgent, she accepted the call. 'Hello, who's it?' She asked, her voice unsteady.

'Karisma?' A male voice came from the other end.

'Yes, who is calling?' The words stumbled out of her as a numbing wave of fear swept over her thoughts.

'It is Dev. I could not call you earlier because I did not have your number. Have you heard of Ronit?' Dev asked, anxiety dripping from his tone.

'No, what is it?' Karisma gripped the phone hard fearing it would slip off her hand unless she did so.

'Ronit met with a serious accident two nights before. The very night my mother was admitted in the hospital. He was with me till late and left around at about eleven. There was a nasty rain storm that evening. I asked him not to drive down that slippery narrow road, but he insisted on going back. They found his bike late in the night, but there was no sign of Ronit by the bike. After a combing search operation finally he was found entangled in the twigs of the thick undergrowth about a hundred meters behind where the bike was. The police think it could either be that his bike skidded or it is a a hit and run case. But the other vehicle had not yet been traced. He was initially admitted in the Sun Shine hospital. He had lapsed into a comatose state. His uncle and aunt had shifted him to a multispecialty hospital outside the state But, there is little hope for him. I am so sorry dear.'

Karisma sat still on the bed, her fingers frozen around the phone.

'Hello, Karisma! Are you there? Hello.'

Dev kept calling from the other end. Karisma heard nothing. Saw nothing. The phone remained stuck inside her grip. A thick curtain of black cascaded down in her front and blocked her vision. She was still sitting there stiff, motionless, her phone gripped in her numb fingers when her parents found her after an hour.

***

'I know what happened to the boy.' A familiar female voice.

'Which boy? And what happened to him?' A male voice, equally familiar. She wanted to listen intently but a storm roared out side and fine, sparkling dusts of white and green spiralled around her blinding her.

'I know you are responsible,' the female voice.

There was a short pause.

'Why do you punish her? What has she done?' the female voice again.

'You know darling she has not done anything. She is taking it on your behalf!' the mail voice was a harsh whisper.

'Please stop this now. I beg of you!'

Something sharp pricked at her arm. She wanted to cry out but the storm subsided and the white and green dusts too settled down. She felt relaxed and at peace.

***

'Look at that blue car. It is tailing us.' The boy said. She was in the rear seat and could not see the boy's

face. She laughed amusedly. 'Drive fast. Shake it off the tail.' The boy laughed and pressed on the accelerator and they drove through the clouds that caressed her wetly and her hair blew and bounced wildly. She looked down. The blue car was just under them and a man looked out of its window. He flicked his fingers as if performing a magic and the bike leaped ahead slashing the jungle of clouds and took a nose dive down and the boy and the bike were thrown out into a deep ravine thousands of feet below. Somehow, may be by some miracle, she did not go down with the boy. She stood at the edge of an endlessly lengthening sandy road screaming and weeping and a storm wind blew hard and the clouds circled her turning from white to grey and then to black. She heard its swish as the car crawled forward to where she stood and turned to look. A man, his face hidden behind big, green-tinted sunglasses and the lower part of his face covered in a scarf waved at her and sped away. Her heart gave a start. She knew the man. Not now but ever since she was a child!!!

The dream kept returning to her nights for about a year. Even after she had re-joined her college and presumably got over the shock. She felt so confused, so bewildered at the repeated visions. What did they mean? She refused to accept that the man who was in the blue car was someone whom she knew closely. But she felt so unsure and every time the dream visited her sleep she started up on the bed, sweating all over and shaking uncontrollably.

Thankfully the dreams stopped their gruesome visit as days shrank into months and months into years.

***

Karisma sat in a basket chair in the lawn of the Sea and Sands club, one of the few deluxe clubs in the town. The club members, who belonged to the elite class and had a heavy lot of money to squander in drinks and gambling, sat under colourful beach umbrellas and enjoyed their dinner under a hazy, gibbous moon that hung indifferently from a mistic sky. An oval swimming pool, screened by luxuriant growths of tall palms shone like a sheet of silvery blue in the shimmering light. She looked vaguely at the beach, at the tenacious waves that bashed hoarsely against the sands as if avenging some ancient pain, and receding away, tired and torn, into the vast green-greyness of the evening sea, then returning rejuvenated and resurgent.

'The sea has a strange character.' Karisma thought bleakly. 'Like a human mind. You try to fling the pangs into it hoping that it will swallow them, suck them into its dark depth, but every time you do that the waves bring them back to you, with greater force, to torment you more. It happens so in the beginning. But as time moves on the sea gets tired of tossing the things back to you and draws them into its bottomless depth where they remain buried. Human mind too, after a certain time-lapse, holds back the pains that it keeps thrusting up in the beginning, buried in its deep recess. But the pain remains, hidden under the placid surface, in a state of dark stupor, waiting to erupt and come whirling up and up to shatter and devastate the calm with its demonic gyrations.

It was almost five years since that fateful night on which Dev called her to share the news of Ronit's accident. She remembered hearing Dev's weeping voice faintly but in the next instant the world had gone blank.

The next thing she remembered were the grueling experiences in the hospitals and with the psychiatrists. But she, as the doctors observed, had been remarkably brave and succeeded in handling her trauma with a positive spirit. She had regained her earlier composure within one year, joined back in her college and completed her graduation. But the pain remained, under the calm, seemingly unruffled surface of her ocean, in its bottomless depth.

***

The entry of Kalyan Kumar, the owner of the Star fishing company, a compellingly handsome man in his early fifties, into her life, was as shocking an incident as the sudden departure of Ronit from it. Her father said that the alliance was proposed by Kalyan Kumar himself after he had seen Karisma in the college while he had visited it as a guest of honour in the convocation ceremony. Her mother had vehemently opposed. 'The man is about more than twenty years older than her. How could you think of marrying your daughter to someone more than double her age? They say that he is a womanizer and an alcohol-addict.'

'Age will pose no hindrance. The man owns

a large number of fishing boats and trawlers and runs a business with an unbelievably huge annual turnover. He is a king in the world of fishing business, and Karisma will be a real queen. And all these talk about he being a womanizer and alcoholic are just hearsay.' Her father had countered. Karisma looked at it resignedly, neither happy nor sad. 'If you say so, father,' was what she said when he tried to explain to her how her life would turn corner once she entered into this incredibly lucky alliance. Karisma smiled bleakly. 'My princess will be a queen now,' he exclaimed, elated at the prospect of being the father-in -law of an influential business magnate.

***

She shifted her eyes to the exit of the restaurant. Her husband was still inside. The three of them, she, her husband Kalyan Kumar and his personal secretary Kiran had come to the Sea and Sands club for a weekend dinner. Kalyan Kumar, like most of other people in the elite circle, was a life member of the club. He was an experienced tennis player and always enjoyed his Friday evenings in the club's tennis court. Kiran was his trusted personal secretary and a good friend of Karisma. In the first year of their marriage Kalyan Kumar and Karisma enjoyed each other's exclusive company in the weekends, but as time drew on, Kalyan Kumar appeared to have got bored in the company of Karisma since she did not share his interests in the business. Neither did she understand tennis or snooker, nor was she a socialite like most of the company executives' wives were. Then Sandhya Kiran, shortened as Kiran, one of the most able and competent employees the company ever had, as Kalyan often described her, joined Kalyan's fishing company and was soon promoted to the post of Kalyan's personal assistant. She stuck to Kalyan Kumar as a shadow. 'You must not take it otherwise, ' he said to Karisma as if explaining to a dumbhead, 'I need her by my side for urgent consultations relating to the business. She is full of brilliant ideas.' Karisma smiled resignedly as she had done when her father had advised her to marry Kalyan Kumar a few years back. She was a princess, that *was* what her father had tried to convince her since she was a child and she was always goaded by an urge to make others happy. So, Sandhya Kiran made her entry into Kalyan Kumar's private chamber and the dreams re-entered Karisma's private nights.

***

She and Kalyan Kumar were on board in a large fishing boat and watched as the fishermen crew at the edge of the deck uncoiled the longlines with baited hooks to set them at different depths of the sea, and then later, trawling the catch back to the boat. The sky was a cerulean canopy overhead spotted with fleecy, white clouds. Suddenly a man shouted from the stern and they turned to look. The face of a woman of astounding beauty bobbed up from the water some five hundred meters ahead of the fishing boat. 'A mermaid,' the fisherman shouted again and they all hurried to the deck to take a look. Karisma gaped ahead as the creature, half-human and half-fish swam fast towards their boat, waving its tail with great force. As she stared on, the sky turned a frightening reddish brown and the wind blew in wild gusts. The creature moved to the right side of the fishing boat and lashed its formidable tail at the starboard. The boat tilted in a perilous angle to the right and she and Kalyan Kumar went sliding helplessly down the tilting deck. Karisma groped blindly for her husband's hand but the strong wind shoved Kalyan Kumar off the deck in a blink. Karisma screamed at the top of her voice but the roar of the sea drowned the sound. Just as she went catapulting over the railing and took a dive, she caught a glimpse of the strange fish-woman's face. It was the face of Sandhya Kiran.

The dream came assuming different forms but always ending at her fishing boat sinking into the turbulent waters, whipped by the tail of the huge, stunningly beautiful mermaid, even to her waking eyes and she staggered under its impact. But she never revealed it to her husband. Certain things are to be kept close to the heart. 'Keep it secret.' Her father had advised her when she was too young to understand Kundan Uncle's show of love, and later her mother had warned her to keep her friendship with Ronit secret. So, she clutched the secret to herself and it ate into her heart like a tenacious worm boring into the soft wood.

The delicate smell of an expensive ladies' perfume brought her back to the present and she looked up. Sandhya Kiran stood by her, carrying a folder crammed with papers across her chest and her laptop bag slinging from her frail shoulder. 'Time to return madam,' she said politely. Karisma looked behind Sandhya Kiran. Her husband was climbing down the wooden steps of the club. The chauffer hurried on to hold the door open and they got into the car. 'Did you enjoy the moonlit evening?' Kalyan Kumar asked. 'So sorry that both of us got busy in discussing the new project and you had to sit alone for a while.' He smiled apologetically. 'It was no problem. You know I like to spend time in my own company at times,' she smiled trying to give her voice a lighthearted note. Sandhya Kiran laughed softly from the front seat.

***

The woman lay in the bed in a hospital cabin. Several tubes fixed to her body were connected to different electronic gadgets that monitored her vital signs. The cabin was apparently noiseless except for the steady beeping from the electronic systems. The rhythmic but weak rise and fall of her chest was the only indication that she was alive. Karisma touched her head tenderly. 'Ma!' she called.

The eyelids of the woman fluttered slightly. 'Want to say something, Ma?' Karisma whispered gently, her voice breaking. Tears trickled down the corners of the woman's closed eyes and her lips quivered. 'Yes Ma!' Karisma whispered into her ears again. The woman's bony hands groped weakly for her daughter's and Karisma let her own hand into her mother's grip. 'Forgive me, my darling.' The woman said in a voice that was barely above a whisper. ' I am a sinner. I am responsible for all you have suffered.'

Karisma's face registered puzzlement briefly and then cleared. 'You are not Ma,' she said. 'You are not responsible. Falling in love is no sin!' Her mother's gaunt fingers closed around her hand tightly. 'I had tried so hard to atone my sin, but he did not forget nor forgive. He punished me through punishing you,' She began to pant heavily. 'Don't speak Ma. Keep calm.' She stroked gently her mother's face. 'No. Let me. I will not have another chance. Be careful. Keep away from him. He will destroy you just as he destroyed me.'

The doctor walked in followed by a white-uniformed nurse. They stood by the bed and scanned the readings on the monitoring screen. Karisma walked out of the cabin and stood by the door, her gaze wandering along the deserted corridor. The tears that had frozen inside her had turned to an ice dagger and stabbed at her heart with a ruthless brutality. She cast a longing, moist glance at the partially visible frail figure that lay motionless in the bed and walked away. Her feet refused to move but she dragged them along the corridor and climbed down the wide steps of the staircase.

***

Kalyan Kumar came for the twelfth day rites. After the guests and relatives departed in the afternoon he sat in the backroom and drank with her father. An oppressive, bitter silence had taken the house under seize. Karisma came out of the house and walked down the narrow sand-filled road that led to the palm and casuarina covered patch of the far end section of the beach. It was like a haven, the only spot where she thought she would find an escape from the biting pangs of her loss. She trudged across the sands and reached a spot, shaded by dense casuarinas and date palms, and slumped down on a sand-mound. She looked at the distant shore where the waves wailed and beat their foamy heads against the callous, unfeeling sands. What loss the waves keep mourning perpetually, what eternal woe? Karisma wondered bitterly. Tears welled up in her dry eyes as the memory of her mother rushed back to her like the surging sea tides and crashed inside her heart.

It was a warm afternoon, and in the pale, yellow light of the departing sun the shadows of the tall palms lengthened gloomily across the sandy stretch. The sea continued to hiss distantly like an ancient reptile in pain and the wind rasped through the palm leaves. Karisma looked around. The sea shore lay empty and lonely and abandoned as far as her gaze could travel. She hid her face in her palms and wept, letting the sorrow that had remained unreleased for days flow out of her. The hard sobs racked her frail body as she vented out her grief. She remembered the stormy evening she had sat here alone, waiting desperately for Ronit who never came back to her. And, now she sat there, weeping for her mother who, too, would never come back.

The sun had dropped beyond the horizon. It was beginning to get dark. Karisma decided to return. Her legs felt as if they had no life in them. She heaved out a deep sigh. Suddenly she felt something like a presence close to her, so close that she could not tell her own breathing apart from that mysterious presence. She went numb and stiff.

'*Karisma*!

She heard a voice; a hollow, disembodied whisper close to her ear. Spider webs crawled down her spine as she remembered the voice.

Ronit's!!

'*Please do not weep. Come to me.*' .

She sprang up to her feet now, her eyes darting frantically around to locate the voice. The beach was as deserted as it was when she came there. She saw something like a driftwood in the sea, some hundred meters away from the edge. She squinted at the object trying to make out what it could be. And then, startling her, a face rose from the water. In the quasi darkness of the approaching evening she could see the face, bold and clear. *It was the face of Ronit! It was smiling at her!*

She ran towards the edge of the water but the object went inside the waters as she reached there. There was no other sound except for the flutter of the wind in the trees and the sibilating waves hitting the shore.

**

Her father ambled into her room, a cup of steaming coffee in his hand. Karisma sat back straight in the rocking chair where she reclined and looked at him in mild surprise. It was unlike father to wander into her room this way, at that hour.

'Were you sleeping, dear?' he asked lowering himself to a leather couch in her front. On asking of Kalyan Kumar, Karisma's father had moved in with them after her mother's death. He had stopped going into the sea in the trawlers and spent most of his time in his room watching television or reading. In the evenings, he invariably visited Kundan uncle's store and had a drinking session with him. There were occasions when Kalyan Kumar found time to spend with his father-in-law, to have a drink with him. But that was very rare. Karisma remained confined to her room mostly except for the evenings she accompanied Kalyan Kumar to the club or attend an official party or a business gathering. Kalyan Kumar kept late nights and usually had his dinner outside. The vast emptiness that loomed over the bungalow would have remained uninterrupted had it not been for the noise of the traffic in the street beyond and the muffled yelling of the kids from the beach, and the hushed conversation of the house staff.

'No father, I was just resting. You want something?'

'No, no! I just wanted to have a word with you. This is such a big house and I do not see you often even though we live under the same roof.'

'You are right father. It is a big house.' There was a vacant expression in her eyes.

'Are you happy, my princess?' He asked fondly. 'I am happy, father,' Karisma forced a smile.

'Didn't I tell you that one day you will be a real princess, living a royal life?'

'Yes father.' Karisma agreed, and again her lips parted in a pale smile.

'You do not look happy, princess. Are you disturbed for something?'

Karisma wondered why her father was querying about her happiness now. There should have been be no doubt regarding that. Wasn't she living the life of a queen, in royal luxury? Was she so obvious? Did her face betray her inner turmoil?'

'You are imagining things, father.' She said trying to sound animated. 'He will destroy you as he had destroyed me!' They were the last words her mother had said, cautioning her. Her father's presence was beginning to disturb her. She cringed inwardly.

'Who is this girl, Sandhya Kiran?' Father asked abruptly. The question caught her off guard.

Wh… why do you ask father? She stammered. 'She is Kalyan's personal assistant. A brilliant girl. An asset to the company.' She added, her emotions under control now.

'Are you unhappy on account of her?' her father asked, ignoring her explanation.

'No father, why should I be?'

He looked at her thoughtfully for a long moment. 'I have put everything at stake to see the gamble pay off. No one is going to ruin that.' He said under his breath. It was an indistinct whisper and it frightened Karisma. The look in her father's eyes softened the next instant and he stood up. 'You know I love you, my princess! And I will always want to see you happy.' He made his way towards the door.

'Father,' Karisma called. He turned to look at her. 'You want to say something, my princess?'

'Please father, do not call me a princess,' it was a choked whisper.

'Why?' He wandered back into the room, looking puzzled. 'What happened?'

'Because it sounds like an abuse!' she stammered. He stared at her for a while, his face hardening.

'It is our secret princess. Haven't I told you that long back? You are my princess and I am the king.' He smiled mysteriously and swinging on his feet strode out of the room.

***

A half-moon drifted lazily through the cottonwool clouds shedding a pale glimmer across the vast lawn of the club. The night was pleasantly warm and a moist breeze wafting from the sea beach beyond the road that snaked along the waterfront drifted in carrying an exotic fragrance in its delicate folds. The fizzy water-columns the fountain spouted shimmered in the lurid light from the elegantly designed light posts hemming it. People, young and elderly, sat in groups in the basket chairs under colourful beach umbrellas chatting over drinks and snacks.

Karisma sauntered out of the tennis court carrying a glass of mocktail and sat down in a basket chair at a distance from the fountain. Here, away from the scintillating blinkers, under the frail, languid moon, she felt at peace. She had been sitting in the tennis court watching her husband at the game. She did neither have much inclination towards nor interest in tennis. After spending a tiresome and unexciting half-hour in the court she decided to leave her husband at the game and come out to the open and spacious lawn that offered a better option of enjoyment.

She looked around the lawn. The crowd was more by the fountain, in the lighted area. But it was partially lonely in that patch where she sat. She noticed a figure, possibly a girl, in a snow- white flowy gown sitting alone by another table in a far corner. There was something like a small coronet on her head that dazzled in the pale light. Her long hair swung over her delicate shoulders in sleek, black waves. She could not see the girl's face but she had an instinctive feeling that she knew her, not as just a formal acquaintance but intimately, and for years! She was faintly curious. She wondered if she was with a companion who was inside the club or had come alone, and at that moment her attention was drawn to a sound of laughter from a table somewhat nearer and her gaze turned in that direction. A young man and a girl sat sipping soft drinks and talking. The girl broke into a tremulous laughter at something her companion said. She felt a sharp prick at her heart as her thoughts went back to the time when she and Ronit used to chat and laugh like that, in the secluded patches of the beach, in the small unassuming eating joints and snack parlours at the outskirts of the town, and during the long drives down the sandy road that lengthened by the beach in a seemingly unending arch.

A shadow fell across the grass patch to her left. It was not exactly a shadow, but a wispy white, transparent thing that edged past her, lengthening forward, like it floated in the air and moved ahead. She stared at it in unblinking eyes, trying to place the smell it left behind as it swept past her.

The shadow, or the figure whatever it was seemed to stop for a fraction of a second and turn and then walked quickly towards the fountain and as Karisma looked on it walked to the column of water-spouts. The white, shadowy figure stopped briefly, turned to look at her and waved at her in a gesture of saying adieu. The small crown on its head glimmered in the diffusive luminosity around the fountain. She had now a full view of the face of the strange character. It was her own face!! Her heart gave a wild lurch and she closed her eyes tightly. When she opened her eyes, the figure was not there, as if it had melted into the water-spray. And suddenly she felt unusually light as if a load that was there weighing heavy on her heart, had lifted off it. She did not know why but she felt relaxed and free.

'Ma'am,' someone was speaking to her. The voice jerked her out of a hypnotised state. It was a uniformed waiter of the club. Karisma looked up at him. 'Yes?'

'Kalyan sir is waiting for you at the dinner table.' He said politely. 'I am coming.' She rose to her feet and followed the man into the club's dining hall, looking furtively back at the fountain. Everything looked so normal, the fountain, the lights and the jesting, laughing flock of men and women under the beach umbrellas.

***

Karisma looked at the disappearing back of her father as he walked out and sighed deeply. She was no longer a small girl now who was held trapped in the persona of a delusive *princess* his father had conjured up, and submitted to the nauseating lechery of Kundan uncle and a few of her friends believing that she was actually a princess born to help her loving, doting father live a life of luxury. And she also knew now why she had done that! The indistinctly uttered, fragmented words of a dying woman in a lonely cabin of a hospital had drawn out a distinct and complete sketch of the abominations that was presented to her year after year in deceptively attractive, glamourous wrappers. That evening, in the palely lit lawn of The Sea and Sands Club, the shadow of the princess that had clung to her soul like a smudge of some muted sin had faded away leaving her clean and contentedly empty.

She knew she had nothing to lose now. She had never aspired to be a queen as her father had wishfully reiterated, nor did she feel like one after marrying the senior partner of one of the distinguished fishing companies of the state. What her father said during his brief and unexpected visit to her room was an unmistakable hint about the absolute hold Sandhya Kiran had over her husband but Karisma never wanted to be possessive nor did she begrudge their closeness.

***

She sipped the tea unmindfully, a vacant expression in her eyes. Things happened in her life with such staggering unexpectedness that they shook her out of her sanity. The words of her mother that meant not much when she had overheard a mysterious conversation between her parents years ago rang in her memory. ...'She is having a problem... You are putting ideas into her mind'. She remembered another occasion a few years later when her mother warned her to keep her friendship with Ronit a secret from her father. Her mind was in a turmoil as if she was flung into a maelstrom that made her whirl wildly, pushing her down and down with progressive momentum into the bottom of a turbulent sea.

***

She finished her tea and pushed the tray away, the breakfast untouched. An oppressive silence shrouded the big bungalow. She did not know where her father was. May be downstairs, washing down the grief with alcohol. Grief? Her lips curved in a crooked smile that could have meant any thing. It could have been one of apathy, sarcasm, anger, frustration.. She propped her head on the backrest of the chair and closed her eyes.

The sands pricked at her eyelids and she closed them

more tightly. She pressed her hands to her ears to keep the shrill whistle of the sand blast out of their reach. It seemed that the sea and the sand storm were howling in a synchrony to drown her feeble screams. She did not know where Ronit was . The angry blasts had swept him away somewhere deep into the forest of casuarina and palms, towards the remains of the ancient structures that stood in scary, desiccated ruins at the desolate patches of the beach out of the reach of her eyes. And the sands swirled around her in angry coils with a vengeful determination to blow her away into some atavistic emptiness between the sea and the sky. She screamed and screamed until she was hoarse and then, a hand touched her shoulder gently and all the noise died. The storm receded and the hissing, ravaging wind became a soft, cool waft of the sea mist that caressed her face lovingly. 'Karisma, do not fear. Open your eyes!' The same hollow, blank voice she had heard in the beach on the twelfth day of her mother's death, whispered into her ear. Her eyes snapped open. And there he was! Ronit! Standing close to her, a look of deep yearning and profound sorrow in his large, expressive eyes. She gaped at him, her mind paralyzed, her limbs stiff, her mouth open. Ronit took a few steps forward towards the sea and turned and smiled. He stretched out a hand, beckoning her. Then turned his face and walked ahead in quick steps. As Karisma watched, bewildered, he entered into the foamy waves and floated forward, one moment visible and gone in the next. 'Wait!' Karisma shouted at the top of her voice but he did not stop and there were more waves, high and howling and they drowned her voice.

'What is it ma'am?' Aruna aunty clambered up the stairs, her breath coming in rasps, fear and concern in her eyes. Karisma was still calling at Ronit when Aruna aunty took her in her arms protectively and ran her hand over her head. 'Easy, ma'am, easy!' she muttered soothingly as Karisma hid her face in her chest and broke into copious tears.

****

For the last one month, since her husband met with that fatal accident, the dreams, that appeared so intriguingly real, visited her solitary waking moments. And every time there was Ronit, beckoning her to come with him into the sea and then disappearing either under the surging tides or in the whirling vortex of wailing sandstorms.

****

Karisma climbed down the flight of stairs to the passageway that edged off the big spacious hall. She cast a passing glance at the hall that looked gloomy and desolate, dimly lit up with the diffusive lighting from the silver chandelier above. She walked down the passageway to its south end and entered a big, well-lit room. The nurse, a young woman somewhere in her mid-twenties, laid down the book she was reading and stood up. 'Good evening, ma'am,' she said respectfully. Karisma flicked her fingers in a gesture of dismissal and the nurse tiptoed out of the room. Karisma sat down in the chair where the nurse was sitting and looked closely at the man lying motionless in the king size bed. He lay almost plastered to the bed. His hands were thin and gaunt and his legs spread slightly apart from each other had a ropey look about them. He opened his eyes at the sound of the gentle rustle of Karisma's dress as she lowered herself into the chair. A strange glint came to the lustreless eyes at the sight of her. He tried to smile at her and saliva drooled out of the corner of his lips that twisted in an ugly, awkward angle. He tried to speak but the sound that escaped his mouth was an indistinct animal moan.

It was for the first time Karisma had entered her father's room after he was discharged from the Amrit hospital. He had suffered that massive paralytic stroke a month and a half back, the night on which she had announced that she had transferred her shares in the company and debentures in the name of Sunil Arya, the company's junior partner. The doctors had little hope of any significant improvement in his condition. Karisma had engaged a couple of nurses from the hospital who worked in shifts and took care of her father. A doctor visited the house twice a week to examine his vitals.

'How are you father?' Karisma asked. Her voice had a formal and indifferent note about it. A brief sparkle came to the eyes of the man who lay helpless in the bed. He tried desperate to move his hands that lay dead and stiff.

'This is the last of me you are seeing father,' she said softly. 'I will be leaving this place. I have no idea what I am going to do but I will not return here. I have made all financial arrangements for you. Aruna aunty will see to it that you are taken care of properly as long as you are alive. There will be no lapse in your treatment.'

The man's eyes darted around revealing how desperate he was and his lips quivered as if he struggled to speak out something but the only sound he made was a muffled groan.

'I know what you want to say father,' Karisma said, a deep agony in her eyes. 'But I cannot continue to live here now. You have to be alone. Didn't you want to live in a palace and own heaps of wealth? I have transferred all the amount to your account and authorised Aruna aunty to do all transactions on your behalf. You have avenged the injustice done to you years ago, though I would not call it a heinous sin as you have always believed and made my poor mother believe it to be one. But what did I do to deserve the punishment you meted out to me, father? Which father could subject his daughter to such devilish exploitation? But of course, you were determined to torture your poor wife for the slip she made by punishing me, by snatching out every damn thing I loved, by utilising me to slake your hunger for money. What a fool have I been to fall for that dirty 'princess' trick you played with me! I have never wanted to be a princess father. I was happy in that small tenement house, with the love of my mother. That was genuine and was not fake, motivated by greed and hostility like yours. And of course, there was Ronit! My Ronit! The only silver lining behind my gloomy clouds of despair. You destroyed that too. I do not believe in the existence of a world beyond this one, or that of a hell or a heaven. Each of us, has to atone his sin through a penance, through self-afflicted torments, like mother did, like I have been doing all these years, my sin was just that I had a look that constantly reminded you of the slip my mother made.' Karisma paused for a breath and looked at the eyes that had sunken into the pale, desiccated face. A few drops of tears trickled down from the corners of the dull eyes. Karisma wiped the tears with the end of her sari. 'There is nothing I could do to help you father. This is your nemesis and you cannot escape it. And I give you my word father, I will not let the truth come out to the open, ever. It will always remain a secret.'

She rose to her feet and cast a long, pitiful look at the inert figure, then turned and walked towards the door. A frantic but low and muffled animal howl rippled across the room, bringing her to a halt. She repressed the urge to look back and strode out of the room, breaking into a tearless, dry sobbing.

***

The pale twilight hung over the beach and the sea like a canopy of translucent grey. And the sand -stretches at the distance appeared like ashen patches, rough and brittle. In the deepening shadow of the evening the tall palms that swayed rhythmically to the rasp of the rising and falling waves were like aliens from some far away planet performing a bizarre burlesque. The casuarinas sighed hard, brooding over some primordial woe.

She felt calm and light, almost volatile, as if a

strong chain that had kept her fettered to the world had snapped, leaving her free.

She knew Ronit would reach there any moment to ask her to come with him as he had been doing all these months.

And this time she would not let him return alone to the sea, she decided and smiled to herself and waited for the hollow, empty voice. Ronit's voice. Her inescapable, inevitable destiny!!

Black Eagle Books

www.blackeaglebooks.org
info@blackeaglebooks.org

Black Eagle Books, an independent publisher, was founded as a nonprofit organization in April, 2019. It is our mission to connect and engage the Indian diaspora and the world at large with the best of works of world literature published on a collaborative platform, with special emphasis on foregrounding Contemporary Classics and New Writing.

9 781645 606994